The Bronc People

THE
BRONC PEOPLE

William Eastlake

Introduction by Gerald Haslam

A Zia Book

UNIVERSITY OF NEW MEXICO PRESS
Albuquerque

FOR MY FATHER

This volume contains the complete text of the first edition, published in 1958.

Second UNM Press printing, 1979.

INTRODUCTION

William Eastlake *feels* the beauty and power of the land. Perhaps because he came relatively late to the Southwest's high, dramatic country, he has not taken it for granted. Instead, he has recognized the land and assigned it a major role in each of his three western novels: *Go in Beauty* (1956), *The Bronc People* (1958), and *Portrait of an Artist with Twenty-Six Horses* (1963). In the most recent of these three novels, he described two riders, their horses, and the setting:

> They allowed their horses to sift down through the delicate lacing shadows of juniper, wither—and cannonbone—high, in blue grama perfumed, the high wide equine nostrils lofting above the gray chamise, plunging in feathered step past all of time, the eroding Todilto formation, the yellowing Wingate and today's earth too, precarious and in almost fluid suspension on a steep, hostile slope. (p. 78)

Moreover, Eastlake often juxtaposes the land's apparent timelessness with human transience to reveal dramatically the subjectivity of temporal perceptions, one of his most persistent thematic concerns. The opening lines from *Go in Beauty*, Eastlake's first novel, indicate immediately the contrast between nature's slow, certain, yet dynamic time, and tense human temporality:

> Once upon a time there was time. The land here in the Southwest had evolved slowly and there was time and there were great spaces. Now a man on horseback from atop a bold mesa looked out over the violent spectrum of the Indian

country—into a gaudy infinity where all the colors of the world exploded, soundlessly.

"There's not much time," he said. (p. 1)

More important still, Eastlake has merged time and space, time and land, in sensing the constant yet often unacknowledged interrelationship between people and the natural world of which they are a part. He has sensed that interrelationship, it seems, not intellectually but shamanistically—he has *felt* it—with expanded perceptions and broadened perspectives. In writing about such things, he often uses a lively humor, whether subtle or bold, to impress important perceptions without having to rely upon didacticism. When an incline is descended in *The Bronc People*, Eastlake places anthropocentricism in proper perspective:

> The mesa here was eroding away in five giant steps that descended down to the floor of the valley where the abandoned hogan lay. Each of the five steps clearly marked about twenty million years. . . . by the different fossil animals found in each. It took the four boys about twenty minutes to descend these one hundred million years, but they didn't think that was very good going. (p. 83)

Eastlake's expanded—perhaps slightly askew—vision of his world, and what Ken Kesey has called his "prairie-hard prose," distinguish his writing. In bringing new eyes and a new style to the enduring Southwest, he has rediscovered old truths and developed unique literary means for sharing them.

Go in Beauty, Eastlake's strong first novel, appeared in 1956 and received favorable reviews. Most notable in the novel was the author's creation of Indian characters who talked like people rather than stereotypes; also praised was what Delbert Wylder has called "the mystic interrelationship between man's sins and nature," suggesting the symbolic depth toward which Eastlake's work would tend.

During the mid fifties, when Eastlake was emerging as an important writer, he discovered New Mexico. His brother-in-law owned a ranch high in the Jemez Mountains. A few visits convinced Bill Eastlake that he had found his place, and in 1955 he settled on a ranch near Cuba, New Mexico, in the country he had come to love. As Richard Angell has observed, "For William Eastlake the high, lonesome country he has been writing about is really home."

The Bronc People, his second novel, demonstrated that a special talent had emerged, for Eastlake had developed a unique manner of portraying the Southwest, one that offended some old-timers but helped many more people truly to see the region for the first time. Bill Eastlake is nothing if not a writer who has nurtured his own special vision and developed his own special style to communicate that vision. As Herbert Gold pointed out when he reviewed *The Bronc People,* the novel made "definite the arrival on the scene of a new, hard, dry, tender, very contemporary talent." Delbert Wylder called the book a classic.

Like all classics, *The Bronc People* is universal while true to its setting. Moreover, during the crucial opening chapter, and in other places, Indians function as a Greek chorus, asking, explaining, and predicting (cryptically in all three cases). In that first scene, as Sant Bowman and the Gran Negrito battle over rights to a water hole, the names of their respective ranches tell much about their conflict: The white man *feels* (Circle Heart) that his need makes the water his; the black man *reasons* (Circle R) that the water is legally his.

The Gran Negrito is killed, and his young son, Alastair Benjamin, escapes (the Indians call him "war surplus"). Eventually he becomes intimately linked to the Bowman family, especially Little Sant, first through the battle ritual that killed his father, then when the Bowmans accept him as their second son. Together, like their fathers, Alastair and Little Sant represent mankind in search of meaning, personifying reason and heart.

If the Circle R and Circle Heart suggest important symbolic meanings, the rodeo in chapter 2 confirms the author's depth of purpose. Rodeos themselves are mythic mergings of humans and animals, both challenges and communions. In *The Bronc People,* the rodeo is strongly ritualistic, with judges who "pulled on their chins and stroked their thighs and squirted down wild brown juice on lesser heads, as wise men will."

And the rodeo ritual is also strongly religious, with Lemaitre (the master) as chief priest. While lesser men make their offerings of greased pigs—". . . like Montezuma's men the golden mantle, like offerings to the god, the animals flashing and screaming, fighting along the arms, upward to the sun"—Lemaitre rides a killer horse and hoists Little Sant in an intense replay of the earlier offerings. The horse, the boy, and the man have acted together and are linked as one, a kind of rodeo Trinity: the Father (Lemaitre), the Son (Little Sant), the Holy Spirit (the wild horse). The rodeo scene is so heavily symbolic that it slips close to parody in places.

Ultimately, after Alastair and Little Sant are joined as brothers, the tension between reason and heart must be reconciled, especially in the young black man. Eastlake introduces a memorable cast of characters to act upon them, the most striking of whom is Blue-eyed Billy Peersall, a one-hundred-and-one-year-old Indian fighter, balanced in the cast by an equally old "white fighter." Mr. Peersall debunks illusions ("Well, we made the wrong arrangements. We should have joined the Indians, fought the whites, the Easterners.") and offers Alastair advice that finally helps him (". . . you can't give anybody anything." "You mean I've got to do it alone?" "Yes.").

That is Eastlake's final message in this rich yarn, or series of yarns, that and the powerful mythic strengths he reveals, for both Alastair and Little Sant may ultimately draw upon their unrecorded, unforgotten past. Don't rely on anyone to do your living for you; rely on your land and on yourself. The problem of faceless, nameless masses who must eventually face alone life's most desperate problems creates much moral tension in modern literature: Despair when mass morality fails. The advice from Peersall's (and Eastlake's) West is to accept the pleasure and pain of individuality from the start, and to know your own special place in all its depth.

William Eastlake has woven a special tapestry in *The Bronc People*. His style is memorable for its crisp dialogue, its effective descriptions, its flashing humor. The reader soon sees that an Eastlake novel cannot be skimmed, that the style is as tight and fine as the weave in a Navajo bayeta blanket, and as beautiful. Yet it is finally Eastlake's recognition of unique southwestern qualities, and his artistic use of them, whether literal or symbolic, that distinguishes his work. His tapestry is rich because he writes of more than merely the land, or merely its people, or merely its history, or merely its magic; it is rich because he blends them all.

Eastlake has constantly sought to transcend the limits of popularly held assumptions and priorities. All of his books seem aimed at answering a question posed by one of his characters, a Navajo medicine man: "Why was I sentenced to earth?"

Gerald Haslam
California State College, Sonoma
Rohnert Park, California

PART I

ONE The two quiet Indians, resting in Z shapes, could watch and hear the shots going back and forth, back and forth, as in a Western movie. But suddenly someone was hurt and it wasn't like a Western movie now.

The two Indians had been watching from the peak of a purple New Mexican butte ever since the big white rider had driven his cattle up to the only active water hole in thirty miles and asked for water.

For two days now this forward-leaning rider with bright silvered trappings that exploded in the sun had allowed his horse to weave slowly in back of the herd; the easily distracted calves bunching to the rear, loitering then leaping ahead suddenly; the mother cows bawling for their young, turning back within the herd only to be pressed forward again in the great shove; the steers sensing the great drought ahead, pausing, tongues hanging, necks sagging, pointing rearward, red-eyed in retreat against the long dry march, quizzical, hesitant and defeated on the flank of the herd, hoping to be bypassed. The white-faced, now dust black-masked, wild-eyed heifers watched the rider, then fled frontward as his rope sang. The insulted, pride-hurt, wide-shouldered, and ball-heavy bull, forced to go now where he had not dictated to go, abused and coerced, lashed and driven toward a mad man-destiny of no water, tolling his big bellow of protest and outrage at the lead of the harem, the cows plodding, patient now, the steers following hesitant, the calves coy, tumbling, skipping sometimes forward, quick

9

and lost—they all bore the brand of the Circle Heart and they had all been without water for two days now.

"Perhaps that's true," the Indian who was on the highest part of the butte said. "But it's the other man's water. And I know the Circle Heart."

"You seem to know everything about everything," the second Indian said.

"I know how the Gran Negrito got this place and I know the Circle Heart."

"Yes, you seem to know everything about everything," the other Indian said.

"And I know how the Circle Heart will get it. They're getting it now."

The two Indians had been right in at the start of everything. They had been there when the two men had begun by talking sensibly. They were right there when they began raising their voices and they were right there when they raised their guns.

"The one who owned the water fired first."

"But not last."

The Indians had seen the man who owned the water go back in the red adobe house. They had seen the other man raise the gate to let his cattle in and they had seen the man in the house break a pane and heard him fire through the window. Then they saw the cattleman drop behind a rock and fire back. The Indians had not seen the man who went in the adobe house take a child from off the bed and put him under the bed before he started firing.

"Is the man inside the adobe house hit badly?" the Indian who was lowest on the butte asked.

"Yes."

"How can you tell?"

"Well, he seems to be firing faster," the other Indian said.

The child under the bed in the house sensed this too. Both of the men were firing much faster now. The boy's father had a lever-action Winchester and he swung the new shells in with a herky-jerky motion of his right arm. The child could not see this from under the bed but he could see the sudden brass empties that dropped around his head and he could smell the acrid gunpowder smell. He could see his father's boots moving quickly from position to new position and the floor becoming slick with something red and bright.

"Somehow I don't want to get in this one," the taller Indian said.

"Do you usually?"

"Yes, I usually do."

"Have you noticed," the shorter Indian said, "that our seat is not too good now, that the war has moved to the other side of the house? Do you think we should move with it?"

"I don't see why not."

The two Indians moved off the butte and, using the very high gray-green sage and orange, bloom-waving Cowboys Delight for cover, got over to the other side of the rincon, where they found a good red rock to sit on. Their pants were very blue against it and their shirts were very yellow. Their wide Stetsons were so beaten up they weren't anything against anything. They both seemed tired.

"Are you bored?" the shorter Indian wanted to know.

"No."

"Have you noticed that the firing has become very irregular?"

"Yes, I've noticed that."

"Have you noticed the man on the outside seems to be winning?"

"Yes, I've noticed that."

"Do you think there'll be a result today?"

"Before the night, yes."

"Then it will be all settled today?"

"No, I don't think so."

"Can you see all right from your seat?"

"Perfectly."

The man who was supposed to be winning was firing from behind a sandstone concretion, almost round, that had come down from the Eocene cliff that circled around and made all of the firing echo. When the firing had started he told himself that all he was doing was answering back. That is, when someone insulted him he insulted back and when someone shot at him, if he had a gun, he shot back. Something like that, but actually without thought. Now

11

he was only trying to pour enough fire, put enough shots, through the window so that he could get away with his cattle. This was the man who was supposed to be winning. He had been hit in the leg, not too badly; he could still move easily and it did not bother him at all. He had been in the last war, and in the infantry, too, but in this kind of fighting it did not help much. He had read some Western pulp stories that were supposed to be about things like this but they did not help at all. The thing he kept in mind was to fire back at the window that kept firing at him. That might stop it. Then he could trail back to the Circle Heart.

The man inside the house, who, according to the two Indians, was supposed to be losing, thought he was doing nicely. Actually, as the small boy under the bed noticed from watching the slipperiness on the floor increase, his father was not doing well at all. He had been hit seriously but did not feel it too much because he was feeling other things more. If only the intruder would leave. If only the first shot he had fired at the white man had had some effect. Now there was nothing to do except keep this up until something happened.

At the beginning he had tumbled a blue box of brass Remington 30-30 soft-point Kleen-Bore cartridges on the low oak table, and all during the fight he would pick them up in handfuls of six, which is what the lever action held, and jam them in the receiver. Now, near the ending, his wide black hand swept up the final six.

"One, two, three, four, five, six," the boy heard him say.

Actually it was the arm that had done the sweeping in of the shells. His hand did not seem to be working correctly any more. The long black arm had gathered the final shells in one big movement—sweep! At the same time a bullet hit into the adobe above the boy's head softly—thwang!

"Son? Son, it's going to be all right." The boy under the bed was too tensed to answer anyone.

The Indians had moved again and they were within a clump of sage on a small knoll now. The two Indians were Navahos and they remembered this place well from their fathers telling about it. This spring-fed, huge circle of green surrounded by mesa was where Many Cattle and Winding Water had hidden their band of

12

Navahos in 1884. This was the place where the whites were not supposed to reach them, the place that the whites would not find. But they found it and burned everything down, the crops and the houses, and they took Many Cattle and Winding Water and their people to the stockade when they caught up with them, starving, at the Canyon de Chelly.

"Can you see all right?" the tall Indian asked. The tall Indian's name was President Taft.

"Very well," the short Indian said. The short Indian allowed the trader to call him My Prayer. They both had Indian names, too—Water Running Underneath The Ground and Walking Across A Small Arroyo. They both wore hats that were not smashed in at the top like white men's hats and they had on army surplus shoes and they both rolled cigarettes without taking their eyes off the spectacle they were watching.

"We could move down a little now, get closer now, without any danger I think," the taller Indian said. The taller Indian had just completed the manufacture of a cigarette entirely by feel and now he placed it in his mouth without ever seeing it. "Yes, I think we could move down closer."

"I guess I'm perfectly happy here," the shorter Indian said.

Inside the cabin that the Indians could see perfectly, the man was beginning to pick his shots. He was trying to place them carefully and he was trying to make each one important, as though each one were his last, which it very nearly was. He had even ceased the herky-jerky movement of throwing the shells into the chamber with a short swing of his right arm and he now worked the lever action more deliberately and certainly, as though he were opening and closing a safe containing precious things. The man he was shooting at was difficult to follow, but, despite the fact that the man was using smokeless powder, the man in the cabin could always tell where the other fired from last but never where he would fire from now, never where he was now. He could always see the two Indians, despite the fact that they kept changing their seats. They always seemed to select something on the rock balcony that gave them a perfect view no matter to which window he went. He had been tempted early in the fight to fire at least one shot

13

close to the Indians simply because they were wherever he looked and because wherever he looked for the white man they were there, complacently, as though there were some law protecting them— two wild things out of season, or two people buying into this incident without payment. Now a shell was too expensive to waste on them. It was a silly idea anyway. Do people always get silly ideas when they are weak? Was it getting dark outside, out there, or was the weakness making everything turn to darkness?

"Son." His voice sounded weak and strange to himself. "Son, remember this." Or was the boy too small now to remember anything of this later, remember ever? "Son, remember this. Are you listening?"

No one answered him at all and then a bullet came through the window and made a strange sound as it slashed through the table.

The man who fired that shot wondered, now that the shooting had slowed down, whether that would hold things for a while, whether he might even now be able to get away, but a shot whee-ed near him as he moved quickly to new cover. He rested the New-Texan 35-caliber short-barreled Marlin saddle rifle between his knees and looked down on the house where he could see no one and wondered whether he would have to wait for darkness to escape with his animals. It was showing no signs of darkness yet. He looked hard at the windows to see if he could see someone there and then he looked up at the Indians who were always there. It would be nice to shoot at them, to do something with someone you could see. He toyed very briefly with the idea of firing at the Indians because they were there so damn comfortably as though they were two civilians inquiring the time in no man's land at the Battle of Gettysburg. Are people this curious? Indians are, I guess.

"Do you think it's right of us to do this?" the taller Indian said.

"Why not?"

"Watching?"

"Why not?"

"It's none of our business."

"Why not?"

14

"You're doing awfully well with the why nots."

"I don't think it will matter at all. I know it will not matter at all. It will come out the way it's going to come out whether we watch or not. It would not have made any difference whether anyone was watching when the whites drove us out."

"We're still here."

"I don't think we are. We're not Indians any longer."

"What are we then?"

The shorter Indian took his eyes off the battle a moment and studied his army surplus shoes. "I don't know," he said.

"Sure we're Indians."

The other Indian put his hand to his mouth and made a warwhoop noise like the one he had heard white children make in the streets of Albuquerque. "Indians! Here come the Indians!" he said.

"We speak Navaho."

"We're speaking it now."

"Then we must be Indians."

"Sure," the shorter Indian, whom the trader called My Prayer, agreed. "Sure we're Indians." And then for the first time he said something in English. "So what?" He ran it together so it sounded like some Navaho word. So whah. Sowhah. Sowah.

"I will tell you sowah," the Indian called President Taft said. "Do you know that, outside of a moving picture, they wouldn't even bother even to shoot at an Indian now?"

"That's perfectly all right with me."

"You don't understand. To them we have become nothing."

"Sowah?" the Indian called My Prayer said.

The white man who had come up fast and tired on a horse one hour ago to draw the first shot observed from his new position that he was close to the Indians. That was all right. If something happened they could testify in his favor. By moving up and over slightly to his right he could join them and find something out.

"Hi!" he said as he moved in ahead of the Indians' rock, still keeping the sage between himself and the house.

"Hello," the Indians said. They could speak four languages, through necessity: Navaho and Apache, which have the same root,

Spanish, which most of the settlers were, and English, which was increasing all the time, and Zia Pueblo, which came in awfully handy in this location. That makes five languages actually, but two of these languages they spoke poorly, so they counted them as one. English and Pueblo were the two foreign languages that counted as one.

"Hello," they said in one of their poor languages.

"Hi," the white man repeated.

"It's a nice day," one of the Indians said.

"Hace buen tiempo," the other Indian tried, not so sure of the white man's nation.

"No, it's a nice day," the white man said.

"It sure is," the Indian who had been correct said.

"Yeah," the white man said.

"You think it will rain?" the Indian who had been wrong said.

"It could," the white man said.

"You think it could not rain?"

"Sure it could not rain." The white man wondered what language he was speaking.

"You think it could snow?"

"Hardly, at this time of year." The white rider felt on firmer ground now.

"Yes, it could snow very hardly this time of year," President Taft said. The white man thought it would be nice if they could start all over again.

"We have been wondering what all the firing is about," the taller Indian said.

The white man pulled down on his cowboy hat. "So have I."

"Isn't it true," President Taft said, "isn't it true about all wars?"

"Isn't what true?"

"That no one knows what they're about?"

"No, it isn't," the Indian called My Prayer said. His partner, he thought, had a habit of trying to be wise by being very simple. "As long as people are involved they're about something."

"Now, that is a bright remark," the other Indian said. His partner, he thought, would go a lot farther if he did not try to be

16

so stupid that he appeared solemn. "I can tell you what this one is about."

"What?" The white man parted the rabbit brush.

"Well, you wanted to water your cattle."

"And?" The white man picked up his gun, held the brush, and looked down on the house.

"Do you have to fire that thing here in front of us?"

"I have to fire back."

"Why?"

"So I can get away with my cattle."

The two Indians looked at each other. "All right," My Prayer said. "Fire away."

There was a soft click in front of the Indians.

"What happened?"

"A misfire."

"Try another bullet."

"The empty shell has jammed."

"Let me see the gun."

The white man below the Indian on the rock passed the gun up to My Prayer, who passed it on to President Taft, who broke off a greasewood twig and inserted this in the ejector while he hit the side of the cartridge case with the big palm of his right hand. The misfire fell out and he levered in another shell and passed the gun over to his partner, who passed it down to the white man.

"I think it should work all right now."

"Thank you," the white man said.

"It's perfectly all right. We're enjoying the show."

"But it's nice, decent of you, to take sides."

"But we're not."

"No, we're not," his partner agreed.

"You mean you'd do the same for that other—?"

"Certainly. Why not?"

"Yes, why not?" his partner said. "After all, why not?"

"I want you to try and remember who started this," the white man said from the brush. "It could be very important and I want to tell you that I don't like this at all."

"You've lost your nerve?" one of the Indians asked.

"I don't want to hurt anyone down there."

"Then why are you firing the gun?"

"So he does not fire at me."

The two Indians looked at each other.

"Oh," they said.

Below, the man that the white man above, talking to the Indians, did not want to hurt was hurt badly. But not quite so badly that he had not noticed the Indian on the rock fix a gun and pass it back down to someone in the brush. So the Indians had taken sides. Now at last he could fire at someone he could see. He raised the gun and rested it on the back of a piñon chair and got the bead right between the eyes of the tallest Indian. He could not pull the trigger. He wondered why. He tried to pull the trigger again and failed. He still had that much strength. He tested his trigger finger in the air. He still had that much strength all right. He lowered the gun and wondered why he could not shoot an Indian. He felt dizziness now and he wiped his forehead and looked around for the boy.

"Son!" he called. He could not remember now where he had put the boy. It was getting very dark. He had better light a lamp. He felt that the Coleman gasoline-pump lantern would be too much for him, so when he saw the tall, glass-chimneyed kerosene lantern, and so close too, he lighted that. He knocked the glass chimney on the floor, where it smashed, but soon he had a tall yellow flame going. Now he remembered where he had put the boy—under the bed. He had something important to tell him. He wanted to tell him to flee, run, get out, go southward again, but then, later on—finally, when he had grown, become a man—to reconquer this, to regain this—this island. This darkness. He waved the lantern weakly but it made no light. Where were all the green fields and the fresh water? Where was a small light to see the big West?

He slipped on something now and went down, the whole glass lantern smashing now where the fragile chimney had smashed before, the kerosene spreading out ahead of small pennants of flame and then licking up the walls, illumining in soft orange the books, the endless row upon row of books; tall books, wide books, thin

18

and fat and leather books, green, red and paper books. The room, the house seemed made of books. Books, stacks of them building new rooms of books within book rooms. The flames eating upward now on books. The man on the floor wanted to tell the boy many many things but all he could say was, "Come back. Come back."

"He seems to have lighted a light."

"Yes, he's lit the light," the other Indian agreed.

"To read those books."

"What books?"

"Just books."

"What for?"

"They say he's a little crazy."

"He's got books of records too. Maybe he lit the light to play them."

"Why?"

"They say he's a little crazy."

"A houseful of books and records in the Indian Country. What's the world coming to?"

"They say he's a little crazy."

"Maybe that's why he took a shot at the white man. Maybe he thought someone was coming to do something about all those books and records."

"Yes. But I've been wondering. I been wondering why he doesn't take a shot at us."

"Why should he take a shot at us? Aren't Indians supposed to be a little crazy too?"

"I mean I fixed that gun for the white man right here in plain sight. He must have seen it." Both Indians dropped off the rock now, down behind the rock where they were out of sight. Now the white man came around the rock.

"The house is on fire!" he hollered. "Here, hold this gun. I suppose somebody's got to go down and try to get him out."

"Why?"

"God, you Indians are lunatics." The white man thrust his gun on them and took off on a long running lope down toward the burning house.

"I wonder what he meant by that?"

"Well, everyone that's different—"

"But our hogans aren't stacked with books and records."

"No, but we're Indians."

"Yes, that's true. We're Indians."

They watched as the white man rapidly approached the house and they both gave a jerk of surprise when he threw open the door and flung himself in. A wide sheet of golden flame leaped out when he opened the door but he went in anyway. Everyone was very strange today.

When the white man went in the front door the Indians noticed something run out the back. It was about the size of a good dog but it ran upright and very fast and soon it had disappeared out of sight over a small rise.

"Maybe we better catch it," the taller Indian said.

"Yes," the other Indian agreed, rising quickly. "It may be all there is left, all we have to prove to ourselves we're not absolutely —anyway, after an absolutely crazy day."

The Indians finally ran it down. They twisted and ran, twisted and ran until, at last, going up a long butte and after losing it and retracing it again and going up and down three arroyos and two mesas, they finally ran it down and carried it all the way to their wagon and put a tarp over it where it would be cool and started up their mules and were off to Canyon de Chelly.

"It's a he and he is black," the taller Indian said. "The man in the house was black so this is a black boy." He touched the tarp as the wagon bumped over a prairie-dog mound.

"Yes. One he is all that's left at the end of a very crazy day."

"We're left."

"Yes, that's true," the shorter Indian said.

"Do you think the white man is left?"

"There are plenty more."

"Yes. But what was it all about?"

"Haven't you seen a movie at the trader's? This was the same thing."

"You mean it was about nothing?"

"Not exactly. It means something to them."

"We've got to be generous."

20

"And understanding."

"Yes."

"I think this was about water. I think it was important to us before the white man came and the same thing is still the same and everything else is still the same."

"It's weird." He used the Spanish words, *"Es sobrenatural."*

"Yes."

"This is still the same," he said, motioning to the rocks and sky and sage around them. "And even this," he said, bending and allowing his hand to run through a wave of orange flame they rode through. "What do they call this flower?"

"Cowboys Delight."

"They call everything by a different name but it's the same thing. And they call everything by a different time but it's the same time. Everything repeats. It would be no different if everything in every language and every time was called Cowboys Delight."

The taller Indian realized that the shorter Indian still oversimplified a very complex thing to appear wise. Nevertheless, there was not much arguing with the idea that if a thing can happen it has happened, that if anything can go wrong it will, and there's nothing *sobrenatural* about this if you realize that there's a law governing everything, including Indians, and it's called Chance, sometimes God, but, according to this Indian, it might just as well be called Cowboys Delight.

"That makes sense."

"Does their shooting it out back there make sense?"

"No. But maybe it makes sense to them."

"Now that they've taken it from us they'll fight over it with each other?"

"I hope there'll be some war surplus left over for us."

"There is," the Indian said, touching the bulge beneath the tarp.

"And I hope everything takes the pressure off us."

"It will," the Indian called President Taft said, staring away. "It's taken the pressure off us for quite a while now."

"Yes, that's true," the shorter Indian said.

21

The name of the shorter Indian was Walking Across A Small Arroyo, called My Prayer, and the taller Indian was Water Running Underneath The Ground, called President Taft. More important to them, they were going to Canyon de Chelly, but still more important, everything happened on a bright, shining, Western day, a clean, ordinary happy, New Mexico afternoon. Even now, as the bright Indian wagon made its way through the rocks, the whole weird warp of the landscape, the entire gaudy, scintillant pattern of the West was still with them, changing yet unchanged, ending but unended. Recapitulant.

"All very well," Taft said. "But what will happen now to the Circle Heart?"

"What will happen to the Circle Heart should not happen to an Indian."

"The Circle Heart?"

"Yes. The children of the Circle Heart."

They went over a hiding undulation in the rolling sage and rock. They could see the Coyote Pass ahead, and the huge fire behind them became only a lingering pattern against the quiet blue sky.

TWO Two years to the week after the wagoned Indians had trailed through Coyote Pass, after the Circle Heart had trailed through the pass, another man trailed through here going in the opposite direction.

Lemaitre was coming back. The native returns. Now he was a city bronc man. Now he was a city cowboy riding out of the East back to the West. From his high mountain road he looked down at the bright red country below, at the incarnadined earth interset with jewels of green alfalfa, green jewels upon a red plain within the dark mountains round. From his high mountain road, red too, his eye could not separate the red adobe-built northern New Mexico town of Coyote from the valley it was made of. He could only see the yellowish, new wood construction of the rodeo grounds; the maze of fence, corral, and tower, virgin but faded— alien to a bright country.

Lemaitre got back in his car—a powder-blue Chrysler Imperial pulling a regal, air-conditioned horse van done in quiet gold, and small-lettered, in caliph flourish, LEMAITRE. He took one last look at the judges' tower rising below before he slammed the door.

The tower of the judges' stand was built of number-five raw timbers, two by twelves that, according to local wisdom, shrank one inch a year. Since this was only the second year of its life the tower still had ten years to go. The corrals surrounding the judges' tower were built of the same timbers, and out in front of all this was an arena one hundred yards by fifty, enclosed by an eight-foot-high hog-wire fence. Behind this were the pickup trucks and the

Indian wagons, and in front of these, their faces pressed against the hog wire, were the watchers—the cowboys and Indians and Spanish-American farmers, caked already with the red dust, watching the prisoned animals in the corrals around the reddening tower, watching particularly the chutes, the final pens from which the animals and bronc people were shot into the arena.

Near the tower a small boy made for the wire fence. He was dressed in a miniature cowboy outfit and had soft, wide-apart, wild blue eyes the color of the sky. His hat was red and his spurs were handmade from finishing nails. His red belt bore the black brand of the Circle Heart.

The first time Sant had heard of the bronc people he was seven. Now, the first time he saw them, he was seven and a week. He crawled between the Indian wagons and under the fence and watched as the announcing man made the announcement.

There was a hush over everyone, as if a fuse had been lit. The big gate of the chute swung open. There was an explosion, and out shot the rider without the horse. They tried it again; the announcing man made the announcement, a hush fell. There was the explosion, and out shot the horse without the rider.

"In case you, some of you, ain't never been to a rodeo before," the announcing man announced, "they was supposed to come out together. Watch again," he said, and someone behind that barricade must have lighted a third match and after the explosion the horse and rider came out together but only for an instant, only for the half second it took the horse to nucker into the earth and sling the man against the fence. The bronc man attempted wildly to land on his face, failed, and crashed all in a heap next to Sant. Slowly he unwound himself from his own wreckage until he reached a sitting and face-stroking, hard-thinking position.

"Why, the bastard!" he said.

Sant leaned over, inquiring with all the profundity of children into the burning red face of the bronc man, "Is it fun?"

Now the announcing man had something else going—the steer-wrestling contest. It seemed the object in this one was to see who could get killed first. A square steer shot out of the chute and made for the other end of the arena, chased by one of the bronc

24

people on his blue quarter horse. Another bronc man rode on the other side of the steer so that the steer ran down an alley formed by the bronc people. Then one of the bronc men fell on the horns of the steer and wrestled him to earth, tied him up, and walked off proud. The next time it happened it seemed it was the man who was tied up because it was the steer who walked off proud. The bronc people retrieved the man, gathered him up as if he were a sordid, soiled, discarded pile of old cowboy clothes, and threw him, not without tenderness, behind the bull chute. Sant found him there reminiscing to himself of better days and ways.

"Isn't this," the bronc man said, "isn't this a hell of a way to make a living?"

"Is it fun?" Sant insisted.

Sant now climbed the board barricade that surrounded the judges' stand until he could look down at the corral maze below. He walked the fence maze, looking down on calf pen, bull pen, steer pen, horse pen, Brahma pen, cowpen, and, yes, here was a pigpen. Whatever did bronc people do with these?

What they did with these was to put a clutch of pigs in a pickup truck out at one end of the field, then all the horse-mounted men came hell for leather, dismounted, grabbed a greased pig, re-mounted, held the flashing object high, like Montezuma's men the golden mantle, like offerings to the god, the animals flashing and screaming, fighting along the arms, upward to the sun.

Sant could not see from his position above the maze what they did with them finally. Maybe et them, he thought, or put them someplace first and won a prize.

He had now reached the tower where the judges sat, way up in ultimate wisdom. They pulled on their chins and stroked their thighs and squirted down wild brown juice on lesser heads, as wise men will.

Sant slowly twisted and twined his way up the tower by the ladder the timbers formed to the seats of the judges. One of the judges leaned forward with solemn weight and raised a finger. The chute was flung open, the watchers yelled, and out plunged a Brahma bull, twisting to catapult the bronc man on its back. The watchers froze. The judge stroked his elk ring and placed a square

25

of tobacco in his jaw before his ice-blue eyes, narrowed hard in awe, froze too.

"If Arturo Lucero Cipriano de Godoy is determined to get hisself kilt—" one of the Anglo judges said and rubbed his horny hands together in a working gesture and finally relaxed as judges must.

By climbing the boards in back of the judges' stand Sant gained the top, the roof, and he looked out at the new world below, feeling within as small boys do, as Cortez did upon that peak.

"Oh Lord! Stay with him, Arturo Lucero Cipriano de Godoy!" Sant shouted.

Away from the arena, toward the mountain, a plume of dust rose from the scar of road to the east. It was the arrival of Lemaitre, king of the cowboys—of the pulp novels anyhow, one of the judges thought, watching it, expecting it, although no one had had the courage to bill it. No one had had the credulity to believe Suds Lemaitre, his cousin—the cousin of Lemaitre the King, whose plume now feathered in the east.

"He said he might make it up on his way, iffen he had a mind to, on his way to see the president," Suds had told them.

"President of what?" someone asked.

"The United States," Suds said.

"Then why would he stop here?"

"We're kin."

"I see. Then he'll stop here when the only place can afford him is Madison Square Garden, the Cow Palace, and the Court of Something?"

"Saint James, he said," Suds said. "But we're kin."

Sant watched the plume increase to tornado size as the entourage neared. Then the plume of fairy-red dust collapsed as the caravan paused, revealing the powder-blue Chrysler and the horse van.

A loud hush fell over the arena as Lemaitre pulled in and parked his caravan, got out and stretched.

"Cousin!" Suds said. Suds was standing at the end of a long line of pickup trucks and he advanced on Lemaitre as a committee of one.

26

"This way, Cousin," Suds said and he conducted him among the abruptly silenced world—even the animals now—to the board ladder that reached to the judges. Sant watched down as the big winged orange hat mounted toward him. Then the face tilted up to check its progress. The clean, hard, slanting jaw of Lemaitre. Big as an ax, so close Sant could reach out a small monkey hand and touch it. The face of Lemaitre.

"Howdy, Pardner." The voice of Lemaitre.

Sant stared back without speech.

The man bent down, entering the seats of the judges.

The rear end of Lemaitre.

Sant, safe now in the center of the roof where he had retreated, moved a miniature grimed hand over an equally grimed face and whispered secretly, "Howdy, Pardner."

The judges, now feeling judged, stood up and fumbled, embarrassed, for cigarettes and whisky. At last a judge who was selected to judge because he read books and had no friends among the contestants—among anyone—leaned forward in sincere diffidence.

"How, sir—" he said. He stared at the man in the bat-winged orange hat, the two-hundred-dollar alligator boots, and the green phosphorescent shirt that lit up at night and in the daytime too. "How, sir, are you?"

"Right smart," Lemaitre said, and he took the judge's seat, sprawled down into the chair, placed the alligators on the railing, and splayed his jeweled hands, the hands that whipped a thousand broncs, on the rough pine arms of the judge's seat.

"Right nice of you to ask," Lemaitre said.

The crowd now had recovered enough to go off, to explode, to stampede, knock their children together, and toss whisky bottles in the sun. The crowd settled into a rhythmic roar, "Lee Mater Lee Mater Lee Mater!" The gaudy man finally rose from the rough pine seat of the judge, approved of what he saw, bowed in brilliant humility, and sat down with a nod that said that whatever they had been doing before he arrived they could continue to do it now.

Sant could watch the gods without leaning over the edge. The two-by-twelve roof boards had sun-crept apart, so the structure was more a lattice than a roof, and he could look down on the shadow-striped gods with ease through the interstices and hear them, if not understand.

One of the judges who did not read things but was awfully social leaned forward and said to Lemaitre, "Sam Tollerfield wants to get hisself kilt. I hope he's no kin."

"All men are kin," Lemaitre said.

God, the judge who read books thought, our hero's a philosopher too.

Lemaitre's eyes narrowed on a palomino that looked fancy. The palomino knocked down the first barrel in the obstacle contest.

"Yes," another judge said. "Yes. We are all everyone's children."

Lemaitre winced and winced again when the palomino touched the second barrel.

"Now, when you meet a king—" one of the judges said. "Now, you are a man who has met many kings. Now, what do you say when you meet a king?"

"Hello," Lemaitre said.

"Now, I mean, do they talk as we're talking now, say the things we say—presidents and kings?"

"Yes," Lemaitre said.

"Well, but you're kind of a king yourself," another judge said. "King of the cowboys. What would they say if they was to meet ordinary people like us?"

"Hello," Lemaitre said.

"I mean if they was to meet us the second time—we'd already had this conversation and they was to meet us the second time—what would they say?"

"Hello again," Lemaitre said.

"What we're getting at," the tallest judge said, "is you mean that if you met us again—" Lemaitre was trying to follow the palomino. "If you was to meet us again all you'd say was hello again? You'd treat us like dirt?"

"Yes, yes," Lemaitre said. "Anything."

Sant retired from his crack to the middle of the roof self-

28

consciously and scratched his ear. They should show more respect for Lemaitre.

Now Sant watched the horses that were swimming in the tight corral below. They had whipped up a circular motion and flowed loose, intertwined and clockwise, without touching the boards, the crimson dirt fluid and spraying out, redding the judges' stand, with a stud's mouth sharklike leaping out and up toward the blue sky, then falling back into the pool of red and flowing horses, as if a fish had been wounded and turned the water thus, the horses churning, still-white teeth snapping and bright in the overwhelming sun, the quiet, whipped dust settling upon Sant from the vortex beneath his feet, his eyes trying to count and failing. Now he selected a white mare and lost her as she was dyed the same pink in the mad, churning, deep aquarium of horses.

"Zowee!" Sant said.

And now the announcing man, whose name, STACEY, was written on his shirt, announced that his father had driven a stage through this country way back when times were desper-*ate*—a stage without wheels, without any wheels, folks. And how was it held up, folks? Well, it was held up by bandits.

"Now," a judge said, "wouldn't Stace go over big in New York City, New York?"

"In New York City, New York. Yes," Lemaitre said.

Sant watched, below, some gaudy-rigged cowboys beginning to work on the killer. The killer horse was not in the aquarium with the other horses but prisoned in a heavy cell of logs that fitted him exactly. They had brought him off the mountain yesterday with seven ropes and twelve horses. He had never been ridden. Rumor had it he had killed five men. Actually he had killed one and crippled another. The killer had been brought off the mountain once before, last year, to sell to a city rodeo, but the city man, the buyer, said, "Hell, that's not a horse, it's an electric chair. It would be an execution, not a bronc ride. Keep the down payment and wait till my truck gets five miles away before you turn him loose."

No one knew where the horse came from. He had suddenly appeared on the mountain one day, full, enormous, black. All the people and half the dogs from Coyote had climbed up to see him.

29

The mangled, bloodied remains of an ancient, high-backed Spanish saddle hung downward around his belly, and a man, quickly killed, went toward him with a rope.

On Spanish fiesta days, when the town was lighted with provoking torches for the feast of San Antonio, the killer was sure to come off the mountain and tear through the streets, scattering the pilgrims and sending the dark-robed people retreating back into the church. Caballo de Muerto? Or He Alone Who Was Free? All the people and half the dogs of Coyote wondered.

The crowd at the rodeo knew what was up. The crowd had quietly turned into a mob, no longer going off in individual shouting, whims, and directions but all intent now on helping the men with the ropes and poles and pickups strain and inch the killer into the chute.

"The great Lemaitre will now favor us country folks with a ride," the announcer said flatly and evenly, and he removed his hat.

Sant looked through the cracks. Lemaitre seemed to have collapsed. He seemed to be holding one hand on the other hand to keep it from moving, but only for an instant. Then he placed the bad hand in his pocket to make it behave and with the good hand he reached slowly up to the Bull Durham label drooping from his electric shirt, removed the sack, and made a cigarette with one hand. He blew out a cloud of smoke and removed the bad hand and it seemed good again. He looked, narrow-eyed, down at the mob and nodded his head.

The bright-crested, swearing, pushing men were trying to work the big black forward into the chute. A fenced alley led from his prison to the chute beneath the judges' stand, but he would not go. They prodded and heaved him forward with ropes, squeezing and pulling until they reached parallel posts at four-foot intervals in the alley, then they placed a log through the fence on the forward side of the post, so the big black could not retreat, and then they swore and heaved him to the next post. In this fashion they finally got him to the chute, whereupon he smashed the log they held him with and backed back to his prison, where he waited. They began again, this time with a larger crew, larger log, larger cussing, gayer hats, and this time three men with three horses pulled ropes from out in the arena until the big black was safely chuted; cussed, sweated, pulled, and prodded until the gates at both ends of the chute were sealed.

"Now," one of the judges said, "we are all ready. We can commence as soon as they get this strap tied around his back you can hold on to." The judge paused. "Like as not they'll try us for murder, and yet it was they"—he indicated the mob—"asked for it. Demanded it."

"Listen," the fattest judge said, "I can raise my finger, turn him back. It will be all right with them. They'll all laugh and go home happy. They'll have had their joke." He watched Lemaitre.

Lemaitre was slumped down in the big pine chair in advance of the judges, slumped there between the people and the judges. To catch the eye of the fattest judge he had to roll back his head and look partly upward and into the face of Sant. Their eyes gripped together a full instant. Then Lemaitre leaned far back and caught the judge's eye, hesitated, then said quietly, "No. No, it's all right."

"You think the people care?" another judge said. "They don't care. They'll take their satisfaction either way."

Sant ceased looking down, looked up at the overpowering sky, and scratched his head.

Lemaitre began to roll another cigarette. "Maybe, maybe not," Lemaitre said. "Maybe we got to do what we're expected to do. The horse is ready, expecting me. The people are expecting me." He looked down. "Particularly the horse. To keep the horse waiting—" he fretted the cigarette and placed it in his mouth—"it wouldn't be polite."

Below, the men were trying to get the surcingle around the horse. Sant watched as they slipped the strap through the crack in the boards beneath the horse's furious belly. The man on the other side of the chute reached in, cautiously, deliberately, to intercept the strap. The horse fired out his hoofs like a shot, and the man fell.

"Who fired that shot?" the announcing man demanded. "He'll be all right, folks," he said as they pulled the man beneath the shade of an Indian wagon, waved fans in his face, and applied things to the slow trickle of blood.

31

"Here's the horse what did the shooting, fired that cannon, folks. Well—" the announcing man paused—"let's have a moment's silence in memory." The announcing man sat down, and Sant watched as Lemaitre worked on the bad hand again, held it to keep it from moving, then finally placed it in his pocket, blew out a huge cloud of smoke and waved it away with his good hand, leaned back and winked up at Sant.

Now another volunteer rushed forward, uncoiled a long piece of baling wire, and fished down between the boards and beneath the great horse and speared the strap and passed it up to the man atop the barricade and above the horse. The man above the horse reached over to the other side of the barricade to receive the other end of the strap.

"Folks, he shouldn't have done it," the announcing man announced.

The horse had fired again, rising up in his chute to twice his height. He jackknifed and shot the man clean over two Indian wagons, a pickup, twenty bales of hay, and a Coca-Cola stand. The man landed and bounced twice in the red dust and then, without ceasing his movement—he was running now—he made toward the hills, followed by his wife, an only child, and an old Indian retainer who chased zigzag and kicking like an antelope, as though pursued—all four of them shouting and shouted to, distant and disappearing, hushed at last in the far hills a mile and one half from where the black horse stood contained, recoiled again, and trembling for other victims.

"Well, folks, that wasn't nice." The announcing man paused and watched Lemaitre. "Maybe we shouldn't ask a man with a city reputation to ride a country horse."

The people laughed.

The announcer seemed to be reconsidering, tapping quietly with a stick on the railing in front of him. "No, folks, I mean this. Let's go home, call it off. You've had your fun."

The crowd booed.

"I wash my hands." The announcing man stepped aside and the show seemed over. People began to move toward the trucks and wagons.

32

"One moment." Lemaitre stood where the announcing man had stood. "One moment. We got one more rider." Then Lemaitre began to climb down the judges' stand toward the chute. The crowd paused, not going to their trucks or back to their wagons but hanging there watching.

Sant beat Lemaitre to the chute, swinging down the tower like a monkey. As Lemaitre neared he saw Sant talking to and stroking the head of the horse. When he got to the chute Sant was down there below the horse someplace, disappeared beneath the barricade, beneath the big black, among those hoofs, still talking soothing horse gibberish. Now Sant passed up both ends of the strap to Lemaitre waiting above the horse. With the same movement of taking the strap, Lemaitre grabbed Sant's wrist and gave it, not a pull or even a jerk, but a flip that landed Sant on a pile of hay ten yards away.

"The horse might get bored with your conversation. We don't want to push the luck."

Now the horse gave a high gyrating lunge that shook the stands as Lemaitre tightened the surcingle and Sant regained the barricade. Some other volunteers, too, now crept up to the barricade with advice.

"Don't," they said in chorus.

"Oh," Lemaitre said, looking down on the horse. "It's too late."

What happened next fixed in Sant's mind as a dream, unconcluding till ever. Not till another country, even, or another land, ever. Not even to the big death of Little Sant. Never.

The horse with one great series of furious kicks was toppling the barricade. As the barricade fell, dissolved in huge splinters, the men leaped clear and Sant remained standing in the air. Lemaitre on his way down to gain the horse plucked Sant and, with no leverage to fling him clear, kept him in his right hand and grabbed the surcingle with his left. Together they shot straight upward into the nearing sun, Sant held even farther upward like some trophy, up and up until they seemed to stall at leaving the earth and glide heavy downward and hit to rise up again and again and again, like some wing-broken bird failing above tree height. Now the horse in huge bird fashion laid a serpentine pattern in the sky so that those on the occasional ground on which he hit fled under the trucks and wagons to watch safely the three up there that all came down together in unexpected places. Like an unexpected dream.

The horse now tried the earth, careening like a mad jet, earth-bound, at sudden right angles and with awful breaks to fling the riders over the mountain. But they seemed now part of the horse, even as they left the arena, flew over the fence like Pegasus, and made toward town. The audience emerged to watch the three nailed together tear around through Coyote before threatening them again with their return back over the same fence to make one final flight in the air. Then the horse quit. The dream seemed over.

Lemaitre stepped off, still holding Sant high and precious, as though they were leaving a rocket to the moon. The mob was still stunned, noiseless, as Lemaitre led the horse with a nose hold into the quiet, gold, air-conditioned trailer and bolted the door with a combination lock, placed Sant in the front seat alongside him in the powder-blue Imperial, and drove off. But the dream was still not over.

Lemaitre held the wheel and made a cigarette with the other hand. Then he looked at Sant.

"We won him," he said.

They rode hushed between huge yellow rocks in the red earth, smelling the pure New Mexico air, feeling the huge space around them, sensing a roof now as they entered beneath cottonwoods at the sulphur springs, then passed between the low clay mounds which looked like melting elephants, then emerged finally, climbing and gliding into bright hills the horse had known.

"He'll get used to being a bronc horse," Lemaitre said. "Fed regular every day and such, catered to and primped. He'll get used to the aquarium." Lemaitre paused. "You think he earned his freedom then. You think we should turn him back loose. You think with all the catering and feed and primping there is nothing worse than not freedom." Lemaitre studied the lost cliffs in the pure distance and dropped the twisted Bull Durham stem into the ash box.

Sant stared ahead in childish blankness with his dream. Then he said as though absent, "I was studying—"

"Yes," Lemaitre said. "But first I'm driving you home wherever you live."

"The Circle Heart Ranch, on your way back to Albuquerque."

"Yes, maybe so," Lemaitre said as though listening for another voice. "Yes. I guess maybe that's it. I guess that's the worst there is."

"The Circle Heart?" Sant said.

"No," Lemaitre said, and he stopped the car and got out and fiddled with the combination lock on the trailer, and then there was a great noise, kind of a smooth rushing of wings into the high hills, and then Lemaitre got back in and said, "Not freedom. That's what it was. That's what *I* was studying."

They rode now through the darkening hills in their shared secret, their mutual conspiracy, as though together they had broken jails for strangers. They had released him who had tried to murder them; against justice, against all man-laws of not freedom, they had conspired together and were linked as one in the act.

"That horse, that's what you were studying, isn't it?"

"Not that horse particular," Sant said.

"My card," Lemaitre said, proffering Sant a small paper. "Maybe one day—you never know—maybe one day you'll want to join the bronc people. Look me up. Lemaitre's the name."

"That's what I was studying all the time. Sant's the name," Sant said taking the card.

The car paused in front of the gates marked the "Circle Heart." Sant got out and watched the Imperial caravan pull away down the long road to Albuquerque.

"Sant's the name. Sant Bowman," Sant said.

The boy started down a cow-trail short cut to the main house, the path beaten hard by the passing herds and the punishing sun. Now he entered a grove, a thicket of tamarisk trees and greasewood brush, and came upon a sudden deer. The buck paused, staring in wild disbelief before he turned, and whipped imperiously off. As the buck leaped he flashed his white card of tail. Now the two, shocking each other in sudden encounter, were fled as quickly as they were joined.

As Sant began to enter the house gate his mother came fluttering.

"Where've you been, boy?" Millicent Bowman, always called Millie Sant, was small and sudden in all her movements. "Where've you been?"

"Up there," Sant said, pointing to the tough sun, the clean distant sky.

"Come, boy," she said, still fluttering. "Where you been?"

"Here," Sant said, taking out the small white card and passing it to her. "Up there," he said still pointing. "Up there where I've been telling you. And I've got that paper," he said, watching the card she examined. "I've got that paper to prove it."

THREE **M**illie Sant listened to a wide catalogue of soft music. That is, she had subscribed at one time or another to every religion in the book and some she had made up. The one she liked best, the one she stayed with the longest, was Theosophy.

"Isn't that the same as Christian Science?"

"No, it is not. Theosophy is the one where you face reincarnation in the form of something maybe you et, so it's important to eat nothing but vegetables. Otherwise you might be a cannibal. If you kill an ant even, you might not be, but you just might be, killing your own grandmother. Murder then."

A refinement on this led her to believe, and support with small money, a man who lived, loyally, in Darkest Africa and played loyally on an organ and was kind to the birds and very careful not to tread on ants and had religious qualms about killing cattle. But he did not have qualms about taking Millie's money to repair that organ in Darkest Africa. Millie dropped the loyal African in Darkest Africa with the ultimate realization that her husband made his living selling cattle in Brightest New Mexico. She even wrote a letter to that loyal man in Darkest Africa (which he must have read, bemused, by candlelight between Bach fugues) asking why he drew a line that discriminated against her husband. Millie had her loyalties too. He did not answer. The hell with him.

Millie's husband, Big Sant, watched her now scurrying with all the inside work that has to be done on a cattle ranch in Brightest Northern New Mexico. He believed in cattle. His hobbies were collecting land and butterflies. But Millie was no butterfly. She

37

grew up in the wide country where women swearing was as acceptable as women forming clubs in Albuquerque. Big Sant collected real butterflies and very real land. Big Sant wore the red-flowering brand of second-degree burns, a brilliant splash of color on an otherwise clearly hacked and wind-leathered face. The Circle Heart was run by a branded man.

Millie was all very pretty, from her carved, tiny face to her neat, unruined figure. Her ability to have any more children had been ruined by a disaster on a horse, but it did not show. The thing that showed most in both of them was open ranching—ranching, ranches, and more ranches, way back on both sides since the day the first settlers came.

Big Sant did not think it fair of him to muse, as he had been musing, to be unfair, as perhaps he was being unfair, about Millie's religions. After all, she wanted children, more children, and what's a woman going to do with all that is pent? What was he going to do with all the land he had got? Little Sant? Wrap him up in a huge education. Get him to forget he had been born to the cows. Get him to forget the tragedy of this land by books, a good education. The tragedies of the Greeks. Sophocles, Aeschylus—there must be a good one there. And then modern nuclear physics. Little Sant could study that one. If he himself had had, he thought, watching Millie, the advantages he could give to Little Sant, northern New Mexico might be all as bright as it appeared. Things would be as nice as cowboy stories, where no woman lives and cowboys are as facile as larks and no man grieves and wooden men gallop across a purple page pursued by wooden Indians. Right proud to meet up with you, ma'am. Do you reckon the future will reckon anyone lived here? Do you reckon they will?

Christ, Big Sant thought, wiping a heavy hand over his scar-flowered face. Oh Jesus Almighty Christ.

Zen, Zoroastrianism, I AM, Theosophy and the reincarnation of the living Buddha all passed in formidable pageant against the grim forces of reality. Beef at fourteen cents a pound on the hoof—down twelve cents. Incidence of fatal Blackleg and ticks among the cattle, 3.2—up 1.2. Which meant fifty-two of his cattle dead this year. The calf drop was nine per cent down, which meant the calf crop was off, which meant there were twenty-six less calves born this year than last. All this, according to Big Sant. According to Millie it became unimportant. Anyway the blows were much softer to her when she was supporting with trivial but important sums the reincarnation of the Living God, Krishnamurti. All the tragedy of ranch life became bearable, including the erosion, the deep wide arroyo that ran through the Circle Heart and became wider with each flood. Including her husband's ever need for more land, including the bright, burning bloom of changing hues of purple that got darker each year and extended down to the loin of Big Sant. Including all the forces of death in life. She had her armed pageant.

She had her periods of transition though, when she just swore. Big Sant could always tell when she was changing armies to oppose fate because she just swore. Curses not loud but deep, explicit and exact, genuine coins minted in the Old West and uncounterfeit.

Millie was even now deciding on battalions.

"If I can't have any more kids and if our one kid—" She threw a ball of dough on the board and stared out the window in a reflective gesture to where Little Sant was seated on a hill. "If our one kid does not become something other than a cowboy— A doctor perhaps. Dr. Bowman will see you when he emerges and he will emerge when he is G-o-d-d-a-m-n well ready."

Fresh legions for old foes. She felt better now and slammed the dough, then kneaded it with new courage. New strength from old wells. Old cesspools marshaled to fling in the face of new droughts—a new dying off of half the herd perhaps—the widening of the arroyos—the deepening scar on Big Sant's handsome body. Come what would come, she had new armor.

"Yes," she said, watching out the window at the boy. She had a clean, boyish, handsome profile.

"Yes what, Millie?"

"Yes, I feel better now," Millie said.

Millie looked out the window again at Little Sant standing on a big butte. He was not much more than a speck of color, and if he was doing or saying anything up there, they would never know. They could not see him staring at the house with his hands on his hips, a miniature statue on a pinnacle of sandstone, a monument of reproof, a memorial statue with a small voice.

"Who says I'm not a really cowboy?"

Sant was nine and he wore the cowboy's shirt, the boots and the chaps—shirt, purple, chaps, orange, boots, bright, and spurs scintillant, flashing the New Mexico sun in a sharp glint from his heels. He called out again from atop the pinnacle above his father's Circle Heart Ranch. He had just had a fight with his mother. He had brought home a dog belonging to someone else and she had made him turn it loose.

"Who says I'm not a really cowboy?" He threatened the house again with his high voice from atop the rise.

"I bet I'm a really cowboy!"

The last dog he had brought home was not a sheep dog and his father had said, "What good's a dog if it's not a sheep dog?" and his mother had said, "It belongs to someone else anyway."

Sant now got bored with threatening the ranch house, and anyway nobody paid any attention. The thing to do was to find some kind of treasure and show them all up and things like that. There wasn't any telling what kind of special treasure to get. Something, maybe, like uranium or gold. He knew where there was plenty of gold, but grown-up people called it iron pyrites even after it looked more like gold than gold did. People want to give a different name to things that they don't find their own selves, so that they can keep people from being really cowboys and things like that.

Sant began to look very carefully for things now from his vantage point on the mesa. He saw the juniper that makes good fence posts, the scrub oak that makes poor fence posts but is easier to get, and the sage and lemita that make no kind of fence posts at all. Now he sat down and decided to look for no kind of things at all and just let his father and mother suffer if they wanted to find him. It didn't do any good to look for anything because if you find it they said it wasn't gold anyway or they said it's not a sheep dog and no kind of dog is good if it's not a sheep dog. Anyway they made you turn everything loose. So why bother to make discoveries and find things?

40

"We found something new," a voice behind him said.

Sant knew it was a Navaho Indian speaking and he knew what kind of Navaho Indian it was and he knew his age, not much more than Sant's own. He even knew his name, which was even more than the Indian himself knew. That is, the Indian threw out a lot of names to confuse everybody, so that he didn't know his own name sometimes, which was Afraid Of His Own Horses. And he must be with The Other Indian. That was some name even for an Indian—The Other Indian.

"What did you find new?" Sant said.

The two Indians came around from in back and sat in front of Sant.

"We found something real new," The Other Indian said. "A white boy that's black."

"Yeah. Cheese and baloney," Sant said. "What do you think I am or something? I don't believe that."

The Other Indian seemed to take this pretty calmly. He sat there with his hands across his knees and stared at Sant with liquid dark eyes. His American name was The Other Indian because they had left him unnamed for such a long time and called him simply The Other Indian for such an eternity that they finally settled for The Other Indian permanently.

Afraid Of His Own Horses is an exact translation of an Indian name and it means afraid of his own horses.

"Sure it does," Sant said.

"What?" Afraid Of His Own Horses said.

"I was thinking."

"You go right ahead."

"A man's got to think."

"Sure he does," The Other Indian said.

Navahos believe that they should send the stupidest boys to school and leave the intelligent ones to take care of the sheep. It was a long time before the Anglos found out (the Spanish-Americans knew it all the time) that by the stupidest the Navahos meant the ones who learned English the fastest. According to the Navahos, Afraid Of His Own Horses and The Other Indian were about the

41

stupidest Indians to come along in a lot of moons. They had to go to school.

"Yeah, you sure did," Sant said.

"What's that?"

"I'm thinking."

"But what about what we found?"

"What about what we discovered?"

"Well, I don't exactly trust Indians."

"Neither do we," Afraid Of His Own Horses and The Other Indian both said.

"Neither does me," Sant said, but he had been plenty confused by the Indians. They always did manage to outsmart him. That wasn't because Indians are naturally smarter than whites and things like that, but because (Sant took off his turquoise ring from one finger and put it on another finger; he looked at the new finger now), but because they always had two Indians just against his own self.

"Show him to me," Sant said.

"You got to pay something," The Other Indian said.

"What?"

"Two arrowheads."

Sant took out one arrowhead from his clip-shirt cowboy pocket, spat on it and shined it up with his dirty hand and passed it to Afraid Of His Own Horses. Afraid Of His Own Horses took it and The Other Indian said, "That will be two arrowheads, sir."

"That's all it's worth."

"A white boy that's black?"

"Yeah. That's all it's worth."

"If you give us two we'll count it as a down payment if you buy him."

"I'll give you all my share of the gold."

"That, sir, we've got," The Other Indian said.

"I'll give you my father and my mother."

"That, sir, we've already got two of," Afraid Of His Own Horses said.

"All right," Sant said and he removed another arrowhead

from his clip-front cowboy shirt and without bothering to spit on it or shine it up in any way he handed it to The Other Indian.

"Remember that counts as first payment if I buy."

"Aren't we very nice?" The Other Indian said taking the arrowhead.

"You got both of my arrowheads."

"I still think we're very nice," Afraid Of His Own Horses said. "Who else outside of us two Indians would do this?"

"I guess you're right," Sant said.

"You want to get on the back of my horse and ride there?"

"Where?"

"That's the secret."

"I guess I do," Sant said.

The Other Indian and Afraid Of His Own Horses mounted their horses they had staked in back of a piñon, and Sant jumped on the back of The Other Indian's horse. He didn't have to put his arm around The Other Indian. He didn't have to hold on to an Indian.

"Why don't you Indians get some saddles?"

"Because we're cowboys."

"Well, you look like Indians to me," Sant said. "Where are you taking me to anyway?"

"No, we are not taking you to Anyway," The Other Indian said.

"No, we haven't been there in an awfully long time," Afraid Of His Own Horses said.

"Not that we have anything against the place."

"No."

"It's just that we've decided to take you to Somewhere for a change."

"I think you'll like Somewhere very much," Afraid Of His Own Horses said.

"Anyway is overrun with tourists now," The Other Indian said.

"Somewhere is the only place to go," Afraid Of His Own Horses agreed.

"Oh, Indians are cards," Sant said, annoyed and bracing

himself on the flank of the Indian's piebald horse. "Indians are cards."

"Indians," Afraid Of His Own Horses said, swinging his horse through the rocks, in the lead, "Indians don't like to be run all together. We're Navahos."

"Then Navahos are cards," Sant said.

"No, we're Indians."

"Well, here's where I get off," Sant said.

"Never get on an airplane at all or get off a horse that's moving."

"Is that an Indian saying?"

"Now it is," The Other Indian said.

In the lead, Afraid Of His Own Horses was twirling a rope for no reason at all, but he was also following an arroyo and inspecting the sides carefully for a very good reason. He was looking for a way down that would work. There are many ways down an arroyo in Indian country but there are very few of them that will work. That is, an arroyo is always cutting and there are very few paths down that last very long before they are undercut by flood waters that tear down every time it rains. Sometimes you get halfway down a steep, two-hundred-foot, narrow path before you realize, or the horse realizes, it is not safe and you have to get off the horse and try to keep the horse from panicking while you attempt to turn it around on a one-foot path. It is something like trying to maneuver an elephant on a two-by-four. These paths are always started by sheep or cattle on a slope that has begun to stabilize on the angle of repose and to build up protection for itself of greasewood, rabbit brush, and sage. Then the arroyo swing begins to make an S and undercuts all that nature has done to recover, all the cattle have done to get a drink, and it foils this small cowboy and these two Indians from finding their treasure. Another thing about the sides of an arroyo is that horses and cattle will never even start down an arroyo path that is undercut if left to themselves. But if left to themselves horses are obviously quite useless. They might go around in circles or squares but they won't go down in an arroyo, and that is why Afraid Of His Own Horses watched for a path which he thought would be a working path to force the horses down.

After rejecting many he finally turned into one and spurred the horse down followed by The Other Indian and, of course, by Sant, who shared the horse with The Other Indian. Sant had to grapple with The Other Indian now, and the Indian's sun-catching *concha* belt burned his hands as they went down the slope. They went all the way down without any trouble. Here the bottom of the arroyo was fed by springs, and to follow the arroyo they had to keep crossing and recrossing the stream that refused to stay in the center but kept swinging from one side of the bank to the other. Sometimes the horses would refuse the soft sand crossing and the Indians would drop down and pull the horses over. Sant never got off the horse. He sat on the horse and told the Indians how to do things. "The customer's always right," he said.

"Well, supposing the customer got pushed off the horse and got drowned?" The Other Indian said, pulling on the horse and knee deep in water.

"The customer would still be right," Sant said. "Right is right. Of course I might not ever buy the treasure anyway. Particularly if I'm not shown any respect."

"We'll show you plenty of everything," Afraid Of His Own Horses said.

They were all on the horses now as they began to wind up out of the arroyo. The lead Indian had on a straw orange cowboy hat above a paint horse. Sant wore his purple cowboy shirt, and The Other Indian had yellow chaps, so that, at a distance, they seemed a flamboyant bouquet, a slow-moving riot of color, strange and tropic, moving through the dry sage to the hills.

"I can't make too great a trip at this time of year," Sant said. "You wouldn't be taking me to New York City, New York?"

"Is that in Indian Country?" the lead Indian said.

"No," Sant said. "The Indians sold it off."

"What do they grow there now?"

"Very tall buildings, I understand," Sant said.

"If you got plenty of water you can do anything," the lead Indian said.

"And the wit and the will and the wisdom," Sant said.

"What's that?"

"Well, it's what you learn at school."

"Well then maybe it's a good thing we never showed up. Can you eat it?"

"No, and you can't ride it," Sant said.

"Well then maybe it's a good thing we never showed up."

"Will you take me to New York or not?"

"No."

"What's the matter with New York?"

"Do you like it?"

"No. I just asked what's the matter with it?"

"Do we have to put up with this for just money?" The Other Indian said.

They were out of the arroyo and had moved across the chico and rabbit-brush country and were well into the piñon when Sant began to sense that the Indians were lost. If you have never seen a lost Indian, remember that very few have. Even these special Indians may never have been lost before. It had probably happened because the lead Indian had been thinking of other things. Of course he blamed it on Sant, the fact that Sant kept bringing things up, but the Indians had kept bringing things up, too, and thinking of other things besides where they were going. Maybe they had stayed down in the blind arroyo too long, maybe not stayed down long enough. Anyway down there you can't see where you are going and when you should come up. But maybe it was because the lead Indian was not much of a lead Indian today. When you are trying to sell something at a high price you don't remember where you are.

"Do you remember where you are?" Sant said.

"I know where I'm going," Afraid Of His Own Horses said.

"But do you remember where you are?" Sant said again.

"But we know where we're going," The Other Indian said.

"But if you don't remember where you are how are you going to get to where you're going?"

The lead Indian stopped his horse. "Is that what they teach you in school?"

46

"Yes. Part of it," Sant said.

"Then it's a good thing we never showed up," The Other Indian said.

"Well, it's common sense as well," Sant said.

"How did you get all those wells in there?" The Other Indian said.

"It's because," Sant said, "I was using a preterit pluperfect clause."

Afraid Of His Own Horses looked up into the pine country and scratched his head.

"You know," he said carefully, "the boy is absolutely right."

"Well, I was only guessing," Sant said.

"Yes, you are absolutely right," Afraid Of His Own Horses said. "We are lost."

"I was only guessing," Sant said. "It is nice of you to admit it."

"Oh, forget I ever mentioned it," Afraid Of His Own Horses said. "I'm just a nice Indian."

"A lost Indian," Sant said.

"Oh, I'm that too. I'm a little of everything," Afraid Of His Own Horses said.

"Maybe if you could tell me what he looks like I could find him—find what we're looking for," Sant said.

The Other Indian looked over at Afraid Of His Own Horses.

"I'd say," Afraid Of His Own Horses said, "he looks particular."

"You mean peculiar," Sant said.

"Yes. A little like that."

"Something like that," The Other Indian said.

"Well, how does he sound?"

"Like this," The Other Indian said. " 'My name is Alastair Benjamin. I presume you are red men.' "

"Well, that's particular all right."

"That's what we been telling you all along," Afraid Of His Own Horses said.

"Yes. What is presume?" The Other Indian said.

"That's both particular and peculiar," Sant said.

47

"Yes, I don't know what it is either," Afraid Of His Own Horses said.

They walked their horses around for a while in great circles, the Indians looking off in all directions but never coming up with anything except comments on the weather, the very low price of wool, and why the sun gets out of the way in the night. This was nothing original, they were both quoting their fathers and it had nothing at all to do with the treasure they were supposed to be looking for, on which Sant had already paid half.

"Listen," Sant said. "Why don't we scatter the way cowboys and Indians do in the movies. We'll cover more country that way. I'll meet you up there at that big white boulder."

"Where do they scatter to in the movies?"

"Just anyplace."

"Well, we know where that is."

Sant slid off the horse. "Well, I'll see you," he said.

After Sant had gone a way he turned to watch the Indians gallop off in all directions.

When Sant got up to the big white volcanic boulder he sat on top of it a while thinking, his shirt a sharp glint of purple, a bright jewel set in a dazzling rock. Looking out over Indian Country he could see Arizona and if he had been higher on the mountain he could have seen Colorado. Two hundred miles in each direction, that is how clean the air is in Indian Country. He could see Cabezon not too far away and all the other cores of the volcanoes that had helped to make this mountain and he could feel the fast wind in his face that was helping to make this part of the mountain disappear. He could feel and especially see an awful lot of things from here but he could see even no hint or suspicion at all of what he was searching for. He could spot some sheep way out there in the purple-blue haze and some hogans, because he knew how to look for them, and he could spot his own ranch house because of the sudden violent green of the cottonwoods that went around it. But he could spot no speck of anything black. That is a color that never appears in Indian Country. There are all kinds of colors but not that. In Indian Country black is rare, exotic, prized.

Sant slid down now off the rock and wandered, searching,

48

into the piñon and juniper forest. Piñon grows straight and short, a stalk of pine in miniature. The juniper twists and turns nowhere, shooting out branches in grotesque attitudes, attempting to fight for space with the overreaching pine that crowds in. Sant walked through this short, dense, dry jungle, stopping suddenly after ten paces to listen and catching only the high, sharp cedar smell of the juniper and the very far-off, distant caw of an unhappy bird. Now he stepped abruptly into an absolutely circular clearing, man-made over a thousand years ago by some pre-Pueblo, basket-making wanderers who always built by digging circular holes thirty feet across and three feet deep with a high center post and thatch over this, now long since rotted. But the circle of earth is so beaten down it is never receptive to trees again. Sant walked to the center of the gently sunken clearing and stood there with hands on hips and studied the tight crowd of trees that pressed around.

"Who says I'm not a really cowboy?"

The crowd of trees made an excellent audience so Sant tried again.

"Who says I'm not a really cowboy?"

"Me."

Sant saw that from nowhere had come someone who stood quietly there in the juniper jungle, a miniature man of very coal black, dressed in rags and pieces, the whites of his eyes immediate and demanding from the quiet shade of the forest. He stood there as though he belonged, as though he were part of it, part of something distant and enduring and native there before the white man, before any man came. And yet there was something comic, too, in this ragbag of color he wore which seemed to belie, seemed to give an audacity, to the somber crowd of forest through which he had pushed to the fore. Now he waited patiently and, despite his size, almost majestically beneath the juniper jungle. He finally made a quick gesture, as though to speak for all, then he started to move into the clearing, extending a small black hand from out of his rags.

"I presume," he said, and there was a sudden flash of white from the mouth of the dark face, "I presume you are searching for me."

49

"I presume," Sant said. He did not know what this meant. He had bigger words for later, when he had time to think, but meanwhile he would not be caught off guard. "I presume," Sant said.

"My name is Alastair Benjamin," the small, dark, gay-clad figure said. "I sent two natives to search, to find me another—another white. I sent out two Indians to look."

"Oh?"

"Yes. They are very reliable, alert, not presuming, active—I am in need of food. I will sell them. Will you buy them?"

"I presume," Sant said.

"Then give me anything, something. They're yours."

"I presume no," Sant said.

"Oh," the dark, tattered miniature that called himself Alastair Benjamin said. He said it suddenly, "Oh," as though he had been bitten. Then he sat down and began to rub his huge almond eyes, and Sant realized that he was crying.

Sant looked around at the forest for some kind of idea. Some kind of big word maybe that, used well, would make the raggedy stranger feel better.

"I remit to say that I am king of the Indians," Sant said. That didn't seem to stop the raggedy stranger from crying so Sant thought he would try one of the stranger's own words.

"I presume to be willing."

That didn't work either so he looked around at the forest and said, "I'm a really cowboy."

That seemed to work better. The stranger almost stopped crying and said, "That's why I ran away, why I came up here, because that's what I am too."

"Well, the first presume we got to do is to eat," Sant said.

That did something. The sobbing finally came to a gentle halt and Alastair Benjamin stood up.

"Maybe we can become partners," he said.

"Partners?"

"Yes. Don't cowboys have partners?"

"Yes, they do," Sant said and he stuck out his hand, and Alastair Benjamin took it and the forest seemed to press, lean forward a little to get a better look.

50

Farther down the slope the two Indians who had scattered were working the badlands, those deep, eroded clay formations with alleys and sudden towering castles in the clouds like a huge undiscovered city. They searched this bright magic maze of legerdemain until they were certain there was no Alastair Benjamin there, then they went back to the rendezvous and from there tracked Sant to the clearing in the forest.

They both slid off their horses, and Afraid Of His Own Horses said, "Well, I see you found him first."

"I presume," Sant said.

"Yes," Alastair Benjamin said. "And I've decided not to sell you at all."

"Sell us?" The Indians looked at each other.

"Yes," Alastair Benjamin said. "I've decided we should all become partners."

"Partners?"

"Yes," Alastair Benjamin said.

"Indians don't have partners," The Other Indian said.

"That's how much you know about Indians," Sant said.

"Well," Alastair Benjamin said, "then we can become enemies."

"We always have been enemies," Sant said. "That's how much you know about cowboys and Indians."

"Yes, that's how much he knows about cowboys and Indians," The Other Indian said.

"I know enough to know that we can't be good enemies," Alastair Benjamin said, "if you got all the horses and we haven't got none."

"You know," Sant said, "he's right, I presume."

"He could be right, I presume," Afraid Of His Own Horses said.

"Then if the other Indian will get on the back of your horse—" Alastair Benjamin said to Afraid Of His Own Horses.

The Other Indian did this, and Sant and Alastair Benjamin crawled on the vacant horse and rode off, leaving the two Indians in the middle of the clearing.

"I wonder how he knew your name," Afraid Of His Own Horses said.

"I don't know," The Other Indian said. "But I think he's got us all presuming too damn much. Where did they go?"

"Oh, they're gone now."

"With my horse."

"I presume," Afraid Of His Own Horses said.

Sant and Alastair Benjamin rode down, hidden, through the long mountain forest, then appeared, visible in the scrub oak, until finally they entered the chest-high sage—a study in grand color on a paint horse.

"Where are you from?" Sant said.

"From the Amenoy Orphanage in Albuquerque," Alastair Benjamin said.

"What's an orphanage?"

"That's a place."

"What kind of a place?"

"Well, it's a place where rich people's kin go."

"And you don't mind associating with me?"

"No. Hardly at all," Alastair Benjamin said.

"Is that the way rich people dress—the way you dress?"

"They dress every kind of a way," Alastair Benjamin said. "That's how you can tell they're rich."

"How does it feel to be rich?"

"It feels okay when you eat," Alastair Benjamin said.

They took the short cut back through the badlands, that other world on earth. You always go down into badlands and then, when you look up, you are hit with another world, a world of battlements and gay cathedrals in the sun—nature bizarre, nature weird, nature at its brilliant best. A gallery, a museum unseen, where you always go down, a city in the southwest, a cellar in the sun.

"An orphanage," Sant said. "Do you have to have a lot of rich kin people to be at a place like that?"

"Yes."

"Is it good, a place like that?"

"They say it is."

52

"Why did you leave a place like that?"

"Because I run away."

"Why did you run away from a place like that?"

"Because I want to be a cowboy."

Sant was neck-reining the great paint horse through the secret way home, the marked labyrinths of the badlands.

"I'm a really cowboy," Sant said.

"I could have told you that the second I saw you," Alastair Benjamin said.

"Then why didn't you?"

"Because I thought you had already presumed it."

"Well, it's always nice to have it presumed out loud by some-body new," Sant said.

"Yeah, I guess it is," Alastair Benjamin said.

Sant was beginning to thread the paint horse now up out of the painted badlands. Sant turned halfway on the horse and faced Alastair Benjamin.

"Why are you black?" Sant said. "You're the first one I ever saw."

"Rich people are black," Alastair Benjamin said.

"Were all your kin people black?"

"I don't know how rich they all were," Alastair Benjamin said. Alastair Benjamin tightened his hold on Sant as they began to go up. "Does a cowboy have to be white? Could he be another color?"

"Sure," Sant said. *"Cómo no?* Why not? With a horse, an Indian, anything, what difference does a color make to a really cowboy?"

Sant felt Alastair Benjamin release his hold, go easy behind him as they climbed the final rise and left the badlands behind them.

"Why were you coming up this way?" Sant said.

"Because this is where I came from."

"Before you were rich?"

"Yeah."

"How do you know this is where you came from?"

"Because I remember they brought me down there by taking

me down alongside this big, long mountain. So that's the way I came back. I just followed the mountain back."

"But whereabouts did you come from alongside the mountain? How did you know where to stop?"

"I remember the earth was red where I came from so I stopped here where the earth began to get a little bit red."

"It's a little bit orange here only."

"Well, that's getting close."

"Yes, I guess it is."

"I kept asking people where the earth was red and they kept pointing up this way."

"Maybe you only wanted to get as far from where you were and become a cowboy."

"Maybe."

"Is that all you remember about the place you were—that the dirt was red?"

"That's all I remember now."

"Maybe you only wanted to get away from all those rich people and become a cowboy."

Alastair drew his hand carefully over his face in thought.

"Yes, maybe. They didn't treat me so good there," Alastair said.

"That's my house," Sant said, pointing to the cottonwoods.

"You mean you got a whole house for just you and your kin people?"

"Yeah. Don't rich people have that?"

"No, they don't," Alastair Benjamin said.

"Cowboys always have it."

"That's why I want to be a cowboy."

Sant made a great circle of the house, always keeping the cup of the hill between the riders and the house. When he had circled the house twice he dismounted in a grove of tamarisk.

"You wait here," Sant said.

"Don't I get to go no farther?" The stranger wiped a dark arm across his face.

"I just don't know," Sant said and he walked off toward the

house, leaving Alastair Benjamin alone on the top of the paint horse hidden in the tamarisk, which is purple in June.

Sant walked into the kitchen that was thick, adobe-walled. It had been calcimined pink; and his mother, in a powder-blue, Sears best house dress, was taking the bread out of the oven. Her face was good, uncalculating, easy, open, and interested.

"Where've you been?" she said.

"Looking."

"Looking for what?"

"Things."

"What did you find?"

"Somebody from an orphanage."

"Do you know what that is, somebody from an orphanage?"

"Yes."

"What is it?"

"Black."

"Well, not always," she said.

"Well, they always got rich kin people then," Sant said.

"Not ever," she said.

"Oh," Sant said. "But can we keep him? All alone I haven't got anyone to be a cowboy with."

"Orphan," she said. She tapped a brown loaf to test it. "Well, that's all right. Black. That's all right, I guess." She walked to the window. "But it's never done," she said. She watched out the window. "Your father has discovered him. He's driving him away, I think. Here comes your father now."

Big Sant looked very tired and he came in and sat heavily in the chair.

"I put the boy in the barn. But we can't take him in, Millie."

"Of course we can't. I know that."

"Of course we can't. But we've got to, Millie."

"Why?"

"He's been beaten, very badly beaten, with a two-by-four across the back. We don't do that to animals. We've got no choice, Millie."

"Well, no, I guess we haven't. But then still—you still better call the authorities. I'll go out and talk to him."

"I've already talked to him."

"That's why I want to talk to him. I want to find out what happened to you. You call the authorities."

"All right," he said.

When she came back, in five minutes, she said, "Well, did you call?"

"The line's not working."

"Well, there's no hurry," she said. "I've got to fix him some clothes."

Big Sant got up now and walked over and sat on the chair Little Sant had just left to go out to the barn. But Big Sant still kept his eyes on Millie Sant.

"He's never been able to keep anything yet. There's nothing he's brought home yet we haven't made him turn loose. And now this. He's certainly not a sheep dog either. He may be absolutely no account at all. Still," he said, "still—" Then he said suddenly, "So he talked you around too?"

"No," she said. "He could never do that. Impossible. It's just that—well, it's simply that, well—" She was tossing around Little Sant's clothes now, holding things up to the light to examine them, to find something that would fit. "Well," she said, "you know what he's like."

"Yes," Big Sant said, placing his cowboy boots on the table and staring at the ceiling. "By now, after seeing, talking with him, we all, everyone knows, I presume."

Big Sant was silent a long moment, watching out the window.

"I wonder if it could be the boy."

"What boy?"

"There were some Indians who said there was a boy in that cabin." Sant stroked the broad purple flower on his face.

Millie jerked her head suddenly toward him as if to swear but then, just as abruptly, her expression became calm and beatific.

"Om mani padme hum. Oh the flower in the heart of the lotus, Amen."

"Amen," Big Sant said.

FOUR T here was never a place or time when time was not involved. It had just fled by—three years. Time had cut deeper the huge arroyo through the center of the Circle Heart. It had caused Millie to accept and reject the idea three times (now it was rejected) that Alastair might have been sent to them as the Living Prophet. Time had not cut the arroyo, though, as much as in former years and Alastair had only been rejected as divine the more he filled her earthly yearnings.

And there was always the brilliant land, the wide country, uncharted and unknown, unlike the seas, unplumbed and undiscovered—unsung. The land with island mesas rising from the gray sea of sage and falling away into the long canyons of the night. The land, towered and pinnacled, sculptured by the fine hand of the wind, painted red with iron and green with copper, fired in the sun. Raging in the sun, quiet in the moon.

And the people of this far country: the gentle Indian, the drunken Indian, the begging and the proud and the last Indian, the Indian who will not be here tomorrow, the final Indian. A nation displaced by a baseball team, a V8 with twin pipes, the sixty-four-thousand-dollar question, a strange god, a wad of bubble gum, and you.

And the cowboys. As long as there are cowboys there will be alive the legend and the dream, the frontier, the hardihood and the hardness, the independence and the myth, the iron line to fall back on. And as long as there are cows there will be cowboys. So the secret, and the miracle, of America lies in the bull. Save the bull and save the country. Nurture the legend. Remember Big and Little and Millie Sant, the keepers of the bulls. Remember our triumphs and our tragedies and remember our humor, the coin that makes both bearable.

Remember the Indians. Turn out the lights. Have we forgotten anything?

You will never have forgotten a long day in northern New Mexico. It is not a memory you lose easily. There are all the strange sights and sounds and sudden beauty.

And there are adventures. Nothing like Camelot. Nothing like the Siege of Troy or What is he to Hecuba or Hecuba to him that he should weep for her. But adventures on a high, dry mesa in northern New Mexico. Like this day, today, as Little Sant watched Alastair coming toward him on a white horse—pale horse, dark rider.

Alastair wore a turquoise Navaho bracelet that matched the New Mexican sky and now, as he dismounted, the crude silver caught the sun and glared.

"You're nonchalant," Alastair said. "What you cogitating?"

"Cogitating?" Sant said. "I've been practicing roping and bulldozing all morning. Is that what's called cogitating?"

"What you got?" Alastair said.

"This," Sant said and he took out a dead lizard.

"You had that last week. What else you got?"

"I got this." Sant took out the card with the name of Lemaitre that had cellophane pasted on both sides of it. "The cellophane is to preserve it," Sant said.

"I seen it," Alastair said but touching it with his finger.

"The cellophane is to preserve it," Sant said. "What you got?"

"Information."

"Information about what?"

"Information about an Indian attack on us whites."

They were both huddled now against the old sod front of the house, the section that had been built—mostly dug out of the slope—by Grandfather Bowman. Sant stared at the yellow pickup truck parked near huge sandstone boulders, again yellow, that formed a corral.

58

"But," Alastair said, "I don't know whether exactly if this attack is speculative or manifested."

"Manifested? How manifested?"

"Killing us whites."

Sant knew he must remain nonchalant.

"How is this manifested?"

"You're being very nonchalant," Alastair said.

"How is it being manifested and all?"

"Throwing rocks down on the secret canyon house."

"You told them they could join?"

"They said they don't want to join no white outfit."

"You told them you were, for example, black?"

"Yes, but they can see different. They know, for example, the way I live, speak the language and all. It's hard to fool an Indian."

"You can't fool an Indian, but you can ambush them." Sant reached for a stick of rabbit brush and began to trace in the hard dirt. "When they start tossing rocks down on the secret canyon house you can bet an Indian will be close to his horse. No chance to ambush them. But when they hunt piñon nuts on the Peña Blanca Mesa later in the afternoon you can bet they'll be what you call nonchalant and you can ambush them. And I bet if you didn't read all those books you could speak English."

"What are we going to do with them after we ambush them?"

"Never scalp an Indian before you catch him." Sant got up and began to catch a pinto horse called Temperature 99. He waved the horse with gentle movements into the corral corner and removed a bridle from the side of the barn. He held the bridle behind his back with his right hand as he talked to the horse and slowly eased the bridle over the horse's head, gently.

"Temperature 99 is dangerous," Alastair said.

Sant threw on the double Navaho blanket woven like a United States flag but with only five stars, and then he threw on the Monkey Ward saddle.

"Not if you ambush him," Sant said. Sant tossed the reins of the horse over the hitching post to keep Temperature 99 from nipping back as Sant pulled hard on the belly strap.

"You got to ambush him first," Sant said.

59

Under the floor of the secret canyon house there must have been two tons of gold. The fact that it was not gold bothered no one at all. It looked like gold. Also at the secret canyon they had a secret language to confuse the Indians. The fact that no one else spoke it was of no importance. They spoke it. They spoke some Navaho, too, and plenty of Spanish, as did their neighbors, but Alastair Benjamin spoke no black, only white and this secret language which the Indians knew Alastair had made up out of his own head, which still made Alastair a white. You can't fool an Indian. Everyone was white or Indian, sometimes Spanish, but that was all there was. You couldn't pull another kind of people out of your hat and fool an Indian.

"Which makes us," Alastair Benjamin had said one early morning while shooting a cornsilk cigarette out of Sant's mouth, "the only white people here." He had lowered the gun and touched a very white handkerchief to a coal forehead. "And I just come awful close to my being the only one left."

When they had got the horses swinging easily and together in a nice lope through the mouth of the wide Baca Arroyo and were approaching the narrow neck of Wetherill Canyon, big, towering, orange and clean up to the sky on both sides, Alastair Benjamin looked up at the slit of hard blue above.

"You still going to be a bronc man when you get grown up?"

"I'm grown up."

"I mean when you get paid for being grown up."

"When I get paid for grown up—yes sir!"

"How much will you charge for a bronc show?"

"Forty hundred dollars or so. I don't know."

"Them movie cowboys aren't really cowboys."

"No sir!"

"They shoot sixty shots from a six-shooter."

"Yeah."

"And they ride through brush country without chaps. That would tear a cowboy's clothes all off."

"Yessir."

"They say Tom Mix and Zane Grey were real cowboys."

"That's because they're dead."

60

"Is Zane Grey dead?"

"I think he is."

They were moving deep into the dark canyon now. The bright walls all became gray on the shadow side. They moved easily at the bottom of the long crack that led even deeper into the heart of the wild mountain.

"You take an Indian," Alastair Benjamin said. Alastair Benjamin ran his arm along the neck of his white horse to reassure the animal against the darkness of the canyon. "You take an Indian," Alastair Benjamin repeated, his soft voice knocked back sharp from the close rock. "Why won't an Indian join our outfit?"

"It's a white outfit," Sant said.

"Will the Indians always be our enemies?"

"I guess so."

"Why?"

"Well, what would there be to do for example if they weren't?"

"Yeah."

"Indians are just naturally Indians."

"And there wouldn't be nobody to fight if they weren't. For example, there'd be nothing to do."

"That's right. I wonder what they do in the city, where there are no Indians."

"Nothing I guess."

"Oh they probably do something."

"I guess they do."

Now the canyon began to widen and let in more of the sky, which allowed the rock to resume its varicolors again, still towering but vivid now and visible, shone upon and shining back, greeted and greeting back, all lighted and lighting in pyrotechnic reds to the abrupt sky.

"You like this better?" Alastair Benjamin asked his horse.

Sant began to work his eye along the sheer face of the left canyon wall to pick up the geological fault that, as they rode on, would become wider. It would always remain about two hundred feet up but soon the slipping formation beneath would become a narrow ledge that a man could walk on, then it would become so wide you could set down a house, which the Old People had done before the white man came. Even before the Navahos came. Alastair Benjamin had been the first white man to see it and Sant had been the first to climb up to it. Climbing up to it was quite a trick. The Old People had used handholds and yucca fiber ropes that they pulled up after them at night or when being chased by the people who must have finally caught them.

"There she is," Sant said, pointing. They both pulled in their horses and their eyes followed the great distance up the side of the wall to where the secret house sat on a secret ledge. Actually part of the house was in a natural cave, but even that part had a roof and wall and window openings, and part of the house was a tower like those that the same people had built in the flat open country. In other words, it seemed as though these people didn't give up a style easily. When they built in the cliff they built the same way they had always built. They weren't going to give up something simply because they were hiding.

"Who you think they were hiding from?" Alastair Benjamin said.

Sant looked away from the house and to the top of the cliff two hundred feet above.

"New people, I guess."

"But what did the new people have against these people?"

"They was here."

"That's all?"

"I guess that was plenty," Sant said and he moved his pinto horse down the gentle slope, and Alastair Benjamin followed on his all-white.

After going up a steep path they arrived now at the spot where they made the two-hundred-foot climb straight up the face of the cliff. The Old People had chipped handholds in the flat rock most of the way up but the earth from the bottom of the cliff had eroded down ten feet since then, or they had used their yucca fiber ropes at the bottom. Anyway there were no handholds on the first ten feet of the climb, so it was necessary for Sant to stand tiptoe on the pommel of his saddle to begin his climb. As soon as Sant's weight left the saddle the pinto moved forward and began to graze, and Alastair Benjamin moved his horse in and followed Sant.

They worked their way up and up the flat burning face of the cliff. They could have waited until the sun left the cliff but then it would have been in shadow—more comfortable but more dangerous—much easier then to mistake a weathering on the face for a true handhold. Shadows hide and they deceive too. But, most of all, shadows come before the darkness of a fall. So they sweated and burned upward in the sun, rapidly like quick monkeys against the moving of the sun. Before the dangerous arrival of the shadows on the sheer face, they went upward like quick monkeys moving fast.

"There," Sant said. "Look down there."

Alastair Benjamin turned his head cautiously downward and saw two Indian boys leading away their horses.

"Now, why would they do that?"

"Because we're here," Sant said between his teeth, and clinging.

They reached a ledge soon where they could sit down. Above them the handholds ceased and they would have to use a rope—the lasso that Sant had carried around his neck.

"Yeah," Alastair said, sitting and watching down, "I been cogitating."

"You been thinking too," Little Sant said.

"Yeah," Alastair said watching the Indians move down canyon with their horses. "I been thinking that the universe is not moral, that things fall upon the just and the unjust equally almost."

"That's what my dad says, but Ma doesn't agree."

"Yeah."

"What does it mean?"

"Big Sant says it covers everything," Alastair said.

"Does it cover us ambushers being ambushed?"

"I guess it does."

"What else do you know?"

"We come a fur piece."

"I know where you got that. From the movie cowboys."

"Yeah."

"Like us, they got a secret language too."

"Yeah, I guess they have."

They had reached the point now in the climb where they had to cross a wide fissure in the rocks. It was about ten feet across. When the Old People built the house the crack might not have been there, or they had used the yucca ropes. Anyway now it was a ten-foot gap with almost one hundred feet of nothing beneath to the floor of the canyon. Sant rose, uncoiled his rope, adjusted the loop, and began swinging it around his head. There was not too much room and it was difficult. He kept his eye on a pinnacle of rock twenty feet above. The thing was to lasso this pinnacle, which was part of a formation that, up there, hung over the middle of the void. You lassoed this and then swung over the ten-foot gap. Sant caught the pinnacle on his first try and winked back at Alastair Benjamin.

"Lemaitre," Alastair Benjamin said.

Sant moved to the edge of the gap now, pulling in the loose rope and coiling it around his wrist.

"Okay," Sant said. "Shove me off."

Alastair Benjamin moved in behind him and gave him a push. Sant swung out over the void and when he reached the other ledge he touched it with his foot and pushed back hard with his leg. Back he came across the gap almost into the arms of Alastair Benjamin. Alastair Benjamin gave him another push, sending him again out over space, and this time he had enough momentum to drop off on the other side. He held the rope. He made a coil of the loose rope now and shot it back to Alastair Benjamin. Alastair Benjamin caught the rope and advanced to the edge of the big drop, coiling the slack rope and tensing himself to jump.

"Be nonchalant," Sant shouted.

Alastair Benjamin wiped the sweat off his forehead and said, "I'm coming." Then he came. Sant was ready for him and shot him back across the gap. The second time he came back he still did not think he had the momentum to land safely.

"Again," he said, and Sant gave him another shove out over space. "Again," Alastair Benjamin said when he came back.

"Land this time," Sant said.

"Landing," Alastair Benjamin said and he landed on top of Sant and they both went down.

"There," Sant said from the scramble and looking down below. "There go the Indians with our horses."

"The ambushers been ambushed," Alastair Benjamin said.

"The bushwhackers been bushwhacked," Sant agreed.

"We can't go back down."

"So we got to go up."

"Who was it stole our horses, can you see?"

"Indians."

"But what Indians?"

"Bad Indians."

"But what's their names?"

"Including the middle name their names is Awful Bad Indians."

"I think one of them is Afraid Of His Own Horses. He's wearing a red baseball cap this season."

"And instead of stealing second an Indian steals horses."

"That's not a very good joke, Santo."

Sant looked up at the cliff above and back down the void where they had come. "I guess it's not too funny," Sant said.

"Afraid Of His Own Horses always hangs out with The Other Indian."

"The Other Indian's a pretty good guy. Are you saying he'd try to break up our outfit?"

"Yeah."

"Yeah, I guess he would all right."

"Shall we get started up?"

"Yeah, I guess we better get started up."

The old handholds resumed again now and Alastair Benjamin went first. They had left the lasso rope dangling. They would retrieve it when they reached the pinnacle twenty feet above.

"I got a feeling," Alastair Benjamin said, "that the shadows are coming on."

"Keep going, Alley," Sant said.

"I don't know whether the next one's a handhold or not."

"Keep moving, Alley."

Well, that one was.

"They've got to be. We can't back, we've come too far and

we can't get caught on the face now. We would be lost in five minutes. The only way now is up."

"I don't know—what do you think about this next one?"

"Just keep moving, Alley."

The next one was okay, but what now?

"Just up, Alley. Always up. We stop and it's all over."

"I think I'll rest."

"You can't rest here, Alley."

"You should have gone first again."

"I can't pass you now, Alley."

"I guess I'm finished, Santo. My hands have gone dead."

Sant looked at his own hands and realized he could not feel them or control them at all.

"Alley?"

"Yes, Santo?"

Sant was quiet long moments and then he said from the now-lengthening shadows, "Alley, I've got hold of a mountain mahogany bush. I've moved over to the right and have got hold of a mountain bush. If you keep moving up I can see the handholds get much larger. If you fall you'll just land in the bush. Get started up, Alley."

He heard Alley move up above him in the shadows. He could not move himself; he would have to hang here and think of another trick to get himself moving, but he could think of nothing, only feel the pain in his deadening arms.

What does a bronc man do? What does a real bronc man do?

Now he felt something brush his face. It was a rope. A bronc man has friends in high places.

Above, when Alastair Benjamin had made it over the ledge, he got the rope and dropped it down to Sant. Now he gave the final heave that pulled Sant up on the ledge too.

"Not that you needed any help," Alastair Benjamin said.

"No. I was okay," Sant said.

They sat a long time resting and recovering and finally trying to capsulize all the wisdom of the ages into one good sentence that might last. The best they could do was: In this country it never rains in June and almost never in August with the exception, any-

66

way as far as last August is concerned, of last year and maybe the year before that. They couldn't remember.

"Anyway, Santo," Alastair Benjamin said standing, "let's get moving."

"*Cómo no?*" Sant said. "Why not?"

It was easy going now along the wide ledge that ran to the cliff house. When they got to the cliff house the first thing they did was go in and see if the gold was okay—iron pyrites they had dug off the side of the ledge that looked more like gold than gold did.

"The gold is okay, Santo," Alastair said.

"Yeah," Sant said, running his hands through it. "It sure is handy to have a lot of gold if you ever want to run away or something."

"Yeah," Alastair said. "Like the trader, Mr. Peersall, says, it sure gives you a lot of mobility."

"What does that mean?"

"It covers about everything, I guess."

"I bet it does. I bet gold covers about everything, I guess. Alley, let's speak our secret language."

They spoke the secret language now, the one that Alastair had invented.

"Santo," Alastair said finally in English. "Let's get out of here."

"Yeah, but how?"

"The easy way."

"You want to take the easy way?"

"Don't you think we've had enough of the hard way for one day?"

"Yeah, I guess we have."

First they checked the house thoroughly to make sure that everything was okay. The house was divided into apartments with woven willow reeds over cedar logs for the roofs. To get from one apartment to the next you had to go through the low doors in a stooping position, so the Old People could dispose of you quickly if you didn't belong. Also you always had to go through another apartment to get to your own, which must have made for interesting living. The whole thing was built in about the tenth century, when the Old People had been pressured off the flat country to down here in the middle of cliffs to make a final stand. There was a cesspool-like hole in the front of the building, called a kiva, where the religious rites were held and restricted to men. They must have gathered down there every evening to ask for something they thought important, but the New People finally got everything anyway.

"They sure built nice buildings," Alastair Benjamin said, staring up at it.

The house was made of flat rectangular stones the Old People had gathered above on the top of the mesa and lowered down here. They were mortared with adobe, but the fact that they were worked perfectly and fitted exactly accounted for the building still standing after one thousand years. Around the building were scattered large pieces of pottery with abstract colored pictures, painted with freedom, which signified nothing except maybe that a thing called art is a deeper part of us than we suspect.

"Well, I guess we better get moving before we get attacked."

Alastair Benjamin allowed his eye to climb above the shallow cave where the building lay and to go all the way up, which was about another twenty feet, to the top of the cliff.

"You think they're going to attack us from up there?"

"Well, you know Indians."

"Yeah."

"Indians never miss a chance."

"Why are Indians that way?"

"Because they're Indians."

"It's not because we're white men?"

"Oh, it's that all right."

"Before you said it's because we're here."

"Well, I guess it's a little of both, but we better get started up."

They followed the ledge until a deer path branched off that led quickly to the top of the mesa—that is, it always had. Now they came to a cutback and the path was gone.

"Indians," Sant said.

"Yeah."

Here the sandy bank was very steep and below fell off abruptly at the stone cliff. The sharp, small hard feet of deer had begun, and maintained by continuous use, a path here; but now someone with a sharp instrument had destroyed it, and to try to walk it would send you sliding and then falling to the canyon floor three hundred feet below.

"Indians."

"Well, I guess we better get started back down."

"Yeah."

When they got back to the Old People's building they sat down next to the hole where the men who lived there used to think, and that's what they did too.

"I wonder," Alastair Benjamin said, "what the women did while the men thought."

"Made these pots," Sant said.

"I guess so. Have you thought of anything yet?"

"Yeah," Sant said. "From here we got to throw a lasso over the top and climb up that way."

"We've done it before."

"But not with Indians up there."

"That's true."

"You think when we got started up they would unhook the lasso?"

"Well, you know Indians as well as I do."

"I'm afraid I do."

Alastair Benjamin looked all the way to the top, shading his eyes. "What makes you think the Indians are up there?"

Sant thought a while and then he said, "Well, I know Indians. I may not know nothing else but I think by this time I should know a little about Indians."

Alastair Benjamin rubbed his nose and tried to think of an interesting way he could contradict Sant. And then a rock fell.

"I guess you do," he said.

They retreated back into the part of the cave that overhung the building but the rocks continued to rain down anyway.

"Just to show us they're there," Sant said. "Just to show us how smart an Indian is. And an Indian's awful smart."

69

"If they was smart they'd pretend they weren't there and when we started up they'd unhook our lasso."

"Well, an Indian ain't that smart."

"I wonder if this is the way they killed off the people that lived here."

"Maybe not killed them. Maybe just got them out of here. This same kind of pots"—Sant touched a pile with his foot—"I've seen at the pueblos where people live right now."

"But why didn't they kill them all off before they got away?"

"I just don't know."

"You mean you don't know everything, Santo?"

"Yeah. Not everything, I guess I don't."

"Now the rocks have stopped raining. You think they gave up?"

"Yeah. The Indians don't stay with an attack very long."

"You sure it's safe now to throw up the lasso?"

"Yeah," Sant said, uncoiling the rope. "Maybe I don't know everything but I should know Indians by now."

"I hope you do," Alastair Benjamin said.

Above, the two Indian boys sat near four horses under some piñon scrub, waiting for the rope to come up. They were giggling. Sant's mother had said that Indians, especially Navahos, were the gigglingest people she had ever met.

"You think they'll be fools enough to throw up that rope?"

"Well," The Other Indian said, "if they don't I don't know my whites. And if I don't know my whites I don't know anything."

"Well," Afraid Of His Own Horses said, "there is a bunch who claim you don't know any—" A rope landed near them. "And another bunch who claims you do."

Before they could grab the rope and make the boys below think they had caught something solid the rope was dragged below again.

"You want me to try this time?" Alastair Benjamin said.

"Yeah. Okay. Try to make her land flat and hook one of those tree stumps we've seen up there."

Alastair Benjamin whirled the rope twelve times around his head before he let her fly.

70

"That puts mojo on it," he said, but it didn't do any good. The rope fell back.

"This way," Sant said, twirling and pumping the loop with a snap. "Like Lemaitre. It puts style into it." He flung the loop with quick grace. "Style," Sant said.

Now he pulled the slack in and the rope went taut.

"I think I've caught something solid," he said. "You want to feel?"

Alastair took the rope and pulled. "It's okay."

"You sure we haven't caught an Indian?"

"Yeah."

"How can you be sure?"

"By the feel."

"How does an Indian feel?"

"With his hands."

"Boy, you're in lousy shape today. I better go first."

Sant took a good grip on the rope, and The Other Indian above dropped the loop on the saddle horn of the horse they had stolen below.

"Something happened," Sant said.

"Yeah, you lost your nerve."

"No, something happened."

"Yeah, you lost your nerve."

"All right," Sant said and he started up. When he got up a way, Alastair Benjamin started up too. Sant turned his head and looked back.

"Don't you feel it's kind of giving?"

"Yeah. Like the tree is bending."

"It feels funny."

"You sure we didn't catch an Indian?"

"Pretty sure."

"Now it's only pretty sure."

"Well, as sure as a man can be. Anyway it's something bigger than an Indian."

"Is it bigger than the both of us?"

"It's funnier than you," Sant said and he began to climb again rapidly now to get it over with.

71

Above, Afraid Of His Own Horses watched the stolen horse brace himself.

"You think he can hold them?" The Other Indian said.

"That's what we're going to find out."

"Maybe we should back the horse up a bit closer to the edge. Make it more interesting."

"Why not?" The Other Indian said.

Sant looked back down. "The rope seems to be stretching."

"If it don't stretch it breaks. You learned that in school."

"We should have stayed there," Sant said and he climbed hard trying to make up for the stretch.

"Well," Afraid Of His Own Horses said, "we can't back the horse any farther without it going over the edge."

"Is that bad?"

"It sure is. Then we couldn't steal the horse again."

"Then why don't you try running the horse forward?"

"Why didn't I think of that?"

"Well, you're not very smart," The Other Indian said.

"Does it strike you that the rope is getting shorter?" Alastair Benjamin said.

"Yeah," Sant said. "What they say about that in school?"

"Indians. We roped an Indian," Alastair Benjamin said, and they both held on as they flew upward fast.

Sant and Alastair Benjamin ended up all in one heap on top of the mesa alongside the tree that they were trying to rope and beneath two of the "gigglingest people"—even for Navahos—that ever lived.

Sant unwound himself to a sitting position and looked carefully at Afraid Of His Own Horses.

"You crazy Indians. Don't you know you almost—?"

"We didn't though, because—well, because—" Afraid Of His Own Horses looked at The Other Indian.

"Because, why, because," The Other Indian said, "if we did that—"

"Let you fall," Afraid Of His Own Horses said.

"Yes. If we did that there wouldn't be anybody left to fight."

"We had that figured out all the time," Alastair Benjamin said.

Sant looked down on the building of the Old People below and then on down to the far canyon floor beneath, blue with distance. Then he removed his small finger from his nose and examined it.

"Yes, that stopped us a lot of times too," Sant said.

FIVE I ndian Country has still got living a real, live Old Indian Fighter.

"I've lived from the age of the horse to the age of the rocket, from the age of real animals to this age of toys. I've—" Mr. Peersall seemed about to deliver a peroration against missiles, an antimissile missive, but he paused. "I don't want to bore you, son."

"Tell us about the gun-slingers of the Old West," Sant said. "Who had the fastest gun?"

"The silliest gun was had by Billy the Kid, the most ridiculous gun was had by Mr. Hickok. Doc Holliday shot number-seven birdshot from a shotgun—he never missed. Mr. Earp lived in Hollywood, died in Frisco. That should finish him. They got those guns now, all of them, preserved in a museum, guns that were never fired, owned by people who didn't exist. Why, they're trying to make heroes out of people claiming they shot themselves into history. They was only, most of the time, trying to shoot their way out of a whorehouse without paying the fee."

"What's that?"

"A place where Navvyhos buy tobacco."

"Oh?"

"Yes. I guess there was only one hero."

"And that was you, Mr. Peersall."

"How did you know, son? Yes, I was the only hero. I was the only hero because I had the only kind of courage that counts. When the Texans in Tularosa wanted to throw all the Mexican kids out of school to protect the white children's pure Texas asses I said

I was a Mexican and would be studying in first grade for a while myself and I would try to see that none of us got bothered. Moral courage. Nothing happened. Moral courage is the only kind that counts. Remember that, and remember, Sant, always hold your hands lightly when you ride, back straight, but always forward. Control the horse with your legs. If you're not part of the horse you're not riding."

"I'll remember, Mr. Peersall," Sant said.

Alastair seemed bored. Every time they went to see Mr. Peersall he was bored. Mr. Peersall never talked about books.

Mr. Peersall claimed that maybe you can get attached to things outside of books—the world. And you can get attached to things that have nothing to do with the world—Indian Country. On Jupiter they say it's so big people can't see each other—never meet up with each other. On Mars it's somewhat different. There are no people to bother you at all on Mars, and you can walk freely about saying and doing pretty much as you please. This is what Mr. Peersall, who ran the trading post and who was actually so old he had fought Indians, said the day before yesterday. This was all apropos of why he stayed in Indian Country since almost infinity—because he couldn't get to Mars, he said.

"Haven't got the time, the money, or the experience, son."

The "son" he had been talking to was Millie Sant. But the old Indian fighter was old and tired and his eyes were bad and he lied a lot because people made him and that's why he called Millie "son." He called people all sorts of odd things. And he threatened the "Navvyhos" still, which the Indians found droll. Alastair anyway said the Indians found it droll. Little Sant found it trying. Big Sant found that he spent all of his time with the cattle and did not have too much time to think about anything much. He brooded down there, Millie said. He brooded darkly, too much.

Up on the vast Martian spaces of the mesa, gay-colored horses moved rapidly, skimming across the wide, flat mesa so that at a distance they seemed borne in the dust they created, seemed part of the heavy white clouds and even the blue beyond. Close they were a roar—four plunging horses tearing the mesa in attitudes of blind speed, splitting the awful silence up there, with jacks jumping up ahead and the buzzards tightening their circles above in anticipation of something happening there below, on a weird, dry, moon mesa of the planet Earth.

"Nonchalant," Sant said between his teeth. "That's all we need."

Sant, straight, white, and wind-burned, rode out in front followed by Alastair Benjamin, who was followed by a red boy, followed in turn by another Indian, The Other Indian. Sant was close to thirteen now, and the others were about that age except Afraid Of His Own Horses, who was fourteen and a half and who was mad now because no one else would do what he wanted to do.

"Don't you think he's crazy, Alley?" Sant said to Alastair Benjamin, turning on his horse.

"Yeah."

"Seeing someone in a shack counting it and knowing where it's hidden, like in a book."

"Even in a movie," Alastair Benjamin said, "would they be giving the Indians two hundred thousand dollars, even in a movie?"

"Yeah, that's right," Sant said.

"Even in a movie it's an original conception," Alastair Benjamin said.

"And they're being nonchalant."

"Oh, Indians are always nonchalant. That doesn't mean anything. Indians are always nonchalant," Alastair said, and Sant increased the speed of his horse and they all, including the Indians, leaped forward suddenly.

"Nonchalant," Sant repeated again. "That is all we need."

They had gotten their other words from Alastair Benjamin or the radio commercials, but this one, nonchalant, they had gotten from an old sign that an Indian had stolen from Route 66 to make a door for his hogan. His door had read: BE NONCHALANT— LIGHT A MURAD. So that Indian family was always known as Murad. And the boy, the son of the father, Sant and Alastair had captured once throwing rocks at their secret house and they had tied him to a stake and lighted a small fire, scattered by Sant's mother, but not before they had lighted a Murad. And he wasn't very nonchalant, Alastair Benjamin had said.

76

"You think, Santo—" Alastair Benjamin had his blue-dyed straw cowboy hat pulled hard over his forehead so that he could barely see and be seen—"you think they could maybe—our Indians, I mean—you think they could maybe not even have two hundred thousand dollars?"

"Yeah."

"But if they have it and we maybe don't get any of it at all? That is, supposing they just ride off and eat it or something all their selves without us?"

"That's what they'll do if we're anxious. We got to be retiring."

"We sure do."

"We got to pretend like we got more than that. That is, we got to act up to our own gold and all."

"Yeah."

"We got to be very uninterested in two hundred thousand dollars or so. Indians can tell when we whites bite too hard."

"When they got us hooked."

"We got to be indiffident."

"You can say that again."

"We got to be indiffident."

"Okay, that's all. What you think, Santo, you think the Indians are listening?"

Sant lifted his hat and half turned in his saddle and watched the following Indians. One of them, Afraid Of His Own Horses, had on his red baseball cap and a white tie over a blue T shirt. He wore stovepipe cowboy boots with white eagles in inlaid leather. He was quite an Indian. The Other Indian was dressed identically except he wore a yellow straw cowboy hat with a high roll and he had no tie on at all. The Other Indian was some Indian too. Both of the Indians rode bareback and rode very well.

"Well," Sant thought out loud to Alastair, "you can't tell about Indians. An Indian could be listening or not listening and no man could say amen."

"Amen."

"An Indian could be dead or alive, breathing or not breathing, fighting or fooling—"

77

"Amen."

"What I mean is we'll both forget about their two hundred thousand dollars."

Alastair Benjamin pulled his blue hat even harder down on his black forehead. "I won't."

"I mean, Alley, we got to pretend to be indiffident."

"Yeah. But you sure you got that indiffident pronounced right?"

"Yeah, I got it right all right."

"Because if that's what we're going to be—"

"I got it right all right. Anyway you know what it means. It means we're not interested in their two hundred thousand dollars."

"You're not."

"Alley, are you with me or with the Indians?"

"Do you want to make it red or white?"

"Yeah."

"Then I'm with us."

"You'll never live to regret it."

"I always have."

"That's not fair."

"Well, you said I'd never live to do something and I said I always have."

"I never thought of it that way."

"Santo, you think there's any danger going with our Indians?"

"Well, if there is my name's not Sant Bowman."

"Well, if it's not Sant Bowman what is it then?" Alastair Benjamin said.

"I don't know, Alley. I just don't know."

"But you don't think we should be worried?"

"Worried? Worried about what? Certainly not whites in front of Indians."

"You mean we shouldn't lose noses?"

"Faces. Or face, I guess it is."

"How about our lives?"

"Well, you've got a point there."

"I didn't want to make a big point of it."

78

"You go right ahead and make as big a point of it as you want."

"Oh, forget I ever mentioned it," Alastair Benjamin said.

"No, you're entitled to your ideas too."

"But not to the aforesaid exclusion of your say."

"Oh, I'll have my say."

"Yes, I guess you will," Alastair Benjamin said.

On the other side of the mesa two men stood on the path that cut through the sagebrush, holding sawed-off shotguns. They were dressed like hunters in plaid woolen shirts and caps and high-top leather woodsmen's boots, but everything was too new and fit too well and the shotguns were sawed off. Three days ago they had robbed a bank in Durango.

"I really don't think the Indians will come back, Mike."

"You think he'll believe that story about us being government men here to distribute this money to the Indians?"

"Well, if you'd been here instead of mailing that Mother's Day card maybe you could have told him something better."

"I never got it mailed. I told you that trading post was closed."

"Then we can forget it."

"No, we can't. The day after tomorrow is Mother's Day."

"And you don't think they'll trace the address?"

"By the time they do that we'll be across the border and into Mexico."

"Why don't you send it from Mexico?"

"Then Mother's Day will be past."

"Did you ever think that of the three guys you murdered they had mothers too?"

"You talk like a cop."

"I only want to talk you out of mailing that letter."

"No. If Mother didn't hear from me on Mother's Day she would go crazy. But I've got an idea. I've been thinking about it. We can run a trip wire from the door of the shack to the trigger of a shotgun that will fire on the person opening the door. That way the Indian and his friends will get a blast in the face."

"And Mother will get her card on Mother's Day."

"Can you think of something else?"

"Yes. Forget your mother."

"You don't know my mother."

"Oh?"

"She's not like other mothers."

"I believe you."

"You really don't believe me. It was just your way of getting me to go on this job." The man's voice now rose like a woman's and he began gesturing with the gun.

"I tell you I believe you, Francis."

"Very well, if you believe me then let's go and mail the letter. The trading post should be open now."

"You don't trust me alone with the money?"

"Well—"

"All right. I'll go along. But why don't we take the money with us and make a run for it now?"

"Because they'll still have a roadblock."

"Then why don't we take the money with us to the trading post while we mail the letter?"

"Because a large bundle like that might look suspicious."

"All right. Let's go."

"But first we got to fix the sawed-off shotgun."

"Of course," the other man said. "After all, soon it will be Mother's Day."

On the mesa, Afraid Of His Own Horses (he wasn't really; it was a family name) raised his arm the way Indians do in the movies and said, "Look. They're leaving."

The group stopped between two huge orange sandstone boulders and watched the two men below. One of them was sitting in the jeep waiting while the other man was doing something carefully to the hogan door. What the two men had called a shack was actually an abandoned hogan. The door was another sign borrowed several years ago from Route 66 and it said: REPENT. THE KINGDOM OF HEAVEN IS AT HAND. JESUS SAVES.

"They were good signs," Afraid Of His Own Horses said.

"Yes. They don't make them like that any more," The Other Indian said.

80

"What does it mean, Santo?" Alastair Benjamin stroked his horse to keep him silent.

"They made good doors," Sant said.

"I mean what does the writing mean?"

"What it says, I guess."

"There's a good one over there," Alastair Benjamin said, reading it aloud. "MOTORISTS WISE SIMONIZ."

"No, it's not a very good one," Afraid Of His Own Horses said.

"No. They don't make them like they used to any more," The Other Indian said.

Alastair Benjamin allowed his horse to move up a little.

"Why does he keep fooling with the door? Is he trying to lock it?"

"Yeah, but he can't."

"But for two hundred thousand dollars you try."

"Yeah, I guess you do. What we going to do with all that money?"

"I guess, like they said, we'll give it to the Indians," Sant said.

"Why?" The Other Indian said.

"Well, you can buy things and all," Sant said.

"What?"

"Rolls-Royces, for example."

"What's that?"

"A foreign car."

"Have you seen one?"

"I've seen pictures."

"Are they good?"

"Oh, they're very good."

"Then I guess I'll have one."

"*Cómo no? Why not?*" Sant said.

Below, the man waiting at the jeep with the other sawed-off shotgun, pressed the horn and hollered, "Hurry it up. For God's sake, get the lead out, Francis."

"Don't get me nervous. You know how I get when I'm nervous." The man called Francis had walked over to the jeep but he didn't get in.

"All right. Take it easy, Francis."

"You know how I get when I get excited."

"Then take it easy."

"I killed those men when I was nervous."

"Then take it easy."

"I'm not responsible when I'm excited. You know what I've done, Mike? You know what you made me do with your hurry, hurry?"

"No. But take it easy, Francis."

"You made me leave my Mother's Day card inside. And the door's triggered to the shotgun."

"Well, that's a laugh."

"I could kill you."

Mike, the man in the jeep, suddenly sobered and stroked the steering wheel.

"Yes," he said. "I guess you could." They were silent for almost a minute and then Mike looked over carefully at the hogan. "There's a hole in the top of that shack," he said. "And it's got curved sides. A man could crawl up the sides and drop down in and get that letter without opening the door."

When the man came back with the letter the other man revved the engine and put her in four-wheel drive but he did not let out the clutch.

"If we take it easy—if we learn to take it easy, Francis, everything will work out."

Now the man called Mike, who looked very worried, released the clutch and the jeep moved forward. Soon they had disappeared in the far red hills.

The boys on their horses watched the two men go off in their jeep.

"Well, what do you think, Santo?"

"Well, I don't know, but the Indians think they're very courteous people."

"Why courteous people? They look like very city people to me."

"Courteous because it's a hogan where Indians died and you

know no one's supposed to go in a hogan after that's happened."

"So they went through the roof."

"Yeah."

"Well, I guess that's courteous all right."

"You sure that's why they did it? They don't look like that kind of people to me."

"Well," Sant said, beginning to move his paint horse forward, "it just shows you can't judge nobody by their looks."

"Yeah."

"My dear sir," The Other Indian said, "shall we get the money?"

"Where did you get that dear sir?"

"Isn't that the way rich people talk?"

"Yes, I guess it is," Sant said, and they began to wind their horses down the bright mesa. The mesa here was eroding away in five giant steps that descended down to the floor of the valley where the abandoned hogan lay. Each of the five steps clearly marked about twenty million years in time. In other words, they had been laid down twenty million years apart, and were so marked by unique coloration and further marked by the different fossil animals found in each. It took the four boys about twenty minutes to descend these one hundred million years but they didn't think that was very good going.

"We'll be all day at this," Alastair Benjamin said.

"The money will still be there."

"Easy," Afraid Of His Own Horses said. "Don't force my horse. Money isn't everything."

"It's a Rolls-Royce," The Other Indian said.

"Well, then, we'll slide down this one." They were on the west sandy edge of an Ojo Alamo formation, vaguely striped in red and orange. Afraid Of His Own Horses, riding without saddle, suddenly turned his horse into it and went straight down. The others waited to see how he made out. When they saw he was down there in one piece waving to them, The Other Indian followed.

"It's easier to do that without no saddle," Sant said.

"It sure is."

"But they'll get all the money."

"Well, they earned it."

"It was going to be distributed to the Indians anyway."

"And we're not Indians."

They turned their horses in eights, pacing the ledge and watching the Indians below.

"They're waiting for us."

"Let them wait."

"It's hard to have Indians for buddies."

"Yeah."

"They expect you to kill yourself."

"Over two hundred thousand dollars."

"Is that how much it is?"

"Yeah."

"It would take you a long time to make that much money at a bronc show. That's what you're still going to be, isn't it?"

"Yeah."

"How much they pay for a bronc show?"

"Forty hundred dollars or so. I've told you that before."

"But you were never so exact."

"Well, now I'm being exact."

"Well, money isn't everything."

"That's what the Indian said."

"They're still waiting. I guess they think we're chicken."

"Well, I guess we better try it."

They went down together and at once, creating a storm, a tornado of ageless dust, a hundred million years in outrage, that followed them all the way down to the level of the Indians.

The two men carrying the letter saw the plume of dust as they entered the trading post.

"I wonder what that was," the delicate-looking one said. "It seemed near the shack."

"Don't get nervous," the man called Mike said. "It was probably a tornado. Don't get nervous."

"Do they have tornadoes here?"

"Sure they do. Small ones. All over."

"What kept you so long?" The Other Indian said as Sant and Alastair became visible in the dying dust.

"Well, it's a lot easier for Indians. Without saddles, that is," Alastair said.

"Sure it is," The Other Indian said. "Well, there it is," he said, pointing. "It was nice of those city people to go through the roof."

"Does it make it okay if you go through the roof?" Sant said.

The two Indians looked at each other. "Yes," Afraid Of His Own Horses said. "We guess it does."

"Then we better go through the roof, I guess," Sant said.

"Everyone else is doing it. I guess that's the thing nowadays," Alastair Benjamin said as he started his all-white horse down the final gentle slope.

The Other Indian shinnied up the side of the hogan first. It was not too difficult. The hogan was built octagonal-shaped of eight-inch cedar logs woven, interlaced, so that the final shape was like an igloo, complete with center hole for the smoke. It was as though these people, Navahos, had made it down from the north a long time ago but had never forgotten their houses, only now they built them of wood, instead of ice. The door, which had always faced east, and still does, was formerly of hides. Now it was usually a stolen sign—SAVE AT THE FIRST THRIFT AND LOAN COMPANY or something like that. This one said, JESUS SAVES.

"I don't know," Afraid Of His Own Horses said as he saw The Other Indian drop through the roof hole. "I don't know whether it's all right really."

"Well," Sant said, "if it's not all right really this is a fine time to think of it. He's already in."

"I don't know really what the Navaho book says."

"It will be okay," Sant said.

"The book is in the minds of the old people and I don't know what it says. I know it says we should never enter the house where a Navaho has died, but you don't enter a roof. You fall in."

"It will be okay," Sant said.

"Oh, that's easy for you to say. You're not an Indian."

"It will be okay," Sant said.

"It was very nice of those city people to remember the book."

"Oh, awfully nice. Shall we join the others?"

"My dear sir, why not?" Afraid Of His Own Horses said.

Alastair Benjamin got down off his all-white horse and joined them, looking up. He removed his powder-blue straw hat. It matched his turquoise bracelet and looked grand and gaudy against his dark skin.

"Well," Alastair Benjamin said, "those city people. I don't trust them. It's a trick. I don't trust them."

"My *compadre* is not the trusting type," Sant said.

"My dear sir," Afraid Of His Own Horses said, "just because a man is from the city—"

"Yes," Sant said. "Just because—"

"Well, all right," Alastair Benjamin said. "But who goes first?"

"My dear sir, my brother is already in there."

"Then you go first," Alastair Benjamin said.

At the trading post the two city men dressed like hunters walked up to the counter and the delicate one dropped the letter in the box.

"Well, Mike," he said to the other man, "that's over with."

"Are you the two men living in that Torreon hogan?" It was the trader, Mr. Peersall. He wore a large Stetson over a big, sunken face and he wore a heavy leather jacket.

"Now we just might be," the man called Mike said. "Which one?"

"Jesus Saves," Mr. Peersall said.

"We just might be," Mike said.

"Yes," Francis said. "We could be."

"Well, I think you better move out." The trader took off his hat and looked at them carefully. "A Navvyho died there. No one is supposed to enter a hogan where a Navvyho died."

"Why?" Mike said.

"Evil spirits are still there," the trader said.

"Do you believe that?" The man called Francis had already walked to the door once impatiently. Now he came back.

"Do you believe that?" His voice was very high.

"I try to go along with their traditions," the trader said.

"Oh, you do?" Francis said. "Well, that's interesting."

"Don't get him nervous," Mike said to Mr. Peersall.

86

"I don't care if I do," Mr. Peersall said. "I'm not busy now."

Francis was biting his lip and turning very white.

"Just don't get him excited," Mike said to the trader.

"At the moment I've got nothing else to do," Mr. Peersall said.

"Come on, Francis," Mike said.

"Don't touch me. Just don't you ever touch me," Francis said.

"Come on, Francis."

"Listen," Mr. Peersall said. "If you people don't want to behave, if you want to stay on in that hogan, I don't have to deliver that letter you just dropped in the box, to the mail pickup at Coyote."

Francis had begun to reach under his coat toward a very bulging long object but now he buttoned his coat again.

"All right," Francis said. "I suppose—I suppose an Indian's got as much right to be a fool as the rest of us."

"Sure he has," the trader said.

"Come on, Francis," Mike said.

The two city men dressed in the new red wool plaid of hunters went very quietly out the door.

"City people or Martians or Plutonians, somewhere from outer space. City people, I guess. City people. They're not bad people for city people," the trader said to the Navahos lined along the far wall beneath the hanging and dusty festoons of hides, saddles, harness, and lanterns.

The Navahos did not respond to this saying of the trader. Then Mr. Peersall abruptly realized with that sudden knowledge you get when you have lived with people who do not communicate much with words, that instinctive learning a trader must have to be a trader—to be in Indian Country at all—he suddenly realized that the two city people had drawn a perfect blank from the Indians, that they had ignored the city people absolutely.

"Well, then, the city people never existed," the trader said. He removed the letter and tossed it into the burning fireplace.

"If they never existed, don't exist, why should we confuse people with their mail, if they don't exist?"

The Indians grunted and their women made a quick shuffling

sound with their feet to assure him he had made a bright saying and they went back to ignoring even him now.

What the trader had done was not an outrage—the tossing of the letter in the fire. It was simply that in this part of Indian Country mail was a thing that had never become a habit, a vice. They had not yet become addicted to a thing that had not as yet traditionalized through long custom. It was still the part of the world where you could tell a person what you thought about him to his face without making magic against him on paper.

The letter burned with a tall cool flame within the dark room, and the Indians enjoyed it very much.

The two small cowboys and the two small Indians were down at the bottom of the hogan counting the money.

"Well, it's all here," Sant said. "Two hundred thousand dollars—such as it is."

"What do you mean," Alastair Benjamin said, "such as it is?"

"I mean that it's patent that it's phony money."

"What do you mean, patent?"

"Just what I said."

"Then what do you mean, phony money?"

"I mean," Sant said, "take, for example, did you ever see money all pressed and in neat packs like this, all crisp and clean? That's not right. That's not money."

"Well," Alastair Benjamin said, "I guess you're right. It must be patent money okay."

"And it's phony too," Sant said.

"Then what shall we do?"

"Burn it," Sant said.

"Wait a minute," The Other Indian said. "What about my Rolls-Royce?"

Sant tilted his porkpie-shaped cowboy hat and thought carefully, closing his eyes to make sure he missed nothing in his judgment.

"Well," he said finally, and still keeping his eyes closed, "the trader man says you got to pay a big price for everything you get out of this world, or something."

"Well," The Other Indian said, "if his saying is going to take

88

away my Rolls-Royce then he better buy me another kind of car."

"That's fair," Sant said.

"Shall we burn the money?"

"My dear sir, please do," Afraid Of His Own Horses said.

"You don't have to talk like a rich man any more," Sant said.

"Okay, then start the fire."

"I thought I heard a jeep."

"You sure it wasn't a Rolls-Royce?"

They all laughed and then Sant began very solemnly stacking the two hundred thousand dollars in a pyramid shape. "The better to make it burn."

"Imagine that," Sant said, "trying to make fools out of us with their phony money and all. I don't even think they're hunters. Why should government people come dressed like hunters when they can wear government clothes? I don't even think they're nothing."

"That's right," Alastair Benjamin said.

Sant put the final sheaf of money on the pyramid.

"Sure it is. Do you want to light it up?" he said to The Other Indian. "Or maybe you, sir?" he said to Afraid Of His Own Horses.

"I'm only a poor Indian again," Afraid Of His Own Horses said.

"Go ahead, light it anyway," Sant said. Sant passed him a pack of matches but it was The Other Indian who took them and lighted the fire. Two hundred thousand dollars makes a pleasant small fire but it smokes a lot.

"Always remember this," Sant said, "in case this happens again. It smokes a lot. Let's get out of here."

Sant bent over and the other small cowboy and the two Indians jumped on his back and crawled out the smoking hole. Sant was still trapped down there until, as an afterthought, as they were mounting their horses, the others decided to go back and get him. The Other Indian crawled in with Alastair Benjamin holding his ankles and they pulled Sant out that way.

When they got on their horses Sant was still rubbing his eyes and he said to Alastair Benjamin as they started off, "Always remember, Alley, how much money smokes."

"Yeah," Alastair Benjamin said.

The two city men who three days ago had robbed a bank in Durango of two hundred thousand dollars and were now dressed as hunters drove their jeep through the square pass, the window in the cliff of La Ventana Mesa. La Ventana means the window in Spanish. The Spanish were the first people here and gave all the mesas their names. They didn't bother to name the valleys because that is where they were standing when they named the mesas and didn't think it was important to name where they were seeing from but only what they saw.

As the jeep rode through this window in the mesa Mike said, "Look, there's somebody in the shack. She's smoking."

"Well, tear down there," the other man said. "The gun's gone off and that's the dust."

The driver drove down the incline toward the hogan as fast as he could go.

"We must have killed an Indian."

"It serves him right."

The driver jammed on the brakes and they both leaped out of the jeep and ran through the door of the hogan as fast as they could go. There was a big roar as both barrels of the shotgun went off. One of the men dressed as a hunter threw up his hands and collapsed immediately and never moved again. The other man was blasted backward and began to stumble blindly through the sage and yucca and greasewood as though he were drunken and searching for something. Then he, too, collapsed and never moved again. Above, in the very New Mexican blue, the gentle, far buzzards began to tighten their circles and move down.

"You hear that shotgun go off?" Sant said. "Maybe those people were hunters, after all."

"I don't think they were," Alastair Benjamin said.

"Then what you think that shotgun blast was? You think they're shooting their own selves?"

"Yeah," Alastair Benjamin said, trying to be difficult.

"My dear sir, why not?" The Other Indian said, trying to be impossible.

"*Cómo no?*" Afraid Of His Own Horses said.

90

"Yes, why not?" Sant said. "If all the rest of you are crazy, why not me? The hunters are hunting their own selves. The killers are killing each other."

They all guessed that this was true or something and then they began racing their horses down the valley as fast as they could race. They went through the window on La Ventana Mesa flying fast, and then they scattered, each trailing off to their different homes way out there somewhere in the nowhere, in that endless New Mexican country that must go on and on in its bright infinity even after they had sped over the horizon, individual specks now, and disappeared completely.

Now the gentle buzzards came on, waving in on a long concentric glide and lighting big and alone in the exact center of the awful silence, and the sky assumed that huge and violent majesty of color it always does in the mesa country as the day, before quickening into dark, gives her grand and splendored welcome to the night. Finally only a hushed pillar of smoke rising from an abandoned hogan gave any sign at all.

PART II

SIX **I**ndians believe that inanimate objects like a stone, a leaf, a bridge, or even a tree have the ability to move. They notice that this remembrance is borne out with proof when they are walking across a bridge path when drunk. When you fish them out of the water, as Big Sant did once at Blanco Crossing, they will say, as this Navaho said, "The bridge walked away from under me." Or when a wrecked Navaho pickup shows up at Sauter's Garage in Cuba, the Navaho will explain that he was driving along drinking quietly when this tree walked up and hit him.

Whites near Navaho Country have even stranger convictions backed up with even stranger proof. For example, they explain to the Indians that the whites own all the good land, the only land with water on it close to the mountains, because when—way back when—the land was surveyed the Indians demanded the worst land. As proof of this there is a signed treaty.

"You mean a tree hit us then too?"

"No," Big Sant said. "The bridge must have walked out from underneath you."

The Indians had a strange belief, too, about the unsolved death of the bank robbers. They said the bank robbers' own guns had fired off and killed them. Indians will be Indians.

There was an even stranger belief held by both whites and Indians around Indian Country and that concerned the Gran Negrito. The Gran Negrito had settled in Indian Country during very strange events about twenty-one years ago. He acquired a ranch called the Circle R, which became known as the Gran

95

Negrito, and built on it a red adobe house, filled it with records of odd long music and books without pictures, ran fifty head of mother cows into three hundred, and held the key to the Circle Heart. When the government springs numbers one and three dried up, the Circle Heart, lying on the long flank of the Circle R, could not trail to its summer mountain pasture without water trouble; so the Gran Negrito on the springs of the Circle R controlled the beat of the Circle Heart.

Now the Gran Negrito was gone. The Circle R was gone—it all belonged to the Circle Heart. The strange belief held about this by both whites and Indians was that, like religion and politics, it was not to be discussed. And the proof of this was that the last time it was discussed someone ended up dead—the Gran Negrito.

Big Sant today was very much alive. He rode his horse all in one with the horse, like a centaur. He carried his brilliant scarred face like a flag. When he rode, it seemed as though he were continually returning from some conquest, carrying this branded face stiffly like a pennant of victory, as though a train of more horses were to follow bearing prize. On closer look there was something wrong. The splash of color repelled. What was triumphant at a distance was now tensed into the tight, reflective face folds of defeat.

Today Big Sant dwelt on secrets and touches.

The secret in creating anything new seems to lie in borrowing all you see and hear about you and adding one small touch. Big Sant's one small touch in cattle ranching was always to carry wire cutters on his saddle string and always to cut the fence rather than go round. He would repair it quickly and it sometimes saved ten miles. No one else did it. It was his one small touch.

Another small touch of Big Sant's was to collect butterflies. No one else in Indian Country did it. He was doing it now. It was another small touch. A lot of other people had gathered new land in strange ways but who in Indian Country gathered butterflies in any way? It was a pretty big touch.

Now he pursued the mighty monarch. Not at the expense of his cattle time. He had already, this day, spent eleven hours pursuing cattle and he was done. He was done for this day anyway. Big Sant would have liked to chase in the direction of home, the

Circle Heart, seventeen miles west, but the great monarch fell in huge circles from cactussed hill to tamarisk. (From morn to noon he fell, from noon to dewy eve, a summer's day.) He fled before the stumbling Big Sant and his faltering horse in every direction but home; he wandered through every ranch but the Circle Heart. Big Sant kept on with the knowledge that, although the butterfly belongs to the same order as the moth, unlike the moth, the butterfly is diurnal, not nocturnal. You have to catch them while the day lasts. They differ from the moths also in having antennas club-shaped, those of moths being fine and threadlike or featherlike; in resting with the wings folded vertically, the moth folding them over the abdomen. Butterflies are not only found close to the Circle Heart. Forty separate species occur within the Arctic Circle. What else? That's all for now, except remember you catch them while the light lasts. They only belong to the same order as the moths, not the same phylum. Sant nevertheless sat down. His feet and legs belonged to the order of man and the same phylum, too, and they got very tired.

You are supposed to be a cattleman anyway, and what do you know about them? The principal beef brands are the Angus and the Hereford. Every schoolboy knows that. Cattle are not native to America but were brought by Columbus on his second voyage. The Western range cattle are in part descendants of the cattle of the early Spanish settlers. Wealth of primitive man consisted chiefly of cattle. The word "pecuniary" is derived from the latin *pecus,* cattle, and the words "cattle," "chattel," and "capital" are related. He did not want to think about that any more. He had better get back to chasing that damn butterfly.

But the butterfly was gone. He had marked the monarch on a Spanish bayonet yucca but now it was gone. All right, he would try the word "cowboy." Cowbird, a small terrestrial or semiterrestrial bird of the hang-nest family, native to the new world. No, I want cowboy, not cowbird. All right, cowboy. The name given Tory marauders, adherents to the British cause in the American Revolution who infested the neutral grounds in Westchester County, New York, and plundered their patriotic opponents. Not many schoolboys know that that's the way the word "cowboy" began. But how

97

about cowboys like you are and Little Sant wants to become? He wants to become a bronc man. All right, but you start by being a cowboy. All right, we'll do cowboy. Name also given to mounted men employed as herders on cattle ranches of the western United States. They were more important and picturesque in the days before the vast ranches were fenced, when their duties consisted of driving cattle to pasture and water, branding them at the roundup, protecting them from wild animals and thieves, and driving them to the shipping point. At the present time their duties are not as dangerous as formerly but cowboys are still fearless and expert horsemen, skilled with the lasso and in all the details of their work.

Well, enough of this encyclopedia word game. You'd better get on your horse and get back to the Circle Heart. Except this—a cowboy never calls that thing a lasso, he calls it a rope. And he doesn't call it a roundup. It's a gathering. And except this—why don't you think about your own life? Why do you have to pick on words? Why do you have to pick on butterflies?

Big Sant rolled a cigarette carefully while watching the Spanish bayonet.

Because I have an interest in things scientific. Because I never had the courage to leave the ranch. I guess that's it. Or maybe it's because my brother didn't have courage to stay during the big drought. Anyway I've always done the work of two men. Little Sant will have an education. He will stay at my brother's when he's getting it. That's the least my brother can do. And speaking of brother, he left when I bought the Gran Negrito, not during the drought. Face it, boy. It wasn't the big drought, it was the big steal, the big murder.

Big Sant removed the cigarette from his mouth. No, it wasn't. It wasn't murder. It was an accident. Two Indians testified to that. And it wasn't stealing. I was just there with the highest bid when it was auctioned, that's all. Another accident. Why didn't you tell the boy then—Little Sant? Because he's not old enough. He might not understand. Murder, stealing? Murder, stealing? All nonsense. It was all legal. And no one knows who Alastair is really. That's not true.

98

He crushed the cigarette in his bare hand until he felt the sharp burn, then he threw the mess on the ground.

"All legal," he said out loud. "Come on," he said to the horse. "It's got me talking to myself."

As he rose, the great monarch took off from the underleaf of the Spanish bayonet and Big Sant followed. He did not pay much attention to the direction it was taking but plodded after it steadily, clutching his net. A cowboy will not carry a canteen, perhaps because he's afraid someone will take him for a Boy Scout, but a butterfly net—there's no law against that.

Big Sant smiled. His mind was getting on to better things now. The great monarch had lofted over the ridge and fluttered down into a green grama valley. Big Sant followed it up and down and over to where it lighted on a pile, a broken and charred pile, of adobes. Sant stopped the horse and stared at the burned house. Now he mounted the horse and turned back toward the Circle Heart.

"That butterfly might take us into the next county," he told the horse. "It might take us clear to Texas and there it would become three times as big as it is now and we might not get it in the net. That's a joke," he told the horse.

Now he spurred the horse, sticking great rowels into the horse's flank. He took two wire fences going as fast as the horse could go.

"It was all legal," he reminded the horse. "All perfectly legal. Oh Christ."

The horse's name was Indian Country and Sant loved the big horse and was annoyed with himself for having caused him to lather badly on the quick trip home. He rubbed the horse down before he went inside and into the bathroom and stared into the mirror over the medicine chest. Indians have a medicine chest, too, but they don't study their own reflection in it. Sant saw in it forty years and a bright brand—forty Christian calendar years. Sant got out the shaving soap and remembered that the Navaho year is divided into twelve months because a coyote questioned the wisdom of having twenty-four. That is, the Navahos recognize only two seasons, winter and summer, and the coyote questioned the wisdom of assigning twelve months to each. You can find all kinds of information like this if you bother to ask an Indian. It helps if you speak the language. Big Sant did. He didn't speak coyote. Very few do. Even coyotes seem to have a tough time with it. If you listen to them carefully in the darkest night you will notice that they repeat the same cry and keep repeating it as though they were not getting through.

Big Sant brought up a coyote once from a pup. Everything was fine; that is, the coyote behaved very much like a dog for one year and everything seemed to be going splendidly. Big Sant always knew the day would come when the wild coyotes would begin calling her from the close ridges. She was a bitch. Then he realized that, growing up in isolation like this, she would not speak the language, and he let her out of the house quite freely, knowing that she would not understand at all what the coyotes were talking about when they called. They might just as well be giraffes up there hollering down. But when the coyotes called from the near ridge Sant's coyote was gone immediately and never came back. The only moral Big Sant could get out of this was that giraffes are different from you and me. Coyotes, too, I guess. She was a bitch all right.

Navahos believe that sickness is due to the magic influence of some divine power and that chants have been ordained for its removal. The first chant may not prove effective in every instance; then a second medicine, found in another chant, becomes imperative, a process that is repeated until the disease has been correctly traced to its source and the medicine will eventually, of necessity, prove effective. The chants can go on all night. They can go on all week.

It could be a very long drink of medicine, Big Sant thought. There must be some simpler way of keeping those he loved closer.

Sant's mind wandered on these touchstones because he had been brought up close to the Navahos, and very close to coyotes, too, for that matter. The Indians and all the animals were very close. People were kind of distant. People were complicated. Unlike coyotes, people have the damndest difficulties understanding each other. He wanted to get close to Millie and help her. He

100

wanted to get close to the boys and help them. He wanted to get close to himself. He had even tried growing a beard but the brand still showed through and people seemed to know what he was up to. He tried cutting it off and defying them. Nothing worked. Millie said she never noticed it. He owed her a lot. He should be afraid of nothing, he told himself as he wiped the razor foam off his chin, watching himself in the mirror of the medicine cabinet which held no chants. Now he hung up the towel and went into the living room.

Millie was reading a copy of Zen, which she put down.

"What's happened to the boys?" she asked.

"They'll be in," Big Sant said. He went over to the shelf and took down a copy of the *Ethnological Dictionary of the Navaho Language*. He was still working on it. He spoke the language rather well but he was interested to see what it was made of.

"They've been planning for some time now to go where they remember. Wherever that is," Millie said.

"That sounds silly," Sant said, sitting down with the book, but he didn't look at the book.

"I thought it sounded silly too," Milly said. "Still, Navahos are silly. We're silly. That dog of ours is quite sensible." They had acquired a sheep dog.

"Yes, as we get older I guess we don't remember what we sounded like when we were kids," Sant said.

"I thought we'd go to Gallup next week," Millie said. "Dr. Graham is going to speak at the Civic Auditorium."

"I was by the old Circle R today," Big Sant said, putting the book aside.

"What do you say about Dr. Graham Saturday?"

"Going where they remembered," Sant said. "They can't remember any place."

"I thought I'd get tickets for Saturday."

"They can't remember that place."

"What place?" Millie said. She paused. "What place would you like? We can get close up for two dollars."

"Get close up," Sant said, taking the book again.

SEVEN **W**hat do you remember?"

"When my grandfather was a kid," Little Sant said, "my grandfather ate buffler meat."

"Tell me more."

"My father eats butterflies." The two boys just stood stock still for a while. "I remember," Sant said, "there was this big horse."

"What big horse? You mean the killer horse?"

"Yes. The horse that I rode."

"I remember," Alastair Benjamin said, "there were all these books."

"What all books?"

"The books that burned."

"Tell me about it," Sant said.

"Tell me about yours again first."

"Well," Sant said, "nobody could ride this horse, but I did it."

"After this fire I was rescued by the Indians."

"Yeah. Cheese and baloney," Sant said.

"Cheese and baloney to your story, too, then," Alastair said.

"Well, I'll believe yours—"

"If you'll believe mine," Alastair said.

They were both all of fourteen years old now. They held the reins of their horses as they sat beneath the shade of a piñon tree and looked out over the bright Indian Country.

"It all began," Alastair said, "I was hiding under a chair or a bed or something like that. Then these spurs came in the room."

"Spurs?"

102

"Well, there was somebody in them," Alastair said.

"Who?"

"This man who kept shooting a gun or something like that."

"Well, was he shooting or wasn't he?"

"He had been shooting I think."

"And then what happened?"

"Then one of those spurs came off the stranger and the room was filling up with smoke and I ran out. Then some Indians rescued me."

"You expect me to believe that?"

"Well, what happened to you?"

"Well, we were at this big show and nobody would ride this horse. It was a wild horse, a killer horse."

"But you rode him, or so you always say. With Lemaitre. You and Lemaitre were partners."

"Yeah."

"You expect me to believe that?"

"I see what you mean," Sant said.

"We both got to co-operate more when we listen."

"Yeah," Sant said. "We certainly do."

They both began chewing thoughtfully on the horse reins they held as the horses watched them and they watched out over Indian Country.

"They certainly gave the Indians a lot of sorry land," Alastair said.

"Oh, it's not sorry land, Alley," Sant said.

"No water."

"Oh, I guess the Indians like it that way. They call it Năhoké."

"What does that mean?"

"The land."

"Well, they certainly gave the Indians a lot of sorry Năhoké."

"Nobody gave it to them. It was always theirs."

"Always?"

"Almost always."

"Who had it before they did?"

"Other Indians, I guess."

"How did they get it from the other Indians?"

"Shot it out."

"Even before there were guns?"

"Well, that's a very good question," Sant said.

"Well, I didn't want to make it too good."

"You make them as good as you like," Sant said. "I guess I asked for it. . . . Do you intend to eat that rein all up?" Sant asked after a minute as he watched where the horses stood. Alastair took the rein out of his mouth and the horse looked away.

"Did you know," Alastair said, "that the Navahos believe they always had horses?"

"Didn't they?"

"No," Alastair said. "The white man brought them."

"They brought the guns too."

"Do the Indians know this?"

"Yeah, they know about the guns," Sant said.

"And the t.b.?"

"They know where that came from too," Sant said. "Are you enjoying the rein?"

"What rain?"

"The rein you're eating up."

Alastair dropped the rein from his mouth and continued to stare out over the Indian Country.

"Boy, this country could use some rain."

"So could your horse," Sant said.

"Yes," Alastair said. "We both got to co-operate more when we talk."

"Yeah," Sant said. "We certainly do."

Alastair fished around on the rocky slope without moving until he found two rocks about the same size but of different colors. He placed one rock between his legs and began trying to drop the other rock exactly on top of it.

"I remember it vividly," Alastair said.

"What does vividly mean?"

"It means most well."

"What do you remember most well?"

"The gun fight."

104

"Oh, that again," Sant said. "Was it before the white man brought the guns?"

"No."

"How do you know?"

"Because there was a lot of noise."

"Other things make noise."

Alastair tried to line up the colored rocks exactly over each other before he dropped the high one this time.

"Blood too?"

"Sure," Sant said.

Alastair dropped the rock but he missed again.

"I guess so," he said. "It's all kind of vague."

"I thought you said it was vividly," Sant said.

"They both mean nearly the same thing," Alastair said.

"Oh," Sant said.

Alastair reached over and plucked a blood-red Indian paintbrush.

"Where did all this happen?" Sant said.

Alastair pointed with the Indian paintbrush. "Out there."

"Out where?"

Alastair was gesturing to infinity with the poison-bright flower. "Out there."

The movement took in the world. From what they could see it took in La Ventana, the Puerco, the Cuevo and the Perro and the Madrid Mesas. All appeared aflame this time of sun, and it took in the deep shadowed land in between. It took in the giant Jemez Range and the quick streams coming down and it covered nicely all the unending sage that wandered south and down to the Arizona peaks rising from their solid foundations like blue, distant, dim cities of a strange faith.

"All that?" Sant said, following with his eye the slow swing of the poison paintbrush. Sant put the rein back in his mouth and talked around it. "Well, that certainly narrows things down."

Alastair put his rein in his mouth, too, picked up the colored stones. He still held the bright Indian paintbrush in his free hand so that he appeared a small, heavy-laden, black, bridled and bitted conjurer preparing to startle the world, amuse anyway the mesa, for money and fame.

"I only want to tell you where I come from, where I first remember," Alastair said.

"Well, you certainly narrowed it down," Sant said.

"I remember the boots," Alastair said. "The boots and the spurs moving from one window to the other 'window, suddenly and mixed up, and I remember the shots."

"Do you remember the house?"

"I remember it was made of mud. Adobe."

"What color?"

"Blood color."

"Red," Sant said. "That's the red country. Gallina, Capulin, and Coyote. Iron."

"Iron?"

"In the soil," Sant said. "It turns everything blood red. That's where I made my first appearance. That's where I remember too."

"First appearance?"

"Yes. Where I rode that horse."

"Then you've been back?"

"No."

"Why not?"

"Because my parents want me to be a gelologist."

Alastair dropped the rein from his mouth. "You mean geologist."

"Is that good?"

"Wonderful," Alastair said.

Sant looked up at the horse and then over at Mount Taylor. "I been thinking," he said. "We could go our own selves."

"Where we remember?"

"Where we remember," Sant said.

"Would they mind us going?"

"They might mind me going," Sant said. "You know they don't want me to be a bronc man. They don't want me to remember. But I can't think of any reason they wouldn't want you to go there."

"No. It's only where I remember."

106

"Only where we remember," Sant said, getting up.

"Well, you can't very well go," Alastair said.

"That's true. I'll just follow you."

"I guess that's legal."

"It won't hurt anyone."

"How could it hurt anyone, going where we remember?" Alastair said rising.

They got on their horses.

"Which way we got to go?" Alastair said.

"We got to follow the Jemez all along the base."

"Even where it makes the U?"

"Yes."

"Why don't we just go over the top there? It would save time."

"No, they got her all fenced off. They got a secret city up there."

"Secret city?"

"Yeah."

"Los Alamos?"

"Yeah."

"To blow up the world?"

"Yeah. It's before somebody else does it."

"Well, that's the way everybody on the outside is," Alastair said.

"You're sharp today. How is everybody on the outside?"

"Very well, thank you. How are you?"

"Crazy now."

"No, today you are very perspicacious, Santo."

"Maybe. But I feel perfectly all right, Alley."

"It will catch you up later in the day, Santo."

"Vamos a ver."

"What's that?"

"We shall see, Alley, what we shall see."

They could not go over the hump of the mountain because that's where the secret city lay and it was fenced off. But they could save some time by going over the Valle Grande. The Valle Grande is a huge cup, maybe twenty miles across, the largest extinct volcano crater in the world. For the last one hundred thousand years it had been the home of thousands of elk; now it was the home of the New Mexico Cattle and Timber Company Incorporated, Keep Out.

Before they got there, though, they had to climb way up. They had to get up on a hogback ridge where they could look down on the Navaho and the Apache country, the Santa Ana, the Zia and the Jemez country. The Navaho country ran way on west and farther even than they could see, on all the way through New Mexico over the horizon into Arizona, Utah, and even into Colorado. They could see all of the Apache country, about six hundred thousand acres of piñon, sage, and cedar fringing the mountain. The Santa Ana and the Zia and the Jemez, why, you could drop a handkerchief on each of them from up here and seem to cover each. They were all pueblos, Pueblo Indian people who never had more land than they could cultivate and they never cultivated more in the old days than the Navahos and the Apaches could steal. The Pueblos remembered in the dim and distant memories of the race how they were destroyed once upon a time by the Navahos and the Apaches, how later they were destroyed by the Spanish. They did not remember what was happening now.

"What do you know about Indians?" Sant said, beginning to twirl his pigging string.

"Well, you take those Pueblo Indians," Alastair said, "that live in these mud apartment houses."

"Yes?"

"Well, when they first saw white men it was the first time they saw horses too."

"And?"

"And they thought they were part of the horse."

"Which part?"

"Yes," Alastair said. "Well, anyway, the Pueblos drew a line about a hundred yards in front of the pueblo and told the white people with signs that they better not cross it."

"And did they?"

"Yes, they did."

"What happened?"

108

"It was terrible. Later they killed all the missionaries and burned all the churches."

"Why?"

"Because they wanted it the way they remembered it, I guess."

"What else?"

"Nothing else. What is that one?" Alastair said pointing down to a square of mud, broken into cubes.

"That one's Santa Ana."

"It looks deserted."

"It almost is."

"What happened?"

"They don't remember."

"How about that one down there?"

"Zia. They're doing all right."

"And that one there?" Alastair said, pointing east.

"Oh, they're putting up a good fight too. That's Jemez."

"What are they putting up a good fight about?"

"I don't know. To keep it, I guess, the way they remembered."

"How do they remember it?"

"The way it was."

"How was it?"

"The way they remember, I guess. Or maybe it was just a lot of baloney."

"That reminds me," Alastair said, "I'm getting hungry."

They were riding through a dense growth of short thick scrub oak now and for a while, as they rode, everything was hidden from their view. Now they emerged on a sheer flat table rock and everything in the world opened quickly before them and below. They were silent a while watching.

"Let them have it," Alastair said.

"Let them have what?"

"What they remember."

"That's big of you."

"What is it they remember exactly?"

"Things."

"Things like what?"

"Things like the world started right here and grew out."

"What else do the Indians remember?"

"Oh, things like the world began in fire and smoke."

"It probably did."

"Yeah."

"What else?"

"That it will end suddenly in quietness."

"Will it? You think it will?"

"I don't know, Alley. I really don't know."

"You don't remember."

"Yeah, that's right. I've got a bad memory."

They sat on their horses very quietly, for a long while resting their horses and looking down over it all.

"Where do we go from here, Santo?"

"Onward and upward, Alley."

"On what and up what?"

"You see that red pinnacle up there with the yellow top?"

"Yeah."

"We don't go there. Now you see that other one on the other bluff, the green one that looks like the tip of a Mexican church?"

"You mean Spanish-American."

"Yeah. We don't go there either. That's copper."

"What is?"

"The green."

"Yeah, I know. We don't go there either. But where do we go?"

"Like I said, Alley, onward and upward." Sant touched his horse and led the way through a trail that seemed to have been hiding, hidden by the sage at the entrance to the scrub oak.

"You can tell about how high you are when you lose the sage, Alley. And we just lost it. That's the last of it. Then you can tell about how high you are when you lose the oak. Then you can tell how high you are finally when you lose the pine, the ponderosa pine."

"Pinus Ponderosa. How high are we then?"

"Then we're in the clouds."

"That's where I am now," Alastair Benjamin said.

"Actually, Alley," Sant said, breaking off a brittle white twig from a budding grove they entered quietly, "you're in aspen."

"Populus Tremuloides. How high is that?"

"It's funny. Sometimes way down, sometimes higher than a kite."

"You are too," Alastair said. "We're supposed to be going to where we remember."

"But I remember all this."

"Yes, but it's not relevant."

"Not what?"

"It don't count," Alastair said.

They went over a piece of ground that gave them the feeling that they were riding over the edge of something, and then, there it was—the Valle Grande. The Great Valley, an enormous, perfect bowl of something, empty and green, twenty miles across in each clean direction.

"Well now!" Alastair said.

A sign posted on a barbed-wire fence said, NEW MEXICO CATTLE AND TIMBER COMPANY, INCORPORATED. KEEP OUT.

"Back to the old wire cutters," Sant said as he got down off the horse and unfastened them from his saddle string.

"I remember this country," Sant said, "when you could ride from the Chama to the Rio Grande without hitting a fence."

"Impossible for you to remember that."

"Someone does and I come from someone and that makes it all one and the same thing."

"Your logic escapes me."

"I'm sorry if something of mine got away from you," Sant said, busy cutting. "Why don't you help me? Maybe you wouldn't be losing all those big words."

"I'll stay up here and watch—stabilize the situation."

"You do that," Sant said. He had the fence open now, and Alastair Benjamin rode through majestically, as though re-entering his kingdom. Sant pulled his own horse through and then repulled the fence. It was hog wire, a sheep repellent with two strands of barbed on top for the big cattle. Wire cutters are a very fancy and valuable tool. They've got gadgets on them for cutting, pulling,

111

turning, and stretching. Sant did all this while Alastair thought important thoughts from atop his horse and idly twirled a pigging string.

"Did anyone see us?" Sant said, regaining his horse.

"Yes," Alastair said, looking up at the sky.

"I mean some human being," Sant said.

"Yes," Alastair said, looking toward the center of the bowl. "That too."

Someone was making toward them, skimming the green grass as fast as his white horse could come. Sant watched the rider coming in on them fast. Indians always stand their ground. Cowboys too.

The rider was coming so fast he had to circle them once before he could stop. He got off his horse in bright Spanish rigging, including yellow tapaderos. He was a tall Spaniard in a black hat and he looked the way a descendant of the conquistadors should. He had a clean, tough, burnt face with small blue eyes watching out. As he got off his horse he removed one of his orange pigskin gloves.

"What passes?" he said.

"*Nada,*" Sant said.

"*Pues,*" the rider said, "then who tore up the fence?"

"Let me first introduce my *compadre,*" Sant said.

"Make it fast."

"If you want to be impolite."

"I'm sorry."

"This is my *compadre,* Alastair Benjamin."

"Very pleased to meet you," the rider said. "Why in the hell did you tear up the fence?"

"If you want to be impolite," Sant said.

"I'm sorry," the rider said, turning to Sant now. "Then why in the hell did you tear up the fence?"

"I can see we're not getting anywhere," Sant said. Sant thought a moment, puzzled and trying to help the rider out. "Aren't you," he said finally, "Arturo Lucero Cipriano de Godoy?"

"Yes."

"Didn't you ride at the Lemaitre rodeo in the red country?"

"Yes."

"Well, I happen to be the one who rode the killer horse."

"That was the Anglo, Lemaitre."

"Well?"

"He was a big Anglo."

"He had me in his hand."

"Oh, maybe he had something in his hand, but it wasn't a person."

"It was me," Sant said.

"It was I," Alastair corrected.

"You mean he carried the both of you?"

"No. I'm a grammarian," Alastair said.

"Pleased to meet you," Arturo Lucero Cipriano de Godoy said. "A little while ago you looked like a fence buster."

"If we've got to be impolite," Sant said.

"I don't care, I only work for the corporation. I don't want my fence busted."

"That's a *non sequitur*," Alastair said.

"I don't care."

"We can't very well allow wild statements."

"You see," Alastair said, "you can't very well work for a corporation that we assume owns the fence and then in the same sentence say that it was your fence that we busted. We can't allow both these statements, can we, without having a *non sequitur*? Can we?"

"I don't care."

"I think you should answer his question, Arturo."

"I don't care."

"We can't very well allow wild statements."

"Not very well," Sant said.

"I don't care."

"I think he may be verging on hysteria. You better let him go."

"You can go, Arturo."

"*Mil gracias,*" Arturo said, taking off his hat. "I thank you from the bottom of my heart for wrecking my fence and then letting me go."

"Let's not be bitter," Sant said. "It's only a corporation."

"Only a corporation is not a fair statement," Alastair said. "After all, a corporation is people."

"Sure," Arturo said.

"All right then, maybe we shouldn't let you go," Sant said.

"I don't care," Arturo said, tired and putting back his hat.

"But you should care," Alastair said. "After all, they pay you."

"But I don't care," Arturo said, smiling insanely.

"How much do they pay you?" Sant said.

"Two hundred dollars a month," Arturo said, sobering now under a sober question.

"That seems fair," Sant said. "Why don't you ride with us to the other rim?"

"All right," Arturo said and he got on his horse and turned it in to theirs.

"What," Alastair said, "what exactly are you supposed to do for the two hundred dollars a month?"

"Please," Arturo said, raising the orange-gloved hand alongside his black hat. "Please."

"That's fair," Sant said. "It has gone far enough. He has more than earned his money. It has gone far enough."

"It's more than true," Alastair agreed, and they rode down the slope toward the center of the vast and very silent, green-carpeted volcano in a small, tight, quiet bunch. Soon they were gone in space. From anywhere on the rim, nowhere could you see anyone, anything. There were clumps of trees down there unseen, and somewhere out there three thousand head of cattle, fifteen cowboys, seven jeeps, twenty-eight horses, five chuck wagons, three bunkhouses, nine corrals, and one stream—all lost, all hidden in pure space like the stars, to be caught only at night when lantern-lit. Now bright daylight hit.

"You can't see nothing," Sant said.

"Anything," Alastair said.

Arturo Lucero Cipriano de Godoy tilted up his black hat with a straight thumb.

"I remember how it used to was."

"How was it?"

114

"*Más que* regular."

"More than ordinary. Go ahead," Sant said.

"A man could have a place, a small place."

"Now?"

"Only a place in a big place."

"What else do you remember?"

"When a man did not have to learn a foreign language."

"*Como Inglés?* Like English?"

"*Sí.*"

"What else?"

"Education."

"That's bad?"

"Very bad."

"Why?"

"Because it takes you someplace else."

"And that's bad?"

"Yes, it is."

"Now that you're in a profound mood," Alastair said, "do you have any bright saying that might solve all the problems of the world?"

"Yes."

"What is it?"

"*No me pregunte. Qué lástima, qué cosa, Dios mío.* I have said it."

"What did he say?"

"Don't ask questions," Sant said.

They were at the bottom of the enormous green bowl now and they watered their horses in the stream that ran there. They all got off and drank with the horses. They took off their big hats as they bent over, holding the hats with bent wrists at a certain angle, bodies pitched forward so that they appeared at prayer. The horses jerked up first, looked around askance as though surprised to find themselves so far from home and down at the bottom of something from which they might never get out. The other drinkers with quicker memories nevertheless looked with awful wonder at the great green cup. When they got up and even on their horses they still watched.

As they started up the other side Arturo Lucero Cipriano de Godoy, leading with a strange hat, a strange horse, wove his arm in a big circle signal and the other horses caught up and passed and they all charged into the hill and up, but not for long. The gallop died into a canter, the canter soon died into a trot, the trot very soon into a walk.

"It's very important really to remember what you remember, Arturo," Sant said.

"Why?"

"Because Alastair and I remember things that nobody won't admit."

"Like what?"

"Like my bronc ride. The one you won't even admit."

"He maybe had something in his arm—a bomb, some gold cup he won, one of them shoats."

"But why not me?"

"Why you? What would he be doing with you?"

"The barricade fell when his horse struck it. I was on it. He snatched me to save me, couldn't toss me away, had to take me on the ride."

"Oh?"

"Something like that," Sant said.

"No, I don't believe it. And what does he remember?"

"A gun fight."

"Yes," Alastair said.

"Who won?"

"We don't know."

"I don't believe it," Arturo said.

"That is, I don't know exactly."

"I don't believe it anyway," Arturo said.

"Would you believe it if I had proof?"

"No, I don't believe I would," Arturo said. "After all, I'm a man. I don't have to believe things."

"What does that mean?" Alastair asked.

"He's speaking English now."

"I don't believe it," Alastair said. "I wouldn't believe it if—"

"If he had proof?"

116

"Yeah," Alastair said.

"Well," Arturo said, getting off his horse in front of a gate. He opened the gate. "Well, good-by."

"Well, good-by," Alastair said as they rode their horses through.

"*Adiós*, Arturo Lucero Cipriano de Godoy," Sant said.

"Don't go to the right," Arturo hollered. "You'll run into the Los Alamos barricade."

"What did he mean by that?" Alastair said as they went through the thick brush bearing to the right.

"Los Alamos means the cottonwood trees."

"Is that what the barricade is made of?"

"No. That," Sant said, pointing to a heavy steel-mesh cyclone fence that suddenly appeared. "That's what it's made of."

"I wonder what those people in there, in the secret city, remember," Alastair said.

"Secrets," Sant said.

They started away from the fence and when they got well into the forest the brush got thicker and the long shadows became solid. They both ducked a very dangerous branch they could not see but only sensed was there somewhere in the deep shadows as they worked their way through thick aspen and alder. The aspen you could always see because it was white and neat like sudden columns of chalk; the other trees gave you trouble. But it was not very long before they were out of the darkness of the forest and they both felt very much better. And it was not very long after that, as they were riding across a blue field of mountain grama, that Alastair said, "Didn't you find him intriguing?"

"Kind of," Sant said. "But he wasn't buying any of what we remember at all."

"Not one bit," Alastair said.

"People are weird."

"Strange," Alastair said.

"Maybe we just attract especially odd people."

"Not that we're odd."

"Oh no," Sant said. Sant twirled his pigging string. *"Un poco, tal vez."*

"What's that mean?"

"A little maybe," Sant said.

"But only to other people."

"Only to other people," Sant agreed.

They approached now an open escarpment in the hills, a bleak torture of giant tangled boulders fallen down from the sleek walled Mesa Verde formation above. The yellow Mesa Verde, scattered here on the pitted floor of the red-and-yellow-striped Kirtland, allowed only an alley through which you could pass.

The two boys rode across scrambled time now; all of the rock formations that were so clean and stark down below had been uplifted and had fallen all around them here so that even an expert, by reading the formations, could not tell what time—how old the earth was here. Their horses moved silently among all the welter of varicolored confusion until they got on the stable earth cover, the bright blue-and-gold and green-shooting and silver-treed slope of the Jemez watershed and entered a deer path, sudden with wild roses and heavy with honeysuckle that garlanded, tight and bright, the dark branches that roofed the trail; entered a quick deer tunnel on a quiet day, and did not say anything at all to each other until they came out on the other side.

On the other side there was a stream, the small beginning of La Jara, which was the last water that fed the Rio Grande and the Atlantic. In a mile now they would be over the Divide and the water would go to the Pacific. But now they allowed their horses to drink, to still rob the Rio Grande and the Atlantic. In another hour of riding they would take from the Colorado and the Pacific.

"It tastes the same no matter which," Alastair said.

"No matter which what?" Sant said, drinking.

"Yes," Alastair said, speaking from the stream. "No matter which way we go we all end up in the same place."

"You're a big philosopher, Alley. Let's get moving." But Sant just sat there alongside the stream.

"Like you say, Santo," Alastair Benjamin said, crouching alongside the stream, too, and staring down intensely at his own reflection in the water. "God, I'm a handsome son of a bitch!"

118

"Your mother's side, I presume," Sant said.

"No, I get it from all sides."

"You got some mule too?"

"Yeah. I'm thinking of making a study of it," Alastair said. "A study of where we come from and how."

"Intercourse," Sant said. "Mr. Peersall said that, and even the missionary admits it."

"Yes, but there are all kinds of intercourse. Social, for example."

"Yeah, but that don't count."

"All right, but we agree that two cells come together?"

"Aren't you skipping a bit?" Sant said.

"All right, but we agree two cells come together?"

"Yeah."

"Making one cell."

"Yeah."

"Then isn't it a fair assumption that the cell that started it all is a cell that is composed of tiny particles of the man's body that started it all?"

Sant began tossing pebbles in the water so that their reflections, their exact images, spread outward in quick waves. "No, it isn't true," Sant said.

"Why isn't it true?" Alastair said, watching the destruction of his image in the water.

"Well," Sant said, "when people have this nonsocial intercourse— Wait a minute," he said, throwing a whole handful of pebbles in the water. "It's got to be social. After all, these people have got to have met each other, been introduced anyway."

"You've got a point there," Alastair said. "I'll tell the missionary it's got to be social. They've got to have met before, I hope.

"Sure," Sant said.

"But what about my statement not being true?"

"Well," Sant said, "if this cell is composed of tiny particles of the body of the man that started it all, supposing the man had lost an arm in battle or something, would the child be born with only one arm? I don't think it would."

"Maybe you got something," Alastair said. "I've got to do some more thinking."

"You certainly do."

"Maybe," Alastair said, beginning to toss pebbles into Sant's reflection now. "Maybe the cell remembers. Maybe it remembers to remember everything the way it was before the battle where he lost the arm."

"Maybe."

"I wouldn't want to have to rework my whole theory."

"You can always get facts to fit anything," Sant said.

"But I wouldn't want to mislead the world," Alastair said.

"Oh, they've been misled before."

"But they don't give medals for that."

"I think they have," Sant said.

"But it would be on my conscience."

"I can't help you there."

"No one can," Alastair said. "No one can. I have got to follow the truth where it leads, to take it where I find it, even if it's against me."

"Sure," Sant said. They both watched their perfect reflections in the water.

"That reminds me," Sant said. "I'd like to find something to eat."

Alastair stood up and looked down on the wide country beneath the clouds that were below them, floating above the long blue mesas like lambs or small puffs of smoke. Each mesa was an island above the earth and each large island was very sufficient unto itself. Each had its own mule deer, a large amount of juniper, jack pine, sage, ground scrub oak, and each its own foxes—red foxes. Some of these islands above the earth had coyotes; the long blue mesas are the last refuge, the final sanctuary, of these beautiful, light-running creatures that the government is determined to exterminate and the islands above the earth are determined to hide. The coyotes with these mesas are winning now because the coyotes are too smart to come down and the government men too lazy and too clumsy to get up.

120

"We got to get to the top of one of those one of these days," Alastair said.

"We been."

"It doesn't look possible from up here, does it?"

"No, it doesn't. But we been."

"When we going again?"

"When we feel like it."

"We can do anything."

"Anything," Sant said.

Alastair allowed his eye now to follow all the many clouds that lightly flowered the sky in each direction. One of them must be darkly shadowing the place where he remembered.

"Let's get going," Alastair said.

Soon they were cutting down the slope sharply but moving blindly through the trees. Then they hit an old and worn, narrow, one-way cattle path that followed along the wide bench of the Jemez. They must have followed this for about five miles or close to one hour, until they came to a clear opening on a sandstone slab escarpment where they could look straight down to sudden green fields below. The green was bright against the red earth. A protective ridge of gray sage sprinkled with the orange of Cowboys Delight and the blue of lupine circled all around the green place in the red earth.

"That's ours," Sant said. "It's part of the Circle Heart."

"This is where I remember. Where we had the gun fight," Alastair said suddenly.

"No. It's ours. It's part of the Circle Heart."

Alastair touched his horse and sped down ahead of Sant. Sant just sat there and watched him go down. He really could not see Alastair for the dust but he could see him finally as he opened the gate to the green pasture and stood holding it for Sant. Sant rode down slowly and went through the open gate very slowly. Alastair fastened the gate quickly and was gone again quickly on his horse, racing the animal to a burned mound in the middle of the green fields. When Sant got there Alastair was sitting on some burned adobes near a rusted iron bed.

121

"This is where it happened," Alastair said carefully and studying it all. "The gun fight. Where I remember."

"No. It's ours," Sant said. "It's part of the Circle Heart."

"Wait," Alastair said. "Over there. That's where the Indians were watching from—those rocks. And here," he said, "here is the bed and alongside the bed, look—shell casings."

"No. It's ours," Sant said. "It's part of the Circle Heart."

"But for how long?"

"As long as I remember," Sant said.

"Here," Alastair said, moving, then standing. "Here's where the window was."

"That orphanage where you were at," Sant said. "There must have been a lot of lonely nights."

"Yes," Alastair said.

"Where a guy could dream of cowboys and Indians."

"I guess so."

"And even of being one himself."

"Maybe. But I remember this."

"Oh," Sant said. "I bet you do."

"You mean you think—?"

"Yes," Sant said. "In the orphanage there must have been a lot of lonely nights."

"Then how about your bronc ride?" Alastair sat down now on the burned and rusted bed. "What about what you remember?"

"Oh that," Sant said. Sant was still mounted. "But this," Sant said, "this is ours. This is part of the Circle Heart."

"You mean that what we remember isn't any good now?"

"That's right," Sant said. "What you remember isn't any good."

"Just because this is yours?"

"That's right."

"Well, I didn't mean to pick on yours."

"Then why did you pick on the Circle Heart?"

"It's what I remember."

"Why didn't you pick on the New Mexico Cattle and Timber Keep Out? They can afford it and it's a nice place too."

"It's not what I remember."

122

"You see, Alastair," Sant said, speaking down from his horse, "whoever controls this controls the Circle Heart. Two hundred permits on the Peñas Negras. Without this water halfway between we couldn't drive to our summer pasture. If we didn't have this we'd have to get it. It's the heart of the Circle Heart."

"What do you mean you'd have to get it? Wasn't it always yours?"

"I think so."

Alastair picked up a blackened brass shell casing and tried, by aiming carefully, to drop it on another shell casing lying there. He hit it easily every time he tried. Now he began tossing shell casings over the hunk of burned adobe wall with an easy swinging motion of his arm.

"Maybe, Santo," he said, "maybe I should have picked on the New Mexico Cattle and Timber Keep Out. I don't know what got into me, picking on your place."

"Your place too," Sant said. "We adapted you."

"Is it adapted or adopted?" Alastair wondered.

"I don't know, Alley. But it's your place too."

"I don't know what got into me, Santo. I must have been crazy."

Sant got off his horse and sat down on the burned bed alongside of Alastair and looked over with him toward the great rocks.

"No, it's just that it's very lonely in an orphanage."

"Yes, I guess so," Alastair said.

"Alley, let's go where I remember."

"Today?"

"Yeah."

"Don't you think we've had enough today?"

"Maybe so. Then let's go back to the Circle Heart."

"*Cómo no?*"

"You're learning Spanish."

"I've learned a little bit every day."

The horses had drag-reined over to the distant fence. Sant was standing now. "I'll get both of them," he said, starting off.

Alastair Benjamin kicked around in the rubble of the burned house looking for treasure but he found nothing. He picked up a few burned books and let them drop. Then he decided to help Sant catch the horses. Sant was trailing them along the fence, careful not to move too quickly, but the horses were very careful to stay just ahead of him. Sant quickened his pace and the horses broke into a small trot. Sant stopped, placed his hands on his hips, and said, "Bastards."

Alastair began to trail the horses as they came across the field and Sant doubled back. When Sant got to the burned house he could see that Alastair had caught the horses in the far corner so he kicked around in the rubble looking for treasure but he found nothing either. Except this, he thought, bending over and picking up a spur that barely showed in the adobe. He wiped off the thick, hard mud and put the spur in his pocket. Now he took it out again and examined it carefully. Near where the sharp Spanish rowel was welded onto the heel piece there was some kind of a brand. Sant wiped it again with spit. It was a circle. Sant wiped it again. Inside the circle was etched a heart. Sant put it back in his pocket as Alastair came up with the horses.

"Any treasure?"

"No treasure," Sant said.

Alastair watched the sky. Big, anvil-shaped black clouds were tumbling in over the mountain already impinging quietly on the gentle blue.

"We got to make a run for it," Alastair said.

"It's too late, we're caught," Sant said.

"Yes," Alastair said, feeling the beginning drops. "But we'll make a run for it."

"All right," Sant said, mounting.

They got out of the green pasture as quickly as they could and put back the gate. Soon they were making rapid time through the dark forest with the rain noisy against the leaves.

"You said something about spurs," Sant said. "You remembered spurs."

"A silver spur. The man lost one silver spur," Alastair said. "But remember from now on we're going to pick on the New Mexico Cattle and Timber."

"Keep Out," Sant said.

124

"Yes, that's better," Alastair said. "It's a corporation, not a person. You don't stir up things."

"Yes. You don't stir up nothing," Sant agreed.

"Then we'll drop it," Alastair said.

"All right," Sant said.

"I'd like to find a cave where we can hide," Alastair said.

"Yeah. Someplace out of the rain," Sant said.

They got their horses out of the forest and made along a stone ledge between two cliffs. Somewhere along here were caves and they began watching the rock wall. What had been gay with vivid colors before was now all dull with rain, and the heavy clouds moved in beneath them as well as above them, blanking out the long valley below so that they moved between two layers of darkness alongside the even darker cliffs, but they continued to watch for a cave, without the protection now of the forest with its noise of the rain. Now there was only a big silence here as they walked their horses seemingly between the dim-lit sandwich of heaven and earth.

"There," Alastair said. "A cave."

The cave was not only large enough for them but great enough for their horses too. But the horses were not having any. They balked at the cave so the boys tied them to each other to keep them from drifting and sat themselves at the mouth of the cave looking out at the forlorn horses and the dark clouds that seemed to be ascending from below.

A deer tripped by with that easy ungainly going-in-all-directions, long-legged clumsiness deer have when they are not running. The deer did not spot the horses till he was among them; then he did not panic but seemed to stare them down as he moved through them and on into the cloud. Actually the deer must have been occupied with something else in which horses did not figure so that the horses did not register yet. Later, in a cloud, the deer might suddenly panic. The deer was a doe. Now there came a buck, a very wide-antlered, businesslike-looking animal except for those antlers. They must give him trouble moving through the heavy brush, but now he moved through the clouds well enough and with the haze around his feet he seemed diaphanous, before vanishing again and cloud-lost.

"They did not pick up our scent," Alastair said.

"No, I guess they didn't."

"I've got a thing about deer."

"What's that?"

"How there got to be different kinds of deer—mule deer, white tails."

"How did there get to be different kinds of deer?"

"Well, they got separated by a river or something. They had different kinds of country, different problems, so they became different."

"But deer could swim that river."

"I know," Alastair said. "For deer I need something bigger than a river."

"Yes, you do," Sant said.

"Maybe oceans," Alastair said. "Oceans separating the land for a while and then letting it join millions of years later. That would do it."

"It sure would," Sant said. "If you could move those oceans."

"Maybe they moved themselves. I'm not going to give up."

"That's right, don't quit, Alley."

"I won't."

"Jesus, I wish the rain would stop," Sant said.

Alastair began to collect a bunch of stones.

"You know, Santo, if a man waited at the mouth of this cave long enough the whole world would go by."

"Yeah."

Within the darkness of the cave Sant and Alastair were getting very low, sitting and watching the rain.

"But if we sit here long enough the whole world will go by," Alastair said.

"I'd rather go out and meet it," Sant said.

"Very pleased to meet you."

"How are the twins?"

"Yeah."

"I'm going out."

"In the rain?"

"Yeah."

126

"Did something happen back there, Santo?"

"No, I guess not. We better get going."

"In the rain?"

"Why not?"

"Cómo no?"

When they got to the place where the tunnel of flowers ran alongside the mountain they decided against going the way they had come. Everything was all wet and dripping in there and what had been bright and alive, riotous, before, was now only gaudy and wrong in the rain. They went up on top and trailed the ridge on an old deer trail. Up here you could sense the first break in the weather. Up here you could look out and over the whole weird, awful land and be in a nice position to enjoy it if anything good happened. They continued to ride the ridge that seemed the top of the world. Up here the two of them were alone and together. Maybe it would be nice if they never had to go down.

"Let's ride her all the way in," Sant said.

"The ridge?"

Alastair touched his hand along the mane of his white horse. "That would be nice."

Now his horse followed a Z in the trail that led him up even higher. He was lost a brief second before Sant spurred his paint and then again quickly they were joined.

"That's the secret-city fence," Alastair said, pointing. "But I don't see any guard and I don't see our tracks. I suppose you've always got to watch out for a trigger-happy guard."

"We're hitting the fence at a different place this time," Sant said. "We'll have to follow the fence down."

The rain clouds were breaking up, dissolving in wraiths and then reforming in less weight, less darkness; but a very quiet, small rain still fell in the manner of rain that will go on falling and has fallen already past remembrance.

"Oh," Sant said. He thought he saw the guard up ahead. Sant and Alastair turned their horses into the brush and disappeared.

"Like Indians," Sant said. "We just move off and leave the white man. That's the way Indians always were, you know. Maybe they'd be with a white party two or three days and then suddenly they had left."

"Maybe they remembered something."

"It could have been that."

"Then let's go where you rode the bronc horse."

"Another day."

"If it's because of those crazy people like Arturo Cipriano de Godoy, remember there's always your father."

"Yes, there was always him."

After four hours of steady riding they were heading down off the mountain now. The rain had eased to be almost nothing, yet the sky was a very deep gray and all the country below was somber in shadow and wet without glisten, green without color. They rode in silence down to the mouth of the long valley. Way up ahead, but visible, were the beginning fences, five barbed-wire strands, horseshoe-nailed to juniper posts, going all around the Circle Heart.

"Yes," Sant said as they brought their gay horses into a trot, "yes. My father eats butterflies."

"You intrigue me," Alastair said. "Tell me more."

"Tomorrow," Sant said. "Today we've had plenty. Tomorrow. I'll remember more tomorrow."

EIGHT **M**illie Sant began working in the kitchen early and by ten o'clock she was finished with Zen. Zen did not seem to fit too well into New Mexico, but to Millie this bright morning made her feel generous and she could not leave any religion without saying some good word for it. She removed from the shelf from between the butter and the beans a copy of Zen Buddhism. She wanted a good word to quit it on. She read from Zen to find a good word.

"When Hui-neng declared, 'From the first not a thing is,' the keynote of Zen thought was struck. This keynote was never so clearly struck before. When the masters who followed him pointed to the presence of the Mind in each individual mind and also to its absolute purity, this idea of presence and purity was understood somehow to suggest the existence of an individual body, however ethereal and transparent it may be conceived. The philosophy of Prajnaparamita, (wu-i-wu) which is also that of Hui-neng, generally has this effect. To understand it a man requires a deep religious intellectual insight in the truth of Sunyata. When Hui-neng is said to have had an awakening by listening to the Vajracchedika Sutra (Diamond Sutra) which belongs to the Prajnaparamita group of the Mayahana texts, we know then at once where he has his foothold."

Millie put the book down.

"He has his foothold in—well, I guess, bull turds," Millie finally decided. That was about the only apt word that ranch life in northern New Mexico had given her to quit the yogis on. Not

129

bad for a young yogin with a high Zen education trapped in the west.

Not too bad, Millie thought, replacing the beans on the shelf and putting Zen in the trash.

"Not bad. It's the best religion I've read in a long time. You can quote me on that," Millie said as she went over and sat on the window box, touched her index finger to her small face, and stared out.

The kids have got to have a religion though. Yes sir, she thought, watching them. They've got to have a religion, some real religion. None of this Zen stuff. Come to think of it, though, they've got to have one of the big three religions so they will fit in with other people and not use bad words and so they'll have a place to look forward to when they die, up there with the big three. Me, when I die, I'll come back to the ranch. I like this ranch very much. Those kids, though, must do things properly. If I had done things properly I would be married to George Hutchinson and working in his dress shop in Gallup. I beat that rap. Big Sant has his problems and only his will to face them with—and there go I. So be it. God save us all.

It was a crystal day at the Circle Heart, a dense clear blue with no clouds at all. Little Sant was working in the corral when Alastair came up.

"He really does," Alastair said. "He catches them anyway. He's catching them now."

"He eats them," Sant said above his pounding on the stock-branding chute. Now he ceased his pounding and cocked the hammer behind his ear. "He eats them."

"Well, he catches them anyway," Alastair said.

"He eats them too," Sant said and he resumed his hammering.

Alastair went back to the hill above the barn where the speckled squirrels had a lookout and where he had been watching from before, and watched Big Sant lumber about in the fields below catching butterflies.

"Eats them?" Alastair wondered.

Later, in a small, dim-lighted room in the great house, Big

130

Sant had the day's catch neatly impaled on a board in front of him with bright pins.

"Can I come in?" Alastair said.

"I suppose so, but I'm very busy."

"Are you going to eat any?" Alastair said.

"Not any of these."

"Aren't those any good to eat?"

"It's not necessary."

"Is it necessary to eat some of them?"

"Yes."

"Why is it necessary to eat some of them?"

"So as you can tell what they're up to."

"Oh?"

"So as you can tell why their color is useful. Most butterflies resemble their surroundings, that is, they have got a protective coloration. But some butterflies challenge their surroundings with big crosses and stripes that holler, Look at me, look at me, look at me now! These are the bitter, nasty-tasting ones. Once a bird has eaten one of these he will never eat another so he keeps looking for those loud markings to distinguish what he should not eat and the bitter-tasting butterflies who can be told by loud markings are safe. Now this system has worked so well that some sweet-tasting butterflies have adopted this kind of loud coloring and it has confused the birds very much."

"I've been adopted."

"Yes. We adopted you."

"Why?"

"That's a different subject. Now we're talking about butterflies."

"Why do you have to eat some of the butterflies?"

"So I can prove that some of the loud butterflies taste good and so I can put down exactly which ones they are."

"Who for?"

"For people who are interested."

"I hope you get some pay for it?"

"No. It's science."

"Don't scientists get paid?"

131

"Not if they haven't gone to school."

"Why didn't you go to school?"

"Because somebody had to work this ranch. My brother had something more important to do."

"You mean it wasn't very important?"

"Yes."

"But you would have liked to have gone to school and become a real scientist?"

"Yes."

"All of those butterflies adopting all those colors and then your adopting me."

"Yes, we adopted you, and that was because, way out here, we figured Little Sant needed someone his own age to be with. Now we have two sons."

"I've got a thing about deer."

"What's that?"

"That we get different kinds of deer because at one time there was one kind of deer and they got separated and then, in a trillion years, naturally they became different."

"How did they get separated?"

"I'm thinking about that."

"It's a very good thing to think about."

"It all began when I was thinking how I got black. We must have got separated from the people who were white."

"It's better when science is impersonal. Try to think about the deer."

"All right. I'm sorry I interrupted your work on the butter-flies."

"That's all right. It's fine. I like to see it. I wish Little Sant took some interest."

"You going to send him to the university?"

"Yes."

"He wants to be a bronc rider."

"Yes. We hope he'll get over that."

"He never asked you why you eat butterflies?"

"No, he hasn't."

"Well, I'm sorry I asked you what you wanted him to ask."

132

"You're my son, too, Alastair," Big Sant said and he slid over a new tray of bright varicolored butterflies that were impaled like the others on a stiff burlap cloth. "That's all right. And you go right on thinking about the deer."

"Well, I was thinking about the old Circle R too. We were up there." Alastair looked around. "I see you've got some burned books."

"Yes. But you go right on thinking about the deer," Big Sant said. "Always try to follow through on important things that might affect your future."

"Okay," Alastair said and he left.

Big Sant buried his flowered face in his hands and stared down at the bright butterflies all impaled there.

Later on in the day, when the big, deep, clear, total blueness of the sky had collected a few high clouds, Alastair and Sant were going around the yellow overhang of the Cuba Mesa on a mission, a mission to a mission. That is, they were supposed to deliver a message to Mr. Sanders at the Torreon Mission from Millie Sant. But they had thought of a better mission of their own which was to go where Little Sant had ridden the killer horse at the rodeo. And now this mission had been sidetracked for a still better mission, which was to trap the trapper. The government trapper was laying out poisoned meat to kill the coyotes and they had just spotted him going up a draw that led to the top of the Cuba Mesa.

"How are we going to trap a trapper?" Alastair said. "We're supposed to be on some other kind of mission anyway."

"We can still do our mission to the mission and go to where I rode the killer horse, too, but we may never get a chance to trap the trapper again."

"It's a unique opportunity."

"Yes. And we may never get a good chance again."

"Yeah."

The government trapper was actually a government poisoner; that is, he did not carry traps but poisoned meat in his saddlebags. Cyanide of potassium was mixed in the meat, which he placed wherever he saw signs of coyotes. It caused violent convulsions in

133

the sleek gray animals and, in not too long a time, they were dead. There are not too many left. The ranchers at one time complained that the coyote was killing their sheep, but now most of them are in cattle and they have stopped complaining but the government has still got the habit of killing coyotes. It's a war. There was one government trapper who used to work the region whom they called Unconditional Surrender Rothrock. He killed eight hundred and fifty-two. A very brave chap. He quit to take a more interesting job at Yucca Flats. Some said he was too lazy to climb the mesas where the last of the coyotes were, others said he got bored killing coyotes and wanted to try something more challenging. Anyway the man below was Unconditional Rothrock's replacement. His name was Charles Enright and he was determined to do his duty; that is, he would climb the mesas. That is, he would go where the coyotes were regardless of the terrain or lack of challenge. As Enright climbed, pulling the horse after him, he would occasionally stop, go back to the saddlebags on the horse, and drop a bait of meat; and the two boys, Sant and Alastair, following at a cautious distance, would on every occasion retrieve the bait and put it in their own saddlebags for later use. The one thing the boys noticed about Enright was that he was not as smart as Unconditional Surrender Rothrock. He did not take the precaution, as did Rothrock, of looking back with field glasses to make sure no coyote lover was following and picking up the meat.

"He's pretty dumb," Sant said, putting the bait in his saddlebag and regaining the horse.

"He didn't go to poisoner's school," Alastair said.

"Do they have that kind of schools?"

"They got every kind of school."

"You know, Santo," Alastair said, "I've been watching him."

"All right, what did you notice?"

"That he's examining the rocks. He seems more preoccupied with the rocks than the coyotes."

"What does preoccupied mean?"

"You know what that word means. You just think I'm using too many big words."

134

"Sure you are. And the danger is that pretty soon you won't be able to use small words."

"Are they better?"

"Sure they are."

"That's very perspicacious of you."

"Sure it is."

"Well then, I've noticed he's interested in the rocks."

"I've noticed that too."

"Well, why didn't you agree with me before?"

"Because you wouldn't speak English."

"Santo, you're a snob."

"What does that mean?"

"It means that you're probably right, that I like to practice big words."

"Well, practice them on your own time."

"When no one's looking?"

"That's right. Sometime, Alley, when we're not trapping the trapper."

"We're supposed to be on a mission to the missionary."

"Missionaries can wait."

"There's something profound in that statement that escapes me."

"Me too. Notice, Alley, our friend is examining the rocks again."

"Friend?"

"Well, studying the rocks is not a good way to catch coyotes, according to Rothrock."

"Well, maybe this is a new way to kill coyotes."

"I never thought of that."

"An innovation."

"I did think of that but I thought it sounded silly."

"Okay, Santo. But it's got me why rocks have got anything to do with coyotes."

"Me too, Alley."

As the trapper, Charles Enright, climbed he marveled that he had come where even the famous Rothrock was unwilling to go, scattering the meat as he went. Now he sat down to study something carefully and he nibbled on the meat bait as he sat. But he spat it out. It didn't taste very good uncooked. The coyotes didn't seem to mind, or the foxes, who must get some of it too. The coyote, he thought, belongs to the dog family. There are several species. Man is only one species. He hadn't remembered this from school, he had looked it up before he applied for the job, thinking they might ask him something. They asked him nothing. Yes, they had asked him if he was willing. He was willing. Charles Enright was one of the few ranchers in the area that still ran sheep. The government thought they knew exactly why he was willing to kill coyotes. Charles Enright owned thirteen hundred and twelve sheep according to the latest tally that his two Navaho shepherds had made on their tally sticks, and six goats to do the leading. Maybe five now. The Indians ate goat when they felt like eating goat. But, Enright thought, pulling on the reins to bring the horse up close to where he was sitting, according to my observations from below I am supposed to be sitting just about exactly where the Nacimiento rock divides from the San José. But now that I am up here I'm not so sure. The San José was sedimentary, laid down about sixty-five million years ago and the Nacimiento around eighty million, but right here the formations seem to have faulted. That is, when that mountain rose over there it pressured the scarp into a down tilt and right here the San José seems like a card cheated into the wrong position in the deck. If I could find a fossil in this lens I am in doubt about, I could send it to the American Museum and they could tell me exactly where I am. Where I was.

"Where is he now?" Sant asked.

"He has just begun to climb up into the San José."

"What is that?"

"That's a formation. Don't you ever read any of your father's books?"

"No. I told you, I'm going to be a bronc rider."

"Well, I'm not so sure he's in the San José myself. There's a bad fault there. She could be out of place."

"Then books don't help much."

"They make you curious if they pose the right questions."

"Well, Alley, I wish you'd be curious about the question at hand."

"Doing the trapper in?"

"Yeah."

"Well, we could shoot him."

"Yeah, we could."

"We could dine him."

"What do you mean, dine him?"

"Well, all this poison meat he's been dropping for the coyotes we got in our saddlebags. We could circle ahead of him, cook it up, and invite him to eat with us. Feed him what he's feeding the coyotes."

"Couldn't they give us the electric chair for life for doing that?"

"Not if it's not premeditated."

"What's that mean?"

"If we don't think about it, it's okay."

"Then we won't think about it. We'll just do it."

"All right. Let's circle ahead of him without thinking."

"And cook up the poison meat without thought."

"Yeah."

The danger is, Enright thought, resuming his climb, that those two boys following me don't know that I know they are trailing me. The danger is they might do something silly. They could do something with the meat that would lose me my job. From the looks of them they are the boys from the Circle Heart. The Circle Heart is a queer bunch. The father catches butterflies. Still, maybe my outfit's a queer bunch too. I catch rocks. Maybe every outfit's a queer bunch if you really know enough about them. I think, though, that maybe the Circle Heart is a queerer bunch than the rest. After all, where did the dark boy come from? At the inquiry, after the fire at the Circle R, it was brought out that the black had no son. Yet President Taft says there was a boy, says he rescued the boy from the fire, kept him several months before the boy ran away—to get back home, that he must have been picked up by the police somewhere and put in an orphanage. Yet Bowman, who was at the fire too, who fired back when he was fired at, says he saw

137

no boy; and who would take President Taft's word against a respected white Christian? And yet the boy they adopted is very dark. Coincidence? Conscience? Maybe he thinks bringing a dark boy into the outfit will make himself easier to live with after he bid in the Circle R so cheap at the tax sale. Maybe he suspects that there might have been a boy in that fire that the Gran Negrito never wanted anyone to see, by some woman he wanted no one to discover. Maybe. Maybe this and maybe that. Maybe I should mind my own business. Maybe, he thought, halting the horse he led and getting down on his knees. Yes, maybe this is the San José. It's too bad they don't have a blood test for these rocks or that I can't find a fossil so that I could be certain of the identification. Bowman has the same problem and I don't mean with rocks and I don't mean with butterflies. But maybe we should mind our own business.

Enright began scattering meat to the right and some to the left. He threw meat above the path and below. This would show all the citizens and fellow taxpayers following how efficient he was. Just as good as Unconditional Surrender Rothrock.

"And my opinions are just as good as President Taft's. I only wish I knew more about these rocks and why the boys are following me. But maybe even President Taft wouldn't know exactly."

"You suppose he knows we're watching him?"

"I think he does."

"Why do you think he does?"

"Because he's acting. He's throwing the meat with more verve than Rothrock."

"Verve?"

"Style. You know I got a theory."

They climbed their gay horses, an Appaloosa and a paint, through even gayer rocks to higher ground beneath a brighter sky, went through a sea of brighter blue beeweed that did not belong at this altitude. Now they gained a deer path that twisted, tortured its way around great stones in a punishing sun.

"So no one is interested in my theory. All right," Alastair said.

"All right, what is it?"

"He is acting."

"Oh."

138

"Yes. He's not throwing the meat the way your father catches butterflies."

"They're two different operations."

"But here there's something acting."

"You mean, as the missionary would say, his soul ain't in it?"

"Maybe. But I still say style."

"Alley, why do you have to contradict everybody including Mr. Sanders, the missionary?"

"Did I?"

"You just did."

"You mean I contradicted him?"

"Before we got there."

"Well, now," Alastair said.

The deer path they followed began to straighten out as they neared the top of the Cuba Mesa. Like all deer paths, this one took the longest distance between two points, but as it neared the top of the mesa the deer decided to cease the game and the path made quickly to a close cover of scrub oak. And so now did the boys on the paint and the Appaloosa.

"Well, now," Alastair said, stroking the paint beneath a juniper, "this looks like as good a place to dine as any."

"Yeah," Sant said, taking the meat they had collected out of the saddlebags. "Yes, it does."

From way up here they could look down on all the land between the mesas and see the sheer sides of many other mesas. They both knew that mesa means table in Spanish, and that's exactly what they looked like. Alastair had found out that they did not rise there in the forming of the earth but that they remained there, these tougher tables in the clouds, when the rest of the land had water- and wind-eroded away. Some of the land that was formerly there between the tables is now in Old Mexico, some of it may be in Madagascar, more of it is at the bottom of the ocean.

"Yeah," Alastair said.

"Yeah what?" Sant said. "Why don't you help me with the fire?"

"Yeah, soon this mesa will be gone too. It's disappearing

before our eyes." Alastair was still atop his horse. "In another hundred million years there will be none of this mesa left."

"Oh, that's terrible," Sant said. "Now you have got me worried. The way you're dreaming up there on the horse it may be gone before we get this fire built."

Alastair got down and gathered some dead piñon and brought it to Sant, who was cradling a small beginning flame.

"Alley, we got to stop worrying about tomorrow and get this nice dinner cooked."

"I wasn't worried about tomorrow. I said it would take a hundred million years."

"As a matter of fact, Alley, it will be only a few minutes before he gets here."

"All right," Alastair said, and he got the frying pan and the bread out of the saddlebags. Sant took the pan and held it over the fire.

"Now get the meat," he said. Sant took the meat, made it into patties with his quick, grimed hands, and settled each patty carefully in the pan he held over the piñon flames. "Now we're in business," he said.

"What we going to use for a table?"

"This whole thousand acres we're on top of is a table. That's what you been dreaming about, isn't it?"

"But supposing we get caught?"

"They can't do nothing because we haven't been thinking about it. We been thinking about something else. We been thinking about tables. We haven't been thinking about poisoning poisoners."

"Yeah, I really have been thinking about something else lately."

"Good. You'll make a good case. Pass me more of the meat."

Alastair passed another ball of meat. "I've been thinking lately that we can't do this."

"We're doing it. Watch."

"I mean even if we don't get caught. We got to live with ourselves."

"Were you planning to live with someone else?"

"I mean our conscience."

140

"Put it in the pan."

"You know what I mean."

"If you can't put it in the pan I don't know what you mean."

They both huddled around the pan watching the meat fry.

"It's about done, Alley," Sant said. "Now we can throw it away."

"Throw it away?"

"Yeah. I scared you."

"Yeah, you did."

"Then that's all. I sure would like to think of some way, though, of keeping him from killing the coyotes."

"Me too."

"Some way we could live with our own selves and someone else too."

"Me too."

Sant cocked his arm to throw the dangerous meat into the brush. "Well, here goes his dinner."

"Wait a minute! Don't throw good meat away, boy." The trapper had come over the top pulling his horse. Now he advanced on Sant and took the pan Sant held. "Don't throw away perfectly good meat," he said, examining it.

"We've already et more than we can hold," Sant said. "We're all finished."

"But maybe someone else. I haven't eaten yet." Mr. Enright wore a big, squared roundup hat above a small, red, inquiring face.

"Oh," Sant said.

"Yes, oh," Alastair said.

"You wouldn't begrudge a man?"

"No."

"Oh, no," Alastair said.

"Then I'll dig in."

"No," Sant said.

"Oh, no," Alastair said.

"Why?" The man went over, still holding the pan, and got out a fork from his saddlebag. "Why not?"

"Because it might be poisoned," Sant said.

"Who would want to poison meat?" the trapper said.

"Some people."

"Sure. Some people," Alastair said.

"Well, I don't think so," the trapper said and he forked a piece of the meat.

"I wouldn't do that," Alastair said. "Like I said, some people."

"Some people such as who?" the trapper said.

"Such as you," Sant said. Sant stood up from his crouched position over the fire.

"Yeah," Alastair said, getting up too. "Such as you."

Enright sat down on a juniper log as the boys stood up. "You think I'm another Rothrock?"

"Another Unconditional Surrender Rothrock," Sant said.

"Well," Enright said and he ate some of the meat, ate it all the way down.

"You're on your own," Alastair said.

"On my own," the man agreed and he ate another piece of the meat.

"All the way down," Sant said to Alastair.

"Yeah, I noticed that too," Alastair said.

"Have you noticed me tossing out the meat too?" Enright asked between bites.

"Yeah."

"Did you notice me mix any poison with it?"

"No."

"Then why should I be afraid to eat my own meat?"

The boys now both sat down on the juniper log with Enright.

"The government," Enright said, "told me to take care of the coyotes."

"That's right," Sant said.

"They gave me the poison and the meat. It's good meat."

"Is it good?" Sant said.

"They didn't tell me to mix the poison and the meat."

"They're not very good about instructions."

"No, they're not," Enright said.

"Still," Alastair said, leaning and looking under the log, "your instructions were tacitly implicit. Is it ethical of you—?"

142

"Yes, it is," Enright said.

"What's that?" Sant said.

"He means I knew my intentions all along and I had no right to take the job."

"Then why didn't Alastair say that?" Sant said.

"The same reason the government didn't," Enright said. "Didn't say it to my face, 'Go out and kill all the coyotes because we have already killed almost all the big cats that prey on them and after you have killed all the coyotes then kill all the rabbits because when the coyotes are gone the rabbits will, of course, explode, and after the rabbits are gone whatever they feed on will be all over the place and then you exterminate that and then the next and the next until we are the only animal alive!' "

"Then you're the opposite of Unconditional Surrender Rothrock."

"You might say that."

"But then that evades the law," Alastair said.

"But there was another law before we ever got here."

Alastair moved a stone with his foot. "What law was that?"

"Nature," Enright said. "The law of nature. It keeps everything nicely balanced. No animal got out of hand."

"We got out of hand," Alastair said.

"Yes, we did," Enright said, and he finished the last of the meat, wiped his hands on his horse that stood by. "Isn't it a beautiful day," he said, looking out. "It was a beautiful trip up here and I think I found out where the San José and the Nacimiento divide."

"Then you're not taking the government money for doing nothing," Alastair said.

"No. I think I've made a contribution they can use."

"In more ways than one," Sant said.

"I hope so, son," Enright said. "Thank you, son, for the dinner." And Enright was off across the mesa, tossing meat above the rocks and below the rocks, around and over the logs, wherever the coyotes might lurk. Just like Unconditional Surrender Rothrock.

"Yeah, I don't know why he did it," Sant said.

"Did what?"

143

"Took the job."

"To save the coyotes, like he said."

"But, like he said, he's got sheep."

"You mean the rabbits that the coyotes used to keep down are eating his grass."

"That's right."

"And that's why he wants to bring back the coyotes, don't want another Unconditional Surrender Rothrock to get the job."

"Yes, maybe."

"But maybe he is an idealist about bringing the coyotes back with no personal gain at all and maybe you're a cynic."

"Yes, maybe. And maybe, like Mr. Peersall says, I'm a realist."

"And maybe, like the missionary says, realism is a corruption of reality."

"Oh," Sant said, getting on his horse and looking out over the country below. "The missionary said no such thing. He speaks English as good as the rest of us."

"Well, where to now?" Alastair said, mounting.

"Home."

"Where the woodbine twineth."

"Yeah. Where my old man catches butterflies."

Alastair led off down the slope. "Where the woodbine twineth is just a phrase."

"Where my old man catches butterflies isn't."

"Santo," Alastair said, allowing his paint to pick and choose in jerky fashion down the slope, "Santo, you've got to be more tolerant."

"If you mean I catch his butterflies, okay if he'll catch my norse.

"Santo, you mean he doesn't give you any encouragement about being a bronc rider."

"That's right. And moreover, he's *dis*couraging."

"Well, you don't encourage his butterflies."

"I try to, Alley. I've worked at them, but somehow I don't follow the train of his mind. Butterflies."

"It's a science. He'd like you to take an interest in science."

"Butterflies," Sant said.

They rode across the very level mesa with Sant roping a rock or a stump when he saw one that was right for roping. They rode mostly through piñon, a tree that produces nuts. They are very irregular in their production and if the Navahos can make a good gathering every three years the Indians are doing very well. Although the Indians don't gather them exactly, the squirrels gather them. The Indians find the nests of the squirrels and rob the squirrels. The same Indians who robbed the pueblos now rob the squirrels.

They rode, too, through an orange sward of pentstemon, then a burst of golden goldeneye and blue bluebells, desert phlox, gilia, and four o'clock, but nearby it was filaree—filaree and yucca. Yucca boiled makes a good soap and the Indians didn't have to rob anyone to get it but the Navaho women had to gather it all by themselves without help from the squirrels. Squirrels aren't concerned with soap.

"Look up ahead there, Alley," Sant said.

"What?"

"See the rainbow?"

"No."

"Well, I'll rope it for you." Sant threw a long rope into the clearing ahead and pulled it in carefully. "There," he said, "I got it."

"Jeez," Alastair said. "You're roping things now that don't exist."

"That rainbow was the Madison Square Garden rodeo, Alley, and I'm going to make her."

"With pluck and luck."

"And practice."

"Even on rainbows?"

"Even on rainbows."

"That don't exist?"

"That don't exist yet."

"Look out!" Alastair dropped his horse off the mesa onto a narrow trail that led below.

"Can we make it down that way?" Sant called.

"You can make her down any way," Alastair said, not raising his voice. "When all else fails you can always fall."

"Down, you mean."

"Well, you can't fall up."

"That's why I keep practicing, Alley."

"You're still on the bronc kick."

"I always was, always will be." Sant joined Alastair now down on the narrow ledge below. "Did you mean that as one of your pure laws when you said you can't fall up? Is that another Benjamin law?"

"Yeah."

"What are some other Benjamin laws?"

"Well, for example, your grandfather can't be your descendant."

"You mean I can never be older than Grandfather?"

"That's right."

"Well, I never did worry about that law. Is there another law that says black people can never be white and vice versa?" Alastair didn't say anything. "Well, I never did worry about that law either," Sant said.

"Follow me," Alastair said, "and don't worry about anything."

Sant allowed his horse to creep along the narrow ledge after Alastair's. "I didn't say anything that annoyed you?"

"No," Alastair said. "This is just a short cut."

"What do you know about girls?" Sant said.

"Very little," Alastair said. "But I'm going to study them."

"And you'll let me know?"

"I'll let you know," Alastair promised.

After one half hour of very slow descent during which they continued to discuss very important things and only the horses worried, they finally made it down to the flat sage and bloom of yucca country where the big arroyos cut in weird angles up ahead.

"Older people seem to take more of an interest in girls than we do," Sant said.

"And it's not an academic interest," Alastair said.

"Yeah."

146

"No, I don't think it's an academic interest," Alastair said.

"Me neither," Sant said.

"But we don't want to condemn before we know more."

"That's right."

"What's right?"

"What you said."

"Yes, I think it's true, don't you?" Alastair said.

"Yeah. Look, I just remembered something."

"What?"

"There's the Circle Heart."

"So it is."

"And I just remembered that we were supposed to be on a mission to the missionary. Instead of that we trapped the trapper."

"So we did."

"And here we are back at the Circle Heart."

"So we are."

"What do we do?"

"Bluff," Alastair said. "Just ride in looking like we been to the mission."

"How does that look?"

"Kind of solemn, I guess, and serious and put in our place."

"All right."

They rode into the yard now of the sprawling adobe house, looking all of those things. Millie Sant stood there in front of the pump house with a dustpan and a piece of bridle in her hand.

"You boys been to the mission?" she called.

"We're going there now," Sant said.

"Yes, we're taking this short cut," Alastair said, and they both rode through the yard and out the other side.

"Lord!" Millie Sant shrieked and retreated back into the house.

"I guess we didn't look solemn enough or serious."

"Or put in our place," Sant said.

When they were absolutely certain they were well out of danger they halted their horses to figure out what to do.

"Did it ever occur to us that the thing to do," Sant said, "is to deliver the message?"

147

They were hidden in a bunch of loose-waving tamarisk along-side a broad saline wash that whitened the dry bed of its course as far as they could see.

"Wouldn't that be too obvious?" Alastair said. Alastair broke off a piece of the bitter tamarisk and ate it. "Yes, too obvious."

"How do we know?" Sant said.

"Read the message."

"Will that tell us?"

"It should," Alastair said.

"Well, it says here," Sant said.

"Where?"

"Well, I haven't found it yet. Have you got it?"

"No. You got it."

"Here it is," Sant said. "It says here."

"That's an odd way to start a letter."

"It says here: 'Dear Mr. Sanders, I'm sending you my two boys.' "

"You see, it is obvious," Alastair said. "That is, it will be obvious to the missionary when he sees us standing there."

"It says here," Sant said, " 'Dear Mr. Sanders, I'm sending you my two boys—' "

"She's being redundant."

"What's that?"

"She's repeating herself."

"No, that was me."

"Well, don't interpolate. Just extrapolate."

"What's that?"

"I really don't know, Santo."

"It sounds pretty good."

"Yes it does. But don't put in any more of your own lines."

"All right. To continue. That means I'm going to start where I left off."

"Did she say that?"

"No. That was me again."

"You better let me read it, Santo."

"All right."

Alastair took the letter and then removed gold wire spectacles from a red leather case, looked at the horse to get the range. The horse looked back and Alastair returned to the letter.

"Now, where were we?"

"I didn't get that far," Sant said.

"Oh, here we are."

"A very interesting letter," Sant said.

Alastair picked up a rock as he examined the letter.

"Okay," Sant said.

Alastair removed the letter as far from his eyes as he could reach but evidently he still couldn't see anything.

"Where did you find those glasses?" Sant said.

"Alongside Route 66. Don't you think they become me?"

"Sure."

"Make me look academic?"

"Sure."

Alastair had the letter turned upside down now. "She doesn't write clearly."

"If you'd take those things off you could see."

"Do things have to be functional?"

"No, but they should work."

"A point," Alastair said and he removed the glasses, held them at arm's length, and looked at the horse through one lens. The horse looked back in unbelief and Alastair returned the glasses to the case and then read the letter all the way through.

"Read it again," Sant said.

Alastair read the letter again, this time out loud.

" 'Dear Mr. Sanders, I am sending you my two boys. The trouble with them is, one of them reads too much and the other never reads at all. The other trouble is, both of them are never home and when they are home one ropes and the other reads. But the trouble about sending them to you is religion. They don't have much, maybe because I don't have any, but everyone else should. I mean everyone else does. And I don't think they should inherit my religion, that is, none. Their father isn't any good either at religion. He is worse than I am. I think these boys should get some religion. Not too much because that's what maybe happened to me. I got too much too young and now can with a good mind subscribe to none. For a while I subscribed to the *Christian Science Monitor*. That's a religion where you subscribe to their newspaper but you don't subscribe to doctors. But after a horse fell on me at Gallina I gave it up. But I think the boys need something to make them more like other boys in case they go to school, where religion is taken for granted. Not that I want everything they do to be taken for granted but I do not want them to be taken for freaks either. What do you say to this? Give them enough religion to make them respectable but not so much that they end up with none. I think you have just the right amount. You help the Indians but you don't make a fool of us in front of them. What do you say to this? Feel them out, my two boys, that is, and see if you can use on them what you use on the Indians. All the Indians in your territory seem nice and one of them, President Taft, seems respectable. Not that the others aren't respectable too. It's just that I don't know the others as well as I know President Taft. If you could make these boys like you made President Taft that would be a fine thing and I thank you. The darkest one is the one that reads books. Sincerely, Millicent Bowman.' "

Alastair tapped the letter with the spectacles. "A good letter," he said.

Sant now had taken to eating tamarisk. He had his cowboy hat pushed back and was leaning foward critically from his seat in the speckled shade and eating tamarisk.

"Was the grammar okay?"

Alastair snapped the lid of the red spectacle case, shying the horses.

"Just about," he said. "When we speak of how a thing is said we aren't concerned actually with grammar. We are speaking of style."

"Are we?"

Alastair touched the spectacle case against his knuckles. "By style one means the ability to communicate emotionally, sentiment but not sentimentality. Sentimentality is the failure of emotion. One frequently uses a symbol to express an unexpressible emotion. The primitive symbol of God is still extant in our civilization. But one finds exceptions."

150

"Does one?" Sant said, feigning sleep.

"Yes. With you it's a horse."

Sant looked sleepily at the horse.

"With me it's truth."

"Oh," Sant said, embarrassed. "I thought it was memorizing books."

"Do I sound silly?"

"Just very young," Sant said.

"I'm older than you."

"Most people are," Sant said. "But they can still sound silly."

"Yes, but because you win an argument doesn't mean you are right."

"Big words don't either," Sant said.

"Listen," Alastair said. "This isn't getting us to the mission."

"Boy, you are so right," Sant said.

"How did we get off the track?"

"I asked you if the grammar was okay."

"No."

"Good," Sant said.

They both lay now in the dappled shade, hidden here against the overreaching sun; even the horses were nuzzled into the tamarisk against the sun and now they began to nibble on the shade above Alastair.

"What I say is," Sant said, "let's go see Mr. Peersall instead."

"Okay."

"You know he fought Indians."

"He's very old. He could have."

"Yes, he could have fought Indians."

"Did he?"

"I think he did, Alley. His stories add up pretty good."

"That's what you would have done."

"Fought Indians?"

"Yeah."

"I guess so."

"Sure."

"And you would have written about it."

"I guess so."

"That's what you got to watch out for, Alley. That you don't end up by being just a writer."

"I guess so. But what's so wrong with that?"

"Nothing, I guess, except you don't do nothing."

"I guess so. But what's so hot about Mr. Peersall?"

"He fought Indians."

They both broke off a twig of tamarisk before the horses got it all.

"Where does he live?"

"Just a piece."

The horses had now eaten away a good deal of the shade.

"What I say," Sant said, "is let's go see Mr. Peersall before our horses make us perish in the sun. There's a word for you."

"All right," Alastair said, rising and hitting the horse above. "Well, anyway it's my own horse," Alastair said.

They got on their horses and Sant took the lead in the direction, he said, of the *casa* of Mr. Peersall.

"Del hombre who fought the Indians. *Luchaba contra los salvajes,"* Sant said, allowing his horse to move well ahead.

NINE ${\bf M}$issionaries and traders—the mercenaries and the missionaries—have one thing very much in common, Big Sant held. They are both exploited by the Indians. Cowboys and Indians know this. Sometimes it will take a trader a whole lifetime to realize that he has spent his life working twenty-four hours a day for the Navahos. Sometimes missionaries will spend all the loose money in Kansas, half the tithes of Salt Lake City, before they realize they have clothed and fed one fourth of the Navaho Nation and haven't got true convert number one. Mr. Peersall, who fought Indians in his youth and should have known better, spent his old age waiting on Indians in the delusion that he was making money, for which he had absolutely no use. Mr. Sanders, the missionary, according to Charles Enright, had spent fifteen years now carrying water, which gave him little time to spread the gospel, if he indeed remembered now what it was he was supposed to spread.

If you keep the white man busy he's quite harmless, the Indian Nice Hands held. The trouble is that there are not enough missionaries being sent to the Navaho Nation. Things are not getting done. Soon there will not be enough water. Soon the Indians will have to go to work. Soon the Indians will lose a little dignity. Soon the differences between the red and the white will only be in the legend.

Mr. Sanders was still a missionary. God bless him, the Indian Nice Hands said.

Mr. Peersall had quit being a trader. "What are we going to do for someone to haul the groceries?" the Indian My Prayer said.

153

"You realize that one day our children will maybe be reduced to trade?"

Now Mr. Peersall, the ex-trader, and Mr. Sanders, the missionary, both lived beneath Luna Mesa. Mr. Peersall had quit the trading post now, more from age than from the realization that he was taken in. He ran a very small still now, the results of which he shared only with a few pet Indians. Rumor had it, according to Big Sant, that the missionary, Mr. Sanders, was behaving queerly now, as though he were pulling out too.

Mr. Peersall was exactly one hundred and one years old. He did not realize who Alastair and Little Sant were sometimes. Sometimes they were his cavalry, sometimes they were hostile and sometimes they were friendly Indians. Sometimes they were arresting officers coming to take him back to Missoula, Montana, where he was born. Cowboys and Indians didn't follow him too well now. None of us follow too well the imaginary life of a very old man. But some cowboys and Indians have an inquiring mind.

"Is it possible," Alastair called, "for a man to still be alive who fought Indians?"

"Sure," Sant said.

"I don't personally know exactly when the last Indians were fought," Alastair mused to himself.

Sant had paused up ahead on the ridge in wonderment at a kit fox and Alastair caught up.

"He's gone now," Sant said.

"Well, I was beginning to figure he was very very old."

"No, he was a young one."

"He was?"

"Yes. I could tell."

"You must mean someone else."

"The fox."

"Was there a fox here?"

"Yeah."

"How old is your Indian fighter?"

"A hundred or better."

"Well, I guess he could have fought Indians."

"Sure."

"He could have fought Indians easily."

"Fighting Indians wasn't easy."

"That's true. But in front of grownups, like the missionary, we've got to make sense. They're not very subtle."

"How do you spell that?"

"Sub-tel. It's got a b in the middle."

"That's what I thought," Sant said. "More nonsense. Let's piss up a storm with these horses."

"You mean—?"

"I mean what I just said. Have you got better English?"

"No. Just more acceptable."

"Are we trying to get accepted to each other?"

"No, but we're going to see the missionary."

"We're going to see the Indian fighter."

"I forgot," Alastair said, and they both touched their horses and fled suddenly toward the purple distance in a moving dark cloud of their own dust, kicking a steady storm of flowing weather in their wake. Just as Sant had said.

"I think that's it up ahead."

"That shack?"

"I think we better start to slow down."

But they could not stop fast enough, and the Indian fighter, standing out in front with a hand shading his eyes, watched them fly by and wondered why he had not been warned of new trouble. They circled slowly as they came back.

"What's up?" the Indian fighter said.

"It's us," Sant said.

"They should have warned me," the Indian fighter said. "I could have hid out."

"I'm General Reno and this is my scout Colonel Benteen."

"They should have warned me," the Indian fighter said, "and I could have cooked a batch of candy. Come on inside. I've got a plan of battle all drawn up."

They hitched their horses to the real hitching post and went into a dark logged house of one room and sat at the rough, only table.

"First of all," the Indian fighter, Mr. Peersall, said, touching

155

a greasy beard and staring at them through the gray cataracts of his eyes, "no quarter."

"Not fifteen cents," Sant said.

"No quarter," the Indian fighter repeated.

"Not ten cents," Alastair said.

The Indian fighter leaned back and surveyed the scene. "What do you want, Love Nests or Oh Henrys?"

"Oh Henrys," they both said.

The old man drew quickly, faster than their eyes could follow, two bars of candy from a drawer and handed them each one. He placed both hands splayed on the table and turned to study in their direction with his clouded eyes.

"There's hardly a man that's now alive that remembers what I remember."

"That's why we're here," Alastair said.

"First off," the old man said, looking up at the ceiling, "they made the wrong alliances."

"What?"

"Well, we made the wrong arrangements. We fought the wrong people. We should have joined the Indians, fought the whites, the Easterners. That's why we come here, mountain men, the plainsmen, to escape all that. And then we joined them to fight the people who were the same, who wanted to live like us—the Indians. I don't know why we did it except we were confused by the color of their skins, the Easterners' skins, their language. Because they were the same color, spoke the same language, we must have been confused into thinking, into forgetting we had come out here to escape them."

"Oh?"

"Yes, we fought the wrong wars against the wrong people. We won the wrong battles, lived, some of us, to see the wrong victory."

"What's it got to do with us?" Sant said.

"Does it have to have—? Yes, I guess it does," the old man said. "All right, supposing you were born free, as some of us were, as some people must be still being born free, what land is there to go to now? What are you going to do now?"

156

"Vote," Alastair said.

"That's about it," the old man said.

"Become a bronc rider," Sant said.

"Yes, that's about it," the old man said. "We lost the wrong war."

"How about this," Alastair said, leaning. "Civilization. You fought for that."

"No," the old man said with thought. "We weren't thinking. We were fighting. We were all young."

"But you accomplished—"

"We defeated ourselves. We—" The old man was tired and paused. "We lost—defeated ourselves. All lost. We got confused." The old man mumbled something, confused again.

"What we want to say is," Alastair said, "we don't blame you."

"Yes, we don't blame you," Sant said.

"It was a logical mistake," Alastair said.

"To confuse civilization with highways and trains and airplanes?" The old man examined his knuckles. "No, we knew about that all the time. We never made that mistake. I tell you I was young. Too young. Too full of piss and vinegar."

"Not Coca-Cola."

"Not then," the old man said.

"How was it, fighting Indians?" Alastair wondered.

"Cruel," the old man said. "They never had a chance. They never had a plan. They fought when they felt like it and quit when they felt like it." The old man fumbled under the table and brought out a Sharps rifle and put it on the table and felt it, no longer trusting his eyes. "It was like you were playing baseball and they had you fifteen to two and then they never bothered to show up for the fourth inning. They felt like doing something else now. They were bored."

"That's no way to fight a war," Sant said.

"No it's not," the old man agreed.

"To what do you ascribe your being out here like a hermit?" Alastair asked.

157

"Money. The lack of it," the old man said, getting away from the rifle and touching his beard.

"Didn't you make any money running the trading post?"

"No, but I didn't lose any either. The Navvyhos always saw to it that I always came out exactly even, that I'd never have any excuse to quit, that I never lost money."

"Remembering what you remember you could go on TV or the movies," Alastair said. "Remembering what you remember."

"No. I remember the wrong things. Fighting Indians. The Indians were hungry and dirty and there weren't many of them and it was like shooting people. Poor people."

"It would be undoing everything they have done on the TV and the movies."

"Yes," the old man agreed.

"They couldn't charge people for remembering what you remember," Alastair said.

"TV don't charge anyway," Sant said.

"You think not, son?" the old man said.

Well, Sant thought, anyway he hasn't said yet "I've fought too many Indians." He always said this in answer to any kind of question when he became very tired or bored with talking about himself and wished the people to leave. He would suddenly cry in answer to something, "No, I have fought too many Indians." It is the prerogative of the famous and the very old, and he was something of both. Now the old man said, "Never shoot a man in the back—his brother may be walking behind you." The old man fingered the rifle and looked at the ceiling and smiled. "Always question authority. It's the way the ignorant have of covering up. Always carry a loaded gun in Albuquerque and they'll treat you nice."

"I never met a man before," Alastair said, "who fought Indians and television both."

"Never go to a fandango without at least appearing to be drunk," the old man said. "Never listen to an old man because his experience is no substitute for intelligence or the lack of it. People being as different as horses there is no use in telling them anything except maybe listen to the wind, watch the stars, observe the moon, feel the sun, notice the animals, smell the fields, hear the birds,

158

listen to what is alive. Alive without talking to excuse or apologize for being alive. My talking's not a very good noise. Here's a good noise." The old man paused and soon a meadow lark tweeped. "There. That's a good noise." The old man paused again. "I must find that bird and thank him for being so damned prompt." The old man lifted the rifle slightly and dropped it as though it were some signal to himself to cease.

"Let's talk about the Wild West," Alastair said.

"No, son. I've fought too many Indians."

Sant rose. "Well, I guess we better be going."

"Go in beauty," the old man said.

"We're going to the missionary's."

"Even there," the old man said.

They got on their horses, and the old Indian fighter leaned feebly on the open door. "That's all this country's got now, missionaries and mercenaries."

"What's that?" Sant said as his horse moved off.

"I said head them off at the pass," the old man hollered.

"We will do," Sant said, and they moved off suddenly, clouding the old man's already clouded eyes in a dark version of the last rider, the last dust, the final memory.

"Wait," the old man thought. "I must thank that damned bird."

Now the boys rode into a sinking sun that oranged and pearled the purple and green-hued clouds in refracted tricks of strange and violent wonderment.

"He said," Alastair said, "something about Albuquerque."

"Who said?"

"The Indian fighter said carry a loaded gun in Albuquerque and they'll treat you nice."

"So he did," Sant said.

"That's where I was in the orphanage, Albuquerque."

"So you were."

"I've got to find out more."

"What more?"

"For example, exactly where I came from."

"Didn't your teacher tell you?"

"I mean where *I* came from."

"It's all the same," Sant said. "As you get older you'll realize that."

"I think I'm a little older than you."

"A little is not a lot," Sant said.

"Are we going in the right direction for the missionary's?"

"Any direction's all right," Sant said. "He's all over the place."

"I mean his house."

"Yes. It's hiding behind that mesa," Sant said pointing ahead.

"What we going to tell the missionary?"

"We won't tell him nothing. We'll just give him the letter."

"You mean he knows everything?"

"Yeah."

"Still, he strikes me as a pretty nice fellow."

"Oh well, tell him hello, good-by—things like that," Sant said.

"You suppose he'll want to listen to what we remember?"

"No."

"No one does."

"That's right."

"Let's not be bitter, men."

"That's right. There he is now."

The missionary was standing with a bunch of something in his arms near a New England, saltbox house, clapboarded and wooden-shingled in the style of another country, the house standing too straight alongside the straight-standing missionary, below the huddled, long mesa, the leaning gray sage. The missionary watched the boys approach, clutching tighter the bunch of something in his arms, watching with the cold glint of a warrior the two enemy horses approach.

"A warrior who no longer believes in the war," Alastair said.

"What makes you say that?"

"He looks defeated."

"No, they all get to look that way."

"Out here?"

"Out here for sure," Sant said.

"Hello, boys," the missionary said. He was dressed in army

160

khaki clothes with open shirt beneath a keen and florid face. He had on white canvas sneakers and a red pith helmet of the kind and shape, if not the color, the missionaries must have worn in the old days. "Hello, boys."

"What you got there?" Alastair said, pulling in his horse.

The missionary looked at what he held. "Wood," he said.

"It looks like rock to us."

"Fossil wood," the missionary said and he put the hard blocks down alongside the white and plastic-green New England house and sat on them. Now he took off his red pith helmet and stared around the world he had made until his eyes lighted on the boys again. "How can I help you?"

"This," Sant said and proffered the letter.

The missionary read it quickly as the boys waited in front of him, holding the reins. The missionary seemed to read it at a glance. Now he glanced up.

"You've come to the wrong person."

"Why?"

"You came to the wrong person, that's all."

"Well," Alastair said, not wanting to push it. "Well, let's see. We admire your tenacity."

"You lasted a long time," Sant said.

"Sixteen years," the missionary said. "Since before you were born."

"Where did you come from?"

"New England," the missionary said.

"That's part of the United States, isn't it?" Sant said.

"Yes it is. It was. I suppose it is. Of course it is. Why not? Yes, it is part of the United States."

"Can we help?" Sant said.

"To what do you ascribe," Alastair said, "to what do you ascribe your desire to convert the Navahos?"

"Damn foolishness," the missionary said.

"Well," Alastair said, uneasy, "well, I mean the underlying —that is, when you were a young man."

"I was just like you."

"Can we—can we help?" Sant mumbled, honestly concerned.

161

"I mean," Alastair said, talking against his uneasiness, "I mean you can't leave the Navahos alone."

"Can't I?"

"Who would—?"

"Who would do their work, be their servant, haul their water, bring them medicine, feed them, clothe them? Who would they have to laugh at, order around?"

"If we can help," Sant said.

"Yes," the missionary said, "you can wait on them a while."

"I mean read the Bible, things like that."

"They are not interested in the Bible, things like that."

"Perhaps patience," Alastair counseled.

"Sixteen years," the missionary said. "I've run out."

"To what do you ascribe," Alastair said, "the lack of interest in religion?"

"Common sense."

"Don't be blastemous," Sant said.

"Blasphemous," Alastair said.

"Common sense. Is that blasphemous? Maybe it is. Report me to the pope."

"Are you Catholic?" Alastair asked.

"No. But report me to him anyway." The missionary looked around at the New England cottage. "Maybe it's just that I've been out here too long."

"Sure," Sant said. "If there's anything we can do to help."

"Yes there is," the missionary said. "Just give the Navahos in this area a little sense of courtesy. A little consideration that I exist as something other than their white slave."

"We understand," Alastair said, "that you did a splendid job on President Taft."

"President Taft is an alcoholic," the missionary said. "He would be respectable, even splendid, to get a drink."

"Ours not to reason why," Alastair said and he nudged Sant. "Say something. Try to help."

"I gather you read the letter," the missionary said. "What did you think?"

"A good letter," Alastair said. "A fine letter."

162

"Did you read the part where she says see what you can do—do for them what you did for President Taft?"

"That was good, I thought," Alastair said.

"You know, before I came here President Taft never touched a drop."

"Well, that wasn't your fault," Sant said sympathetically.

"He means," Alastair said, "you have got nothing to do with anything."

"Did I?"

"Sure," Alastair said. "Now the missionary was saying—?"

"I was saying that my coming here imposed on the Navahos a cultural dichotomy."

"Oh, no," Sant said.

"A contradiction," the missionary said. "An impossible choice between life and death as they had known it, understood it for centuries, and now, something radical." The missionary paused, put back his red helmet. "What am I doing confiding to children?" he wondered aloud.

"If we can help," Alastair said. "If only to relieve your mind, to talk to another white."

"Yes," the missionary said, staring up at Alastair. "Yes." And then he said quietly, "I suppose so."

"We're here to help if we can," Sant said.

"But you must be—you must try to be rational," Alastair said.

"I suppose so," the missionary said.

The clock of sun told them in silent splendor of another lost day, told them in a change of abrupt and quiet magic. The sun wavered there in a final call, in penultimate moment, in impatient finality and pause before Finis. The mesas and sage were all in shadow and the New England house in gloom. The boy Sant raised his arm in gesture. The missionary touched his chin. Somewhere off there a coyote sang. Alastair Benjamin touched the ancient stone upon which the missionary sat and said, "What you going to do with this, now?"

"Now, with this wood, I don't know," the missionary said. "Later."

"Later what?"

"Build a house that belongs here," the missionary said. "Something that's native."

"How about adobes?"

"Adobes are good too," the missionary said.

"I have a theory," Alastair said.

"What's that?"

Alastair tossed pebbles, pieces of rose quartz, in an embarrassed gesture, toward a sagging cedar.

"It's that when people hurt you you've got to get revenge," Alastair said.

"That's brilliant," the missionary said. "What else?"

"What I mean is," Alastair said. "What I mean is, nothing else."

"Oh, you are brilliant today," the missionary said.

"Yes, he is," Sant said.

"What I mean is," Alastair said, ceasing his tossing and stroking his cheek. "What I mean is, if the Indians or someone hurt you, or even if they hurt your father, if you didn't do something to even it up you would get to think you were crazy or—"

"Or what?"

"Or reasonably adopted to ignore it."

"Adapted is the word," the missionary said.

"No, I'm not getting those words mixed up now. What do you think of the theory?"

"Very little," the missionary said.

"Not much," Sant said.

Alastair put one of the stones in his mouth and talked around it. "But it is a theory."

"No," the missionary said. "Actually it's an observation."

"Is there a difference?"

"Very little."

"Not much," Sant said.

"As long as you don't call it an opinion."

"Maybe that's it. Maybe that's what it is."

"Sure," Sant said.

Alastair looked concerned.

"What I want to know," the missionary said, "is what the hell are we talking about?"

"Do you always use words like that?" Sant said.

"Only lately," the missionary said. "Since I was saved."

"Saved?"

"Saved from being a missionary."

"That's sacrilegious," Sant said.

"No, it's the truth," the missionary said. "It came as a revelation. The revelation that I was about as qualified to be a missionary as President Taft. It came while I was walking the top of the Luna Mesa."

"A revelation is only the culmination of experience," Alastair said.

"I tell you a revelation is a revelation. This was a revelation in reverse, that's all."

"Is that possible?" Alastair wondered.

"Anything is possible," Sant said.

"Well," Alastair said, "but we need a missionary here. You suddenly can't—you suddenly can't walk out on us."

"My mother would say we done it," Sant said.

"You suddenly can't walk out on the Indians," Alastair said.

"Can't I?"

"You suddenly can't walk out on yourself then," Alastair said. "After all these years."

"We change."

"But the truth," Alastair said. "The truth doesn't change unless the evidence changes. And nothing changed."

"That's right," the missionary said. "Nothing changed. The Indians, everything's the same since I came."

"Patience," Alastair said.

"Patience your own damn self," the missionary said.

"Temper, temper," Alastair said. "One doesn't want to do what one would regret later."

"One doesn't care. This one," the missionary mimicked Alastair.

"My mother would say we done it," Sant said.

165

"Let's go into the house and talk this over quietly," Alastair said.

"I won't go into that house any more. That Puritan house," the missionary said. "That New England house."

"Come, come, it's a nice house," Alastair said. "A nice house."

"It doesn't belong here. I don't think I belong here."

"You come along quietly," Alastair said, "and we'll see what we can do to help."

"Leave," the missionary said.

"But we can't leave you in this condition."

"My mother would say we done it," Sant said.

"You leave me as you found me," the missionary said.

"I guess that's all right then," Alastair said, mounting his horse.

"I don't know," Sant said. "My mother will say—" But he mounted his horse anyway.

The missionary rose from his stones and handed Alastair the letter. "You have been a help," he said. "Just talking to someone, it's been a help."

Alastair put the letter in his jacket. "I'm the dark one she mentions. The one who reads books."

"I gathered that," the missionary said. "You come back."

"Good-by," Sant said.

"The both of you come back."

They rode on a way before they looked back. The missionary was sitting on his stones now but he was still waving.

"Doing anything alone for sixteen years is hard on a man," Alastair said.

"Very true," Sant said. "He does this about every five years. After all, you can't expect anyone on this earth to put up with being the slave of the Indians without revolting occasionally."

"Has he been revolting long?"

"I don't know. But he'll get over it."

"As long as he doesn't burn his place down."

"Or the Indians don't. They've done it before. If it gets dull they might do it again."

"Why would they do it though?"

166

"Oh, they can still revolt too."

"You mean three hundred years ago they burned all the missions down."

"They burned one down not too many years ago."

"Yes, I guess they can still be revolting then. I was intrigued," Alastair said, "by what he had to say about Albuquerque."

"He didn't say anything about Albuquerque."

"It was somebody else?"

"It was the Indian fighter."

"I certainly would like to know more where I came from."

"Get off it," Sant said. "Please get off it. If you get off it I'll tell you an old joke that's pretty good."

"Okay."

"Well, this guy from here whose father I know was in Mazatlán, Mexico, in a *cantina*. That's Mexican for a bar. This Mexican was saying that in the United States they give a foreigner everything free. A free bed, a free breakfast in bed, free nice things to wear, even free jewelry. 'Have you ever been there?' the guy from here whose father I know asked the Mexican. 'Have you ever been to the United States?' 'No,' the Mexican said. 'But my sister has.' "

"All right," Alastair said. "But why don't you want to talk about *my* father?"

They eased their horses around the final bend of the Peña Blanca Mesa. The land toward home would be all flat now save for the old volcano cores that stood as though on a strange planet, and an occasional rise where the antelope watched and sometimes a lonely juniper and sometimes pine, sage and, rarely, a willow weeping downward to an arroyo. The moon rose cold and they became a small army in shadow, multiplied and moving homeward along a trail that had shadowed Coronado too, Billy the Kid, the plumed Indian, and all the great shadows of the buffalo. All gone, shadows into final shadows without any sign on the land, any mark at all. Now Sant made a gesture in the air to quicken the pace.

"All right, Santo," Alastair said. "It's not a bad joke. But I'd still like to know—"

"Tomorrow morning," Sant said. "Everything can wait until tomorrow morning."

167

TEN **O**ne week later it was a very nice morning, a New
Mexico morning, a crisp and sage-smelling and San Juan flower,
red-blooming morning, a morning all alive with every growing
thing; the gilia, the Cowboys Delight, the filaree, the Indian paintbrush, the *añil del muerto,* and the fireweed, the evening primrose,
the verbena, and the desert pentstemon, all exploded, all coming
around to the opinion to bloom at once and all of a different
opinion on what color the morning showed—all in sudden riot.

"You know—" Big Sant was having an opinion too. The two
boys were seated on the adobe porch beneath him.

"You know, I don't know," Big Sant said. He tilted back his
broad hat from a broad, bright-splashed face. "I don't know where
you came from. Is it so important?"

"Yes," Alastair said. "I think so."

Big Sant looked out over all the flowers growing wild out
there, all scattered out there by seeds borne on an indifferent wind,
growing in an indifferent earth, fed by a could-not-care-less sun,
but watched now by careless but caring blue eyes.

"Yes, I guess people care about where things, especially
people, especially their people, come from. That's all right, but—"

"But if you know, I'd like to know," Alastair said cautiously.

"I don't know," Big Sant said. "That Indian, President Taft,
he did claim to know when he was alive. He did claim to know
there was a boy in that house. It's not impossible it was you. Still
it's not impossible it was any one of a million unfound boys—if
there was a boy."

"When he was alive? Who?"

"President Taft."

"He's dead?"

"Yes. He was sick for quite a while before he died. Whisky."

"You're sure he's dead?"

"Pretty sure. They're going to bury him today."

Alastair scanned the sky in seeming abstraction, the sky in big blue, big solid, pure blue absence of anything. Alastair now joined this absence in seeming absence, watching the vacant sky vacantly.

"Well," Alastair said, "will there be any of his friends there at the funeral?"

Millie Sant emerged now and sat in the middle of the silence, sat up above Sant and Alastair and looked down on them from where she sat even with Big Sant.

"There is no life, truth, intelligence, nor substance in matter. All is infinite mind and its infinite manifestation for God is all in all," she said.

"Will there be any of President Taft's friends there at the funeral?" Alastair insisted.

"President Taft didn't have too many friends toward the end. After he took up Christianity," Big Sant said.

"Ye shall know the truth and the truth shall make you free," Millie Sant said.

"Will it?" Alastair said.

"The Indians tend to isolate the different," Big Sant said.

"Whose truth?" Alastair said up to Millie Sant.

"What do you mean?" she said.

"You just said that the truth would—"

"Oh," she said. "That's just some saying left over from my Christian Science days. I was just kind of not thinking out loud. Whistling."

Little Sant whistled low. "Alley wants to find someone who knows something about him."

"My Prayer will be there," Big Sant said.

"Who? Where?" Millie Sant said.

"My Prayer, the Indian, will be at the funeral of President

169

Taft, the Christian; at the missionary's who doesn't know which way to jump."

"That reminds me," Millie Sant said. "Did you two boys get to the missionary's last week?"

"Yes," Alastair said. "And we're going again today too."

"The Indian fighter should be there," Big Sant said.

"What do you mean the missionary doesn't know which way to jump?" Millie Sant said. "You boys spoke to him last week. He was all right, wasn't he?"

"He didn't know whether to build of adobe or petrified wood," Little Sant said.

"Something wrong then. What's wrong with his fine New England house? We need a Christian structure here."

"He said it didn't belong here."

"All right, all right," Millie Sant said. "So he's quitting too. Because the rest of us don't wear shoes is no reason the shoemaker should quit. Or I guess it's as good a reason as any."

"It's the Indians who let him down," Big Sant said. "A missionary can be living among one million heathen in New York City and yet they come out here to convert fifty Indians."

"They are the exotics," Alastair said. "The Indians."

"Yes," Big Sant said. "They are the trip around the world in a fourteen-foot boat. They are the elk a New Mexican hunter will pursue in Alaska when he could shoot one out of his own window."

"The exotics, I presume," Alastair said.

"You said that," Big Sant said.

Alastair took off his hat and scratched his ear. "I was trying to put it cogently," he said.

"How many of my books have you read, Alastair?" Big Sant asked.

"All of them twice. Including the ones that are partly burned."

Big Sant winced, then looked over at Millie Sant, and then down at Little Sant. "And you?"

"None of them. Twice."

"Wouldn't you like to talk like Alastair?"

"Like Alley?" Sant mused. "No. I'd rather be understood."

170

"But after a while, when he grows up he'll get over those big words and he'll still be smarter than most," Big Sant said.

"I'd still rather make sense," Little Sant said.

"He's got a lot of his great-grandfather in him," Millie Sant said. "He was a mountain man."

"I'm going to be a bronc man," Little Sant said.

"Well," Big Sant wondered out loud, "I wonder what happens to a bronc rider after he's thirty-five?"

"What happens to a mountain man after he's thirty-five?"

"Yes." Big Sant took off his hat and tapped it reflectively on the adobe step. "Yes. You are like Great-grandfather."

"Who am I like?" Alastair said.

A dove, an Inca dove with white wing tips and mauve breast, landed in a close cottonwood, one of the chain of cottonwoods that ran around the house. The dove called furtively in a sharp, clean trill until another dove landed too. Now the Inca doves measured each other in silence until a swarm of Inca doves, the whole covey, made a circle in the sun and alighted on a near long branch. Now all of the doves eyed the people sitting on the steps of the adobe house.

" 'From the first not a thing is.' But of course that would leave out my children. It would leave out this wonderful ranch. It would leave out those doves," Millie said.

The Inca doves zoomed off at some secret signal, made a flowing turn in the sun before they were lost in the sun.

"What about me?" Alastair said.

"Yes, well," Big Sant said. "At the funeral My Prayer will be there and he was there."

"Where?"

"At the fire."

Sant extracted a burned spur from his pocket and passed it up to Big Sant.

"Yes. I was there of course," Big Sant said, fingering the spur. "But I saw no child."

"Who fired the first shot?" Alastair asked.

"He did."

"And the last?"

"I did."

"Why?"

"Fear, I guess," Big Sant said. "Isn't that why every shot is ever fired? But I think his was directed at the whole human race. I was only firing at him."

"And you hit?"

"I must have."

"And your books in there?" Alastair said. "Were some of them his?"

"Yes," Big Sant said. "Those slightly burned or those that smell of burning."

"The one that has written on the flyleaf 'Revenge is the only certain thing you can ever get—the only sure thing'?"

"Yes, that was his."

"Why didn't you tear that flyleaf out?"

"Because I had no right."

"It was written on the burned flyleaf of Mr. Shakespeare's *Hamlet,* wasn't it?"

"I think that's where it was written," Big Sant said.

The air turned crisp now, as it will in New Mexico on a sunny day in October when a cloud obscures the sun. They sat there in the deep shadow in the sudden cool of October as the Inca doves again circled close in the autumn warning of winter. Soon the doves' circle would become greater and even greater until the last wide final circle of fall before they shot south for Old Mexico and the fleeing sun.

"As I said," Big Sant said, "they will all be there, everyone who ever remembers anything about it; and all those who made something up, they'll be there too."

"All those that made something—?"

"Yes," Big Sant said. "Everyone had an opinion."

"Well," Millie Sant said, "you mean you're going to let those children—?"

"Go to the missionary? Isn't that what you wanted?"

"Last week," she said.

"What's wrong with today?" Alastair said.

"I hear tell there's a man dying there."

172

"He's dead," Big Sant said.

"You mean President Taft has passed away?"

"President Taft is dead. I told you that."

"Well, I wasn't listening," Millie Sant said. "Well, I suppose everyone should ought to go to President Taft's funeral. Except me."

"Except you?"

"Yes. I don't believe in funerals. I gave them up."

"Oh?"

"Yes," she said. "Dead is dead."

"You used to believe this was the biggest thing that ever happened to a man."

"Yes," she said. "But now dead is dead."

"Well, Millie," Big Sant said. "How many religions have you gone through?"

"One."

"I thought it was five."

"They were all the same. All one."

"Maybe it's better when you've got one."

"I have," she said. "Respect for other people's religions."

"But where's the poetry and the mystery?" Alastair said. "It says that women need that."

"I used to need it."

"I wish you would go to the funeral," Alastair said. "I need people to help me with things."

"How do you expect," Big Sant said, "how do you expect the missionary to carry on if you don't support him, Millie?"

"Carry on what?"

"Well, he tried to help our country."

"All right," she said. "I'll go to President Taft's funeral. Yes," she said. "All right. I'll go."

And she went, riding in the front bucket seat of the Willys jeep alongside Big Sant with the boys in the back and the dogs chasing them till they crossed the cattle guard, where the dogs gave up.

Millie Sant hung on, and the jeep took off over the hills following a very dim wagon trail.

"What does it mean for me?" she said, raising her voice for Alastair. "What do the Dead Sea scrolls mean for me?"

"Well," Alastair said, leaning his chin forward on her bucket seat. "The Dead Sea scrolls are ancient religious documents whose recent discovery in a cave in Transjordan throws a new light on scholars' interpretation of the Old and New Testaments."

"What do they mean for me?" Millie Sant had to holler above the noise of the grinding jeep as it went into four-wheel drive. "What does it mean for me?"

"Well," Alastair said loudly in her ear, "it's the most important discovery in many centuries. The Dead Sea scrolls may completely change the traditional understanding of the Bible."

"Well, does it have anything to say to me?" Millie Sant hollered.

"Well," Alastair said in her ear, "it's directed at all those who are concerned with religion and archaeology."

"And what?"

"How people lived before we were born," Alastair said. "And it's valuable for both the scholar and the layman."

"Which am I?" she hollered.

"Yes, who am I?" Alastair said.

"I can't hear you," Millie hollered.

"No one can," Alastair said.

"Where did you get all that information?"

"The trading post. *The Dead Sea Scrolls,* paper bound. Signet Mentor, thirty-five cents."

"Thirty-five cents. That's cheap enough," she said. "Where are we going?" she hollered to Big Sant as the jeep went up an almost vertical cliff, heaved and groaned finally over the top.

"Is it a good book, Alastair?" she said, quieter now.

"I don't know," Little Sant said. "I don't know whether we're going the right way."

"Well, for one thing," Big Sant said, "you don't follow the wagon trails. You navigate. In the night you can use the stars but in the day you line up landmarks. If you follow an Indian wagon trail to someplace, you finally begin to realize the Indian wasn't going anyplace."

174

"Just a Sunday drive," Little Sant said.

"Yes," Big Sant said, using the small levers alongside the transmission box to shove her back into two-wheel drive. "You got to remember to use the four-wheel drive as little as possible. It's hard on everything."

"Horses is better than jeeps," Little Sant said. "They're in four-wheel drive all the time and they don't mind it at all. And another thing about horses," Little Sant said, "if you're lost and you drop the reins they'll take you home."

"If I let this steering wheel go, how do you know this jeep won't go back to the factory?"

"Or the war it remembers."

"Which war was it?"

"The Second World War."

"I wish we'd make this conversation more relevant," Alastair said.

"Like how?" Little Sant asked.

"Like talking about what we're going for."

"Getting there first is more important."

"The first thing I'm doing," Big Sant said, dodging the jeep between five junipers, "the first thing I'm doing is lining up with Cabezon Peak. About halfway there is the Indian fighter's shack and then we'll bear due north to the missionary's."

"There's the Indian fighter's shack now," Millie Sant said. "Maybe he'd like a ride to the funeral."

When they got in front of the shack Big Sant stopped the jeep and Millie Sant got out and went inside the shack. It was hard for her to see at first but then she could make out the dim form of Mr. Peersall sitting up straight and formal in a cowhide chair, watching a small still percolating whisky in the corner.

"I thought you might like to ride with us to the funeral, Mr. Peersall," she said.

"I am at the funeral, Millicent."

"Taft's funeral, Mr. Peersall."

"Did the president die? Why, the old son of a bitch, dying before me."

"Yes."

"You know, in the old days I shot him several times. It never seemed to bother him a bit. Now, finally, I got him with whisky."

"You fed him whisky?"

"Yes. We drank together in the evenings and talked about old massacrees."

"You're only trying to shock me," she said. "Now come along to the funeral."

"I'll take along some ammunition, Millie. You never can tell." He slipped a half-pint in his leather jacket. "You never can tell what sidewinder will show up at a formal function like this—a fandango like this. Wars and rumors of war," he said as she led the way through the door. As he hit the blinding sun he nodded toward the jeep. "Who assassinated the old gentleman? The function will be hopping with secret-service men." As he finally seated himself in the jeep and signaled to shove off he said, quietly, "He was a good Indian and he made a great president."

"You're only trying to shock me, Mr. Peersall," Millie said.

"Maybe I am, but maybe my memory isn't so good."

"Your memory," Alastair said. "Can I ask you a question, Mr. Peersall?"

"Yes, you can, son."

The jeep faltered and skipped and then began to settle in some loose sand that had drifted in the bobtail cut, a narrow canyon east of Cabezon that took you up on the escarpment where the mission was. They went into four-wheel drive and they all felt on firmer ground as the jeep moved forward steadily again.

"Can I ask you a question, Mr. Peersall?"

"I said you could, son."

Alastair wiped his chin in thought and studied the dashboard where it said DO NOT EXCEED FIFTY MILES PER HOUR IN HIGH GEAR. DO NOT EXCEED FIFTEEN IN LOW. DO NOT EXCEED THIRTY MILES PER HOUR IN THE INTERMEDIATE.

"Well, Mr. Peersall," Alastair said. "What do you remember about me?"

"Stop this thing," the Indian fighter whispered to Big Sant. The jeep stopped.

"Up there," the Indian fighter said in a husky whisper, "up

176

there and to your left, standing in front of that red concretion. Antelope."

They all watched the delicate animals cautiously, as though staring hard might frighten them.

"They'll pick us up in a second now," the Indian fighter said. "Then they'll come down here. They are the curiousest animal that ever was."

Soon the antelope did notice the new object on the bobtail cut and soon they were down examining it. The people in the jeep had to remain motionless, almost without breath, so the Indian fighter could study the animal which was as curious as himself.

"All right," the Indian fighter said. "Blow the horn." At the blast of the horn the antelope exploded away, gone in sudden nuclear magic.

"Beautiful animals," Mr. Peersall said to everyone. To Big Sant he said, "Proceed." And turning to the two boys in the rear he said, "What were you saying?"

"The Wild West," Little Sant said. "What was it like? What were they like—the bad men?"

"The bad men?" Mr. Peersall mused. "The bad men? Well, the West was unorganized, not much law. When there became law and organization the bad men went into business. Now they've become presidents of banks and medical doctors. Now they're legal."

"You're only trying to shock us, Mr. Peersall," Millicent said.

"Now they've got Elks, Rotarians, instead of the Prescott gang. Look. You see that signal?" The jeep had made the top of the mesa and Mr. Peersall was pointing to the rear rumps of the fleeing antelope. On all of the rear rumps of the fleeing antelope there had suddenly appeared huge white targets. "That white spot the antelope cause by contracting their muscles. It makes the white rear hairs stand on end and flicks a danger signal to all the other herds. Soon all the herds on the mesa will be running."

"A telegraph," Alastair said.

"What, boy?"

"I want to ask you a question," Alastair said.

"Go ahead, son."

"What do you remember about me? Where I came from?"

"Where's your brand?"

"Where's my what?"

"Without a brand it's very hard to tell. Even then it can be faked."

"How?" Little Sant asked.

"Well, you can easy see how you could make an N into an M or a heart into a circle heart, things like that. Don't you read any pulp novels? Of course if you cut off the hide you can tell by the marks underneath that the brand has been changed. Haven't you seen any Western movies? However—" Mr. Peersall paused as though about to render a decision—"however, we had a boy worked for us on the Hashknife outfit who cut a piece of hide off the cow where the brand was and sewed the hide back together again before he put his own brand on so that, even by skinning the animal you couldn't tell he stole it. Now, when people will go that far, and that's a fact, how can we ever trace humans? They're running around loose without any brand at all."

"Loose?"

"Yes. And even when branded it was not unusual to see calves of certain brands following cows of different brands."

"What about me?" Alastair said.

"What about the Hashknife?" Little Sant said.

"It was one million acres of land the railroads got free from the United States government to build a railroad. They got bored with the idea of a railroad and decided to run cattle instead. When they talk about a free country they're serious."

"Wait," Alastair said. "Don't you recollect anything President Taft might have said about me?"

"He was given to earth-shaking platitudes."

"About me?"

"About you?" The Indian fighter had to think about this now and he pulled his mustache.

"What about the Hashknife?" Sant said.

"Well," Mr. Peersall said. "Then every cowboy stole from the Hashknife, even those that worked for them. That's how most of

178

the ranches in the West were begun. So when they talk about a free country they're serious."

"All right then," Alastair said. "So it's a free country."

"That's right, son."

"But that still doesn't answer my question."

"But it explains how the West began."

"But it doesn't explain how I began."

Mr. Peersall didn't know what the dark boy was up to so he retreated back to the West, where the other boy lived.

"Actually," he said, watching the West go by, "actually, they got free not one million acres but two because on the grant along where the tracks were supposed to be they were given alternate sections, and as there were no fences at the time, and as and whereby the company objects most strenuously to entry upon its lands of any herds or droves which must necessarily occur when they cross from section to section, we must preserve this land of ours against all comers. And so the freedom was compounded. They took all the land. The land of the free became the freest land in the world."

"More," Little Sant said. "But put some action in it. No more speeches."

"Yes," Mr. Peersall said, trying to recollect where he had left off. "No, it's not that those antelope were curious. It's just that, as well as being the fastest hoofed animal in the world, they also have the best eyesight. That's why they come so close to us. They only trust their eyes, nothing else."

"But what about Wyatt Earp and the Ringo Kid? What about all them?"

"They only trusted their eyes too," Mr. Peersall said. "Nothing else. Those who thought stayed back East."

"And who was the fastest gun in the West? Hondo?"

"Me," the Indian fighter said and he laughed quickly. "Blue-eyed Billy Peersall. Me."

Little Sant reached up and touched the gun arm of the old Indian fighter.

"Me." Blue-eyed Billy Peersall laughed a bit louder now as the jeep went down the western slope, the wind and dust making everything dim. "Me," he said again quietly beneath the din of the jeep, conjuring up all the dim memories of the wild and slandered West. "Me," he said. "Blue-eyed Billy Peersall. Ask any girl at Alice Boardly's old fandango in Taos. Ask them if they remember Blue-eyed Billy Peersall and the fastest gun in the West."

Alastair gave up and settled back against the rear of the front seat and watched the country retreat. But Little Sant was not going to be put off the track.

"Tell us about—"

"No," Mr. Peersall interrupted. "I've fought too many Indians."

Sant now was quiet and settled alongside Alastair, watching the West disappear.

ELEVEN avahos will gather at the drop of a dollar. That is, they will gather for most anything. They do not appreciate a dollar as much as they should—there's no respect there—but they will even gather at the drop of a dollar. The Navahos love a gathering. They will not gather for a funeral; it's too late, the damage has been done; they should have gathered sooner. Still, if a man was a Christian, as President Taft was, we should gather. It's a chance to show we're broad-minded. It's a chance to study a primitive culture. It may even be an opportunity to get drunk. Let us gather. And on the third day they gathered and there was never such a gathering as this in the history of the Checkerboard.

They danced the sweetie sweetie. Sweetie sweetie was the local, Checkerboard, name for a *yebechai*. My Prayer was an older Indian who did not dance the sweetie sweetie any longer. He was at an age in life when a Navaho becomes a member of the orchestra, while the young Indians who pay dance the sweetie sweetie. To dance the sweetie sweetie you need to be young and have ten cents. A girl touches a man and, if he does not dance, he must pay ten cents, or if he accepts her command, he pays ten cents. The sweetie sweetie costs ten cents no matter what you do, if you are young and have ten cents.

My Prayer, as a member of the orchestra, arrived early and was reinforced with three and a half bottles of Four Roses to stay late. He had on blue wrangler jeans and a red-and-green-striped pajama top and his hair was done up in a bun in the back of his neck, as a man's should be. Many of the young men, My Prayer observed, had their hair cut very short in the manner of Navaho delinquents. They would also, he knew, by moving slowly, try to slow down the beat of the chant in the manner of Navaho delinquents. In the old days this would have got them a bullet up their ass and they wouldn't be Navaho delinquents any more. Now My Prayer watched the reservation police watching him from the periphery of the great circle and he knew there was no opportunity now to save the youth of America. Let them go to hell anyway, My Prayer thought. I remember my grandfather telling me the day will come when we can't shoot any more whites and we'll all go to hell. My Prayer did not think the word hell. He used the Navaho word *hajinai,* which is identical and frequently used at sweetie sweeties.

My Prayer gave a few bangs on the drum as a gesture of impatience as he waited for the Indians who were still streaming across the mesa toward the mission. This was only the second time they had played for a sweetie sweetie at the mission. Still, this was the first time a Christian Indian had died from the Checkerboard area. The Checkerboard area was an extension of the Navaho Reservation. It was every other section of land near the Jemez Mountains that the railroads didn't get, that the Jicarillo Apaches didn't get. The Apache Reservation was close. Some of them would probably try to horn in on this sweetie sweetie. My Prayer gave the drum a big whack and all the close Indians jumped back a little because they knew this was not the start of the sweetie sweetie but My Prayer annoyed with somebody—probably the Apaches. Actually My Prayer had just glanced at the missionary's house. The New England clapboard, green-and-white, three-story monstrosity made him bang the drum. Inside the house, he knew, rested the body of President Taft. President Taft was a very old friend of his. He had known him when. He had known him when he was only Water Running Underneath The Ground. He had known him before the old trader at Torreon had made him President Taft. The trader had made two other Indians presidents at the time, to keep down hard feelings. He had made one Indian from the Heeka clan President Lincoln and another from the Dohi clan President Washington. Washington was killed in a brawl in

182

Gallup many years ago, but his wife survived to have a child by Abraham Lincoln. All the presidents had always been friendly. President Taft had survived to become a Christian and get drunk without fighting. Evidently the Christians do not believe in fighting unless it's properly organized into a war.

My Prayer banged the drum again to frighten those that had jumped before, to wake up the prairie, maybe put a little life in President Taft, but mostly to applaud himself for all the very bright things he was thinking.

Now you take the missionary. He's a pretty nice fellow. It's a shame that he's thinking of giving up this Christian business. What's a man going to do when he's put his whole life into something? What's he going to believe, and will the whites take him back or are we going to be stuck with him? They say he is going to build a hogan or something from adobe, that he'll burn down the tall wood house. He's been here fifteen years converting one Indian. Now that Indian's dead. It's too bad. More of us should have signed up. We Indians are too damned independent. It wouldn't hurt a bunch of us at all to sign up, to say we're saved or saving something, whatever it is they want us to say. We Indians are too damn unco-operative. He thought this in Navaho but he banged the drum now in a universal language of protest that everyone understood—banged it against all the Indians who didn't become Christians. Imagine having to write back to this Boston or someplace, after fifteen years, "Nothing doing yet. Hold on. Be patient. Send more money." Imagine what the other Indians would do to me if I was away for fifteen years to convert the whites and showed up again with only their President Taft.

My Prayer beat out a little Navaho rhythm now on the drums to buck himself up and to dismiss his idle thinking. He didn't get into anything solid yet, it was too early. After a few riffs he put down the drumstick to examine the early arrivals. Of course all the Indian ladies, and especially the young squawlets, were examining My Prayer. My Prayer was very famous for banging on the drum. As with Arturo Toscanini among the whites, age did not diminish My Prayer's attraction; genius, as well as being universal, is timeless. Banging on a drum, besides being noisy, is virile—to an Indian lady. My Prayer shrugged off the soft eyes fastened on him. Fame is not so much fleeting as too late, not so much a spur as a bit. It kept all of the men watching you too. My Prayer watched back at the new arrivals. Now a jeepload of whites arrived. My Prayer shook his head, annoyed.

One of those getting out of the jeep, he thought, is Blue-eyed Billy Peersall, the old Indian fighter. As an old white fighter, I respect him. I wonder if he lies as much as I do about the old days. Well, if you tell the truth you can't compete with the moving pictures in Gallup. Cowboys and Indians were supposed to have done certain things, I guess, and if you tell the little Indians you didn't do them they think you were not much of an Indian. The other white following out of the jeep is Sant Bowman. He is the one Taft and I watched having a gun fight before the cabin burned down. It would make a good movie. Then there's the boy, Little Sant, and the wife, Millicent, of Big Sant. It would make a good poem. Now there's the black white boy, Alastair, who wonders whether he is the boy we picked up after the cabin fire. Black white boy, Alastair, he repeated. He thought again, I've got to stop thinking that if you're not red you must be white. There can be other kinds of people and Alastair is one. But if he's not white why does he talk and act like one? No, black is just another color of white. After all, he doesn't speak Navaho, he doesn't speak Apache; he speaks and dresses white and so did his father and so did every black man I ever saw. I never met a black white who spoke Navaho and I never met one who spoke Apache. I hope they don't bother me today about the gun fight. President Taft has already said all we know about it. Almost everything. What we didn't say is not what they would want to hear. It wouldn't make a good movie. It wouldn't make a good poem. It's not what they would want to know. They always would blame me for telling the truth. I suppose the old Indian fighter has learned that, but I must tend to my music. My Prayer began to bang the drum slowly.

The missionary stood erect alongside the straight house that stood on a slight rise, and looked down on all the people arriving. It looked from here as though the Indians were trying to start a sweetie sweetie. What else could My Prayer be doing with the

184

drums? It was part of Prostitution Way, an Indian rite that always began with a sweetie sweetie. He had President Taft's body in the house. It was probably, he thought, the last time the house would be used for anything. He felt badly that the final use of the house would be as it had begun fifteen years ago, with a sweetie sweetie. The failure of a mission.

It looked from here as though there must be trouble. It looked from here as though people are different. It looked from here as though Navahos might have trouble if they went to New England, built a hogan on the commons and tried to convert people to Navaho beliefs, and it looked from here as though the opposite were true. It looked from here as though the thing that made the New Englander believe what he believed never happened in Indian Country. You could buy a few, bribe a few, but, he thought, the thing that loaded a very proper Bostonian with guilt only made an Indian question your sanity. Take My Prayer, banging on that drum. He wants to help. He probably feels sorry for me. He is organizing the sweetie sweetie because he feels it's the correct, the proper thing to do. He just doesn't know what's proper in Boston when a person dies. He doesn't know there's any other way than a sweetie-sweetie way. Indians are tough and they know they're not in the center of Boston but in the heart of Indian Country and they're going to make it stick. Mr. Sanders wondered, watching down, whether he had been a complete failure, as he had wondered unceasingly for many dark nights now, sleeping outside the New England house. Out here it made a problem without a cellophane wrapper, without a crush-proof box, without tail fins, without anything to help that helps others.

Now he watched the party of whites unwind from the jeep. Perhaps they would help him stop the sweetie sweetie and make the Indians pass in front of the bier properly. And then maybe they had problems of their own. The whites that were brought up among the Indians didn't seem to take the Boston kind of problem seriously. The problems they had of their own seemed to have something to do with that black boy, and maybe they would feel that having the Indians stop the sweetie sweetie and pass in front of the bier wouldn't help anything at all. The missionary looked up at the

185

high house he didn't like to enter any more. The failure of a mission.

Down below, the word had been passed around by the faithful, or, rather, something said had been passed around, and distorted in the repeated saying, that beer was going to be passed around. What had originally started as a command by the missionary to stop the sweetie sweetie and pass before the bier had been corrupted by wishful-thinking Indians into, The missionary is going to pass out beer if we stop the sweetie sweetie. All the Indians began to move toward the New England house, and the missionary, wondering what someone had wrought, stepped inside the house to maintain order in the line. Inside discipline.

The Indians entered the kitchen door and entered the living-room door and the whites stood by the living-room door wondering what was up.

"They've got a dead guy in there," one of the Indians said.

"No beer," another Indian said, and they drifted back unhappily toward the stamping ground of the sweetie sweetie.

My Prayer continued to bang the drum loudly. He had not capitulated to the bier-beer rumor; he maintained his dignified beat. Anyway he was a Four Roses man. He was an Indian Fighter man too. That is, he drank the old Indian fighter's home-made liquor, which was called Old Indian Fighter. President Taft had turned out a batch of the stuff once they called Old White Fighter but it wasn't any good. The failure of a still.

My Prayer nodded to the other orchestra members as they moved in and began their practice chants. The orchestra consisted, as all Navaho orchestras consist, of one or two drummers and as many male chanters as were sober. They were in excellent voice, My Prayer thought. They must have been to Gallup recently. My Prayer thought that if a man fornicated enough he could do anything well. It was his *mystique*. My Prayer was the poor Indians' D. H. Lawrence without the consumption but with the coterie, the cult. Even religion was on his side. That is, three medicine men said that fornicating, or *edesh il,* does no harm. My Prayer took this as a solid endorsement of his theory. It was his letter from Rome, his cachet, his diploma in dentistry, his argument with the

186

missionary. They had apparently passed a law against it in Boston which had passed through all the white kingdom; but, my children, you are not in Boston now. *Edesh il.* Forever *edesh il.* Most Navaho words sound as though they were formed by wind rushing around their back teeth.

Yes, My Prayer concluded. But he couldn't conclude anything when someone was chanting off key. My Prayer pointed his drumstick at the weak Indian and it was better now. Yes, My Prayer thought, but the youth corrupt early. Of the young perhaps those two over there were the worst, the ones with the short haircuts, Afraid Of His Own Horses and The Other Indian. They leaned coyly against the post in secret dream while watching the girls. They had associated too much with the whites. They were always hanging around with that Little Sant and that dark Alastair and there was no telling how far they were gone in white nonsense. Soon they might even take an automobile and kill themselves.

The orchestra seemed ready now and My Prayer touched the side of the drum for their attention. This was not quite necessary because My Prayer always began the sweetie sweetie with a long solo on the drum that would drown out Niagara Falls. All watched and waited with respect—awe. My Prayer was an old Gallup man. What New Orleans was to the blacks and whites, Gallup was to the Indian. If you got your start in Gallup around the turn of the century under old Twenty-three Burros you were pure and true and clean in your drumming without any falseness, any of the frills of the northern reservation people. My Prayer was a galloping Gallup man and he was driving now real good.

The missionary stepped out of the New England house and up to the band of whites.

"I wouldn't mind," he said, "I wouldn't mind their ceremony so much if they'd take care of this first."

"What?"

"The burial."

"Why?"

"Why—well, it is the proper thing."

"Why?"

"Why—well, it is, that's all. You know that. You're white."

Young Alastair pulled up his pants and nodded in agreement but no one said anything.

"And well—," the missionary said, and then he faltered.

"And well what?" Big Sant said.

"And well he's beginning to smell," the missionary said.

"All right," Big Sant said. "How deep do you want it?"

All the whites pitched in to dig the hole. They were told to dig it deep enough so the coyotes wouldn't get it and Blue-eyed Billy Peersall set the depth at seven and three-quarter feet and stood alongside the hole measuring while the other whites dug. After two and a half hours' working below in the darkness where they could hear the distant Indians chanting about something else, they finally satisfied Billy Peersall that the grave was coyote-proof. Now those at the bottom were pulled out with ropes and they went up to the mission-house porch to receive a cool glass of water, except the Indian fighter, who drank from his own bottle because he was very tired from measuring. Now an Indian from Cabezon by the name of Almost Never Talking came up and said that a drunk Indian had fallen in the grave and the side had caved in somewhat and there was no way to get him out and furthermore he seemed very happy and quiet down there after fighting above and why bother him. Why bother?

"Was the drunk Indian President Taft?"

"No. It was another drunk Indian. This one was alive."

"We were saving the grave for a dead Indian. President Taft," Mr. Peersall said, putting down his bottle.

The whites trooped back to the grave with their rope, and the Indians began to troop over too. It seemed another rumor had started. This time the rumor was that the missionary was trying to bring President Taft back from the dead. They could all see the whites hollering down into the grave and dangling the rope. So the rumor was not false. They could see the attempt being made with their own eyes.

"Let him alone," one of the Indians said to the missionary.

"It's drinking that caused it," the missionary said. "And he's got to be helped."

"It's a little late," the Indian said.

188

"We will do what we can to save him," the missionary said.

All of the Indians knew or had heard second hand or third hand that the head of the missionary's religion used to bring people back from the dead and now they guessed the missionary was going to try his hand at it. The least they felt they could do was to show respect for the other religion by remaining silent, which they did now while carefully watching the missionary and the other whites do their damndest.

First the whites tried dangling down a rope and hollering, "Grab this." Of course nobody grabbed it and the Indians shifted their weight on the other foot and waited for what next.

Next, one of the whites fell in the hole. He was trying to see to the bottom of the hole and the loose edge gave way and he fell in. Now they dropped down two ropes and told him to tie one to the other man. When they pulled the body up the Indians inspected it. The man was alive all right but it wasn't President Taft. It was another Indian. They all went back to the sweetie sweetie annoyed.

Alastair Benjamin, the dark white boy who had arrived with all the other whites, came over now and sat beneath My Prayer. My Prayer looked up at the pure sky and tried to lose himself in his beat. An artist has got to be different from other people—he's got to have more talent. A rich man has got to have more money than other people and an artist has got to have more talent.

So, My Prayer thought, beneath this baton is not only the dark white boy and a hundred loyal Indians but a thousand sleepless nights that every genius knows.

Now Little Sant went over and sat next to Alastair Benjamin beneath My Prayer and watched up at the man above the big drum.

"If I'm not," Alastair began between beats, "if I'm not being—" after another beat—"I'm not being—" after a loud bang—"if I'm not being too inquisitive, who am I?"

The song ended. He could have waited. My Prayer acknowledged the stamping of the crowd with a raised arm, as though he had completed many scalps, a gesture without humility, without recognition, even, that they were there. He could have been alone on the mesa with his kill and his gods.

The big Bowmans were off comforting the missionary, and

Mr. Peersall had taken a stand on a small rise overlooking the wide flat mesa and all the scene. If he had had his Sharps repeater he could have been mistaken for a picket, for a guardian of the rite and the right. Nothing that he saw had changed much in the almost century since he had first seen it except that damned house. The house appeared set down in rudeness, in contempt—in rudeness of everything that appeared there and in contempt of everything that was believed there. A house set down in righteousness and accompanying blindness, set down to affirm The Truth, not a truth. A house rampant with gold crosses and palm-leaf clusters, alien to this moon.

"Wait a minute," Mr. Peersall told himself. "They've got a right. The Christians have got their rights. Just because I'm not a Christian." When Mr. Peersall acknowledged he was not a Christian people wondered whether he was a Jew. Indian blood then? Or maybe a Unitarian or a Buddhist or something?

"No, I'm just Blue-eyed Billy Peersall. I've tried to be all of that and I've helped people without the need to sell them what I believe and I'm William Peersall, which is quite enough, quite a job right there, quite a bit to cope with still on this earth without making a bad guess at who occupies the universe."

Mr. Peersall brushed a fly off a beaten but unbeaten face. "Blue-eyed Billy Peersall, sometimes known as. Hell, what I'm getting at," Mr. Peersall said aloud, "is, if they want to dance, let them dance. They're not changing money in the temple. They're not—" Mr. Peersall paused and removed something from his pocket for the stomach's sake.

Mr. Bowman and Mrs. Bowman, Big Sant and Millie Sant, were close to the house trying to comfort the missionary.

"I only thought," the missionary said, "I've only been thinking that I'm leaving anyway. I'm getting out soon. They know this. That is, I think it's known. You'd think on this last occasion— No, it's not respect I want. I've never demanded that. I was careful to remember always, careful to remember I had no right to demand anything. Now, you'd think on the last occasion they'd pause before rubbing it in, if they were human. You'd think they'd

190

allow themselves to forget for a few of these last minutes anyway that they're Indians."

"Can you forget Boston?"

"No," the missionary said. "But can't we all remember we're human?"

"They'll quieten down," Millie Sant said. "Maybe, if we ignore them."

"Listen," the missionary said. "You can't ignore that. The end of the world. Listen."

"The children, Sant and Alastair, seem to be enjoying it," Big Sant said.

"Children, yes, they'll enjoy the end of the world. That's always been known." The missionary took off his red sun helmet and drummed on it, unconsciously following the drumming of the Indian drummer. "Always been known," he said, drumming with the drummer.

"There," Little Sant said, looking up at My Prayer as the chanters took over. "That was all right."

"Very all right," Alastair said. "You know, do you mind, Mister Indian, if I ask you a question?"

"Don't call him Mister Indian," Sant said. "You wouldn't want him to call you Mister White Boy."

"That's true," Alastair said, still watching up at the big face above the drum.

"Call him Water Running Underneath the Ground."

"How about My Prayer?"

"That's okay too."

"What other names has he got?"

"Well, he's got a secret name, a war name. All Indians have outside of their Indian name and their white name; they've got a secret name."

"What's his?"

"I said it was a secret."

"I heard someone call him the Galloping Gallup."

"That's just another white man's name," Little Sant said.

"Well, how do I get his attention?"

"This," Sant said and he picked up a rock and dropped it, not too hard, on the Indian's toe.

The Indian looked down.

"Who am I?" Alastair said. "That is, now that President Taft is dead you're the only one left who was there at the fire after the shooting. Am I the one you rescued?"

My Prayer looked down quizzically and annoyed and curious too.

"I don't know," My Prayer said. "All white people look the same to me." And he resumed his drumming, began to bang the drum grandly over the heads of the two boys and in front of all those Indians.

"You know," the missionary said, "I think he's saying something."

"Who?"

"The drummer. I've lived here long enough to know he's saying something. Telling the Indians something with his drums."

Mr. Peersall came up in back of the group that was seated around the open grave. "Yes, he is," Mr. Peersall said.

"What is it, Mr. Peersall?" the missionary said, turning quickly, his abrupt movement sending dirt into the open grave. "What is it? I've got to know."

"It's too late. They've done it."

"Done what?"

"Moved the body. Taken it from your house to his hogan."

"Oh." The missionary turned back to the grave, his motion sending a small rivulet of sand into the hole the whites had dug. "Yes, I should have known better." He watched over at the hogan, cut logs and mud, hexagonal and almost camouflaged against a short tower of rock a thousand yards away. The hogan his retainer, his convert, had built to be near the Word—or the handouts, the missionary wondered. Yes, he thought, I should have started right, begun properly, made him face that door west as missionaries have always made them do, always started by making them give up that first Indian superstition that the door must face east in the direction of *their* gods. I made my first mistake fifteen

192

years ago. But maybe I made it twenty years ago when I became a missionary. Maybe, perhaps, then this was all inevitable.

"Well, don't worry," Millie Sant said. "They're not going to eat it. They're not cannibals."

"They're going to burn it," Mr. Peersall said. "Along with the hogan, they're going to burn it."

The missionary purposely now pushed a little sand into the grave. "A heathen rite," he said.

"Their rite. Their right," Mr. Peersall said, wondering up at the sky.

"I hope they're not doing this to shock us," Millie Sant said.

"Or to finish me off," the missionary said, wondering into the ground as the Indian fighter had wondered into the clouds. Parting is such absolute sorrow, such dirty work.

"Patience," Millie Sant said. "Wait and see what they do first. Patience. Watch and listen."

A big solitary bang came from the drum, an alone bang preceded and followed by silence. All the Indians now moved toward the hogan with the door facing east.

The Indians grouped around the hogan in the manner of flies settling, groups of them here and there in bunches and singly; in large groups and in ones, twos, and threes; in laughter, some of them, and others in expectation, and most in wide, pointed cowboy hats and in narrow pointed cowboy boots; many, including the men, in squaw boots and bright headbands. All of the Navaho women had rubbed iron oxide from the sand cliffs into their cheeks, as Navaho women will for a celebration—a wedding or a death or spending borrowed money. They looked like painted china dolls. They looked very pretty to another Indian.

Mr. Peersall realized now that the Indians were going to do this right. He knew they believed that when an Indian dies there are two ghosts to be coped with by the Indians who are left. One of the ghosts, the good ghost, goes up into the sky and that is okay, but the other ghost hangs around and can be very annoying. It helps if you burn the hogan and it helps if you burn some of the things with the hogan that the dead man loved. The ghost likes that. Burning a live hunting dog with the Indian helps because

193

then he can go hunting. However, Taft never did go hunting much lately. Now that you could buy corned beef in a can at the trading post there wasn't much point to hunting. The Indians are not romantics. Then burning a live woman would help. As every Navaho knows, it keeps the ghost from sleeping with your wife, which is nice. But for a long time now the Navaho women have objected to being burned alive to sleep with a ghost. The Navaho women seem to take their religion with a grain of pemmican. Burning an Indian body in his own hogan too will give the dead Indian's bad ghost a sense of where he lives, a sense of belonging. Of course he will always try to follow the Indians home after a funeral, but if the door is quickly slammed in his face there is a good chance the ghost will go back to where he belongs. That is why it's ideal to burn a real dog and a real widow or something nice along with the Indian. It's especially ideal, the old people claim, to burn a woman. But Mr. Peersall knew the Navaho women were no longer keen on this. Mr. Peersall wondered what the modern Indian would go with to make the ghost feel better, to make him stay at home. Now he knew. One of the Indians went slowly up to the door and dropped a full quart of old Four Roses inside. It was old My Prayer. He understood. He would understand. My Prayer felt certain now that the bad ghost would not follow him home. Everything that must mean anything to the ghost of President Taft should be inside the bottle that would always be full in the afterworld.

Take the way they are piling brush up now around the hogan. That is to keep the bad ghost inside the hogan until all the Indians can get safely home without being too closely followed. Two things are distinctive about the Navaho. (Mr. Peersall wished he had his Sharps rifle to lean on while he was thinking; he felt naked.) One thing was their fear about death, this continuous fear before and after the event. And the other thing was their continuous unfear about sex before and after the event. A Navaho boy will, if he is normal and healthy—there are queer Indians—but if he is normal and healthy he will *edash il* a Navaho girl any chance he gets. When she is going for water is a good chance and it's a very good chance when she is tending the sheep. So cowboys are likely to find, all over the prairie and anyplace on the mesa—particularly near the bubbling springs or the amazed sheep—Navahos *edash iling* until they are blue in the face. Navahos seem to like to do this very much.

Mr. Peersall leaned on a scrub oak in lieu of his Sharps rifle but it wasn't the same. Nothing was quite the same any more. He liked to remember that he was able to remember everything as it was.

The two Indian boys still sitting near the orchestra—the drum had not moved, still played on—they liked to remember everything as it was going to be. They could not live in the past because they had no connection with it. They could not live in the present because no Indian had any connection with it. So they liked to remember everything as it was going to be. Everything was going to be a big blank, so they lived from hour to hour, drifting from dying week to hopeless month through unrecorded and unremembered years. They did not know what the older people were up to, burning down the hogan. They didn't much care. They didn't know what the white people were up to with their rites. They didn't care at all. They were caught exactly in that hiatus between the death and the resurrection of a race. That maybe was the blank, the big blank, in the minds of the two boys lolling there, physically equidistant between the red group at the burning and the white sad knot at the missionary's. With, not, and for neither, unwanted and unbothering—uncaring. Their names were Afraid Of His Own Horses and The Other Indian.

"Who am I?" Alastair Benjamin asked.

The Other Indian looked up and down at Alastair Benjamin. "The hell you say," he said.

"What I mean is," Alastair Benjamin said, "what I mean is, My Prayer was there but he won't say. You haven't heard him say anything, have you? Something he maybe wouldn't tell a white man?"

All Alastair got was that big blank from both of the boys.

"What I mean is," Alastair said, "now they're having this burning it could have been the same thing. What I mean is, it could have been the Indians also that—"

Alastair was still getting the great blank and he finally turned away.

"The hell you say," Afraid Of His Own Horses said.

The Other Indian watched Alastair Benjamin diminish. Another white problem like a white-school problem—if you have eight apples and John has four apples. No one really had any damn apples at all. Why was Alastair—anyone—worried about the past when there was no damn future. Yes, there was this nice blank. There were those nice girls over there now and there would be a nice blank tomorrow. Afterward did not exist and they hoped Alastair Benjamin would recover some of his marbles tomorrow and not go around mooning Who am I? Hell, you're a white man, aren't you? What more is there? What more would he want to know?

"He is, though, an awfully odd color, don't you think? For a white man?" The Other Indian said.

"They come in assorted colors."

"Parece," The Other Indian said. "It seems they do."

"And they got weird problems. In assorted flavors."

"It seems," The Other Indian said.

They both strained to see some kind of a ghost pop out of the burning hogan and they both remembered, as all the Navahos grouped around did, *not* to remark the ghost. A ghost will sometimes take the form of a coyote or a bear or even a snake. Sometimes even a— My Prayer beat heavily on the drums. My Prayer knew what other forms ghosts could take. He had seen it happen. A ghost running from a dead man's pyre can take the form of Alastair Benjamin.

The steady bang of the drums increased in a rolling and mounting objection to thought—a furious and inchoate beat that lost the listener in a new world of other gods.

"Like I have been trying to say all along," Big Sant said. Big Sant was standing near the white house with the other whites. "Like I've been trying—"

"It's not Christian Science," Millie Sant said.

"What?"

"What those Indians are doing." Millie Sant watched. "No,"

she said. "What those Indians are up to is no true religion. It's not written down, not financed."

"Not financed," Mr. Peersall agreed.

"Like I been trying to say all along," Big Sant said, "it's not whether it's written down or whether it's financed, it's simply that we're outnumbered two hundred to one."

"At least," Mr. Peersall agreed.

The missionary, Mr. Sanders, took out his ballpoint and wrote on a close rock while thinking of something else—ARCHIBALD SANDERS.

"What I've been thinking is," Mr. Sanders said, "does might make right?"

"Outside of a speech hall, it generally does. Yes," Mr. Peersall said. "That is, when we had the Indians outnumbered two hundred to one we always noticed some difference in the result."

The missionary wrote YES on the rock and then crossed it out.

"I always had the faith," he said, "that right makes might and in that faith I would always do my duty as I saw it. Does that sound silly now?"

"Yes," Mr. Peersall said.

"You're a bully," Mr. Sanders said.

"No. I just have trouble sometimes figuring out what's right."

Mr. Sanders wrote YES again on the rock and then he crossed this out and wrote ARROGANT BULLY.

My Prayer banged on the drum and watched over at the white people. He saw one of them writing on a rock. Most Indians, wrong or right, contend that writing is the white man's way of laying a ghost. An Indian will quell a ghost by building a neat pile of stones, the dog will plant his ghost by pissing on it, and the white man by writing on the queer pile of rock KILROY WAS HERE. Actually the ghost the whites planted most on the rocks of Indian Country was JESUS SAVES. The Indian will probably always go with his neat pile of rocks, maybe with marked trees, the white man with his written business, and the dog will always piss on all three. If there was some moral, some *anaji,* here My Prayer could figure out none. He got back to planting his own ghost with his drums.

Big Sant watched from the group of whites with more especial concentration than anyone else. He thought that nothing extra, nothing but flames would fly out of the hogan. But after what the Indians claimed, after the last burning, it would do no harm to watch carefully.

My Prayer watched for the match expectantly because an old friend was in there and they had both been through this before when they were both on the outside. None of the whites believed what happened then and he was happy to see there were many watching now. In case something happened now there would be many witnesses.

Nothing happened. The hogan burned with a long, high, bright flame as tall as a ponderosa and lighted all the Indians into silhouette, but nothing happened.

"Something happened all right," the missionary said as the flames began to retreat back into the ground from where they seemed to rise.

"What happened?" Big Sant said, concerned.

"The Indians had their way, that's what happened," the missionary said. The missionary, Mr. Sanders, worked his hands together in thought, watching the quieting blaze. "I guess we had better cover over that grave with logs before an Indian falls in."

"We can throw back the dirt," Big Sant said. "Make it permanent. I guess no Indian will ever use it."

"This Indian maybe," the missionary said carefully.

"Why is everyone trying to say something shocking today?" Millie Sant said.

"No, this Indian won't," Mr. Sanders said, still speaking carefully, and dazed. "Maybe this Indian won't. Maybe he'll go the way of all Indians." Mr. Sanders threw a helping twig toward the fire. "In a nice blaze."

"You see," Millie Sant said, "when you go back to Boston everything will be all right again."

"Yes," Big Sant said. "They'll all be exactly like you. No problems."

Mr. Peersall fingered an imaginary Sharps. "Exactly like you," he agreed. "That's all right," Mr. Peersall corrected himself. "There's not nothing necessarily wrong with people being like you." Mr. Peersall still did not think this sounded generous. "We got to be tolerant," he concluded.

"When you get back there," Millie Sant encouraged, "your faith will be restored. You'll get real Bible back there. No body snatching. There's real Bible back there."

"Where?"

"Boston. Boston Bible. Isn't that where you come from?"

"Yes," Mr. Sanders said bleakly.

"Why you can go to a ball game every day if you want," Big Sant said. "Any time you want."

"The Braves have moved to Minneapolis," the missionary said.

"Then you do know what's going on," Big Sant said hopefully. "I thought something might have happened to you—been out here too long."

"Oh, I know what's going on," Mr. Sanders said. "Watch the Indians dance." Watch the Braves dance had been his first thought. "Watch the Navahos dance and howl their chant. I know what's going on. I know what's happening. That's where all the difficulties lie."

"You'll see," Millie Sant said. "In a little bit you'll find yourself."

"It will take a little time," Big Sant said. "Let's cover up that grave before an Indian falls in."

All the whites went down to cover up the grave except Mr. Sanders. He just sat there studying the fire. Now he was joined by Alastair Benjamin, who sat alongside him and studied the fire too.

"We've both got the same problem now," Mr. Sanders said.

"What's that?" Alastair said.

"Finding out who we are."

"You too?" Alastair asked.

"Me too," Mr. Sanders said and he tossed another twig toward the fire.

At the grave everyone worked very hard. That is, Big Sant worked very hard filling it in now that there was no body. Everyone else watched. No one to help, Big Sant thought. Even some Indians who were bored by the fire came over to watch. The sweetie

199

sweetie was still going on, the drum continued, but these watching Indians were too old for sweetie sweeties now. Mr. Peersall stood as straight as a very worn ramrod addicted to whisky above the grave watching down at Little Sant beneath him, watching up.

"What's a good book to read on the Wild West, Mr. Peersall?"

"Andy Adams' *Log of a Cowboy*."

"Nothing else?"

"No. That's all."

"Who was the best bronc rider that ever lived, Mr. Peersall?"

"Mr. Peersall."

"Anybody else?"

"No. That's all."

"If I try very hard can I become a great bronc rider, Mr. Peersall?"

"Not necessarily."

Little Sant made a big circle on the loose ground with his foot. "Why not?"

"Talent. The lack of it," Mr. Peersall said.

Little Sant wiped out the circle again with his booted foot. "Oh," he said and then he drew a cross with his foot. "What would you say distinguishes you most?"

"Lying."

"I mean very truly, Mr. Peersall?"

"I was all right at busting horses," Mr. Peersall said. And women, Mr. Peersall thought. Blue-eyed Billy Peersall said, "Yes."

"Yes what?"

"Yes, horses," Mr. Peersall said.

"Who was the best horse buster that ever lived?"

"Lemaitre."

"I rode with Lemaitre," Sant said. Sant fumbled quickly at the lips of his pants pockets as though drawing guns. He drew from this a dirty card.

"Sure you did," Mr. Peersall said.

"And I got this to prove it," Sant said, passing it up to the man above.

"Sure you did," Mr. Peersall said, examining the card that could have been given away with every box of Cracker Jack.

"I got that Cellophane on to protect it," Sant said.

"Sure you did," Mr. Peersall said, returning the card that could have been given for sending in five whisky tops. "Sure you did."

"Nobody believes me," Sant said.

"So you rode with Lemaitre," Mr. Peersall said.

"Yes, I did."

"Sure you did," Mr. Peersall said.

Little Sant strode away, not making circles or crosses or anything any more, just kicking the dirt as he went. When he got to the first two people who looked the way he felt he sat down beside them within the noise of the music and all the shadows the dying fire made.

"They have no souls," Mr. Sanders said finally.

"No, they haven't," Alastair agreed.

Sant noticed that without any shoes it was obvious that the Indians didn't need any, but he was in such a mood he went along anyway. "Very true," he said. "Yes, just bear in mind that I'm better than fourteen years old now and I don't have to look up to Mr. Peersall or anybody else."

"Very true," Alastair agreed.

"And I don't have to do nothing but ride a horse proper."

"That's all," Alastair said. "Nothing happened."

"What do you mean, nothing happened?"

"Nothing ran out of the hogan."

"Did you expect somebody would?"

"I didn't know."

"Let's dance."

"What about the missionary?"

"Forget the missionary," the missionary said.

"Will you join us?"

"Why not?" Mr. Sanders said.

"Look," Millie Sant said. "Look over there. The missionary. He's going to dance. Oh my God," Millie Sant said.

Mr. Peersall sat down on a grama clump near the edge of the unused grave. It was the first time he had sat down since the sweetie sweetie began. "It's all right, Millie," Mr. Peersall said.

"Big Sant," Millie Sant said. "Darling, Mr. Sanders is going to dance. A pagan dance. My God," Millie Sant said.

"It's all right, Millie," Big Sant said, sitting down alongside Mr. Peersall. "It's all right, Millie dear."

"By God, that's a crock of crap," Millie said quietly. "By God, I still know right from wrong."

"What's up?" Mr. Peersall said.

"He's betraying us," Millie Sant said, still thinking about it, still trying to figure it out.

"You can't betray someone who never believed in you, Millie," Big Sant said.

"Yes, that would be a crock of—" Mr. Peersall was interrupted.

"Don't be so vulgar. Do you have to be so vulgar?" Millie said, her voice rising.

"You said it, Millie dear."

"It makes no difference," she said sincerely. "Do you have to repeat like children every damn thing you hear? Men! Oh my God, men," she said quietly now. "It's all right if I said it. It's all right if I said it, I guess, but don't be like children—vulgar to be vulgar. Men are like children. He's betrayed us, and don't say that, just because no one believed in him— That's a crock—"

"Millie dear."

"All right. Very well," she said.

At the stand for the band, a small rise on the flat mesa hung over with juniper and surrounded by silver sage flowering in gold and smelling sharply and pungent always, My Prayer played on without pause, emitting his beat that wafted with the wind, prevailed with the prevailing breeze, loud, and when the wind went wrong his beat carried into the canyons, lost.

Yes, My Prayer thought, watching out above his boom, as long as I can make great magic, as long as I can keep a good beat, I will have the world, this little world, firmly held by the *ziz*. I don't know why one kind of magic must always give way to another kind of magic, why the missionary and I can't live together, why the red man and the white man can't live in the same world without speaking to each other. As soon as we spoke, the day we spoke, that was the beginning of the end. That was the day the white man began to love the Indian to death. A white man can never commit a crime and forget it. When we stole this land, when the Navaho stole this land from the Gallina people, the Navaho forgot it. Except for some rather pleasant memories of the war, the Navaho forgot it. When the white man stole this land from the Navaho Nation he has got to compound the crime in order to forget it. He's got to love us to death. Love is their way of not giving back something they have stolen. Take that white man over there, Blue-eyed Billy Peersall. He is the only white man ever known who hasn't tried to love us. He doesn't even like us—he tolerates us. I wonder if the white man will ever learn that that is all any defeated people ever want—to be tolerated. To be allowed to be different. Love is their way of intolerance. Love is their gentle way of grabbing you firmly by the *ziz* and twisting until an Indian hollers Uncle Sam. The whites never did anything wrong that wasn't made up for by this love. Their love is like a gentle *ziz*-twisting thing. Their love.

Now My Prayer got back to the sweetie sweetie, the dance, the reason for being. He would try hard now not to go back over all those reasons for not living. He would stick with the true love, the dancing, the music, the sand painting, the *edesh il,* the stars in a very black sky, and the way the world looks in the very early morning in Navaho Country and in the evening and at noon. All these true things which were mostly music. That is my true thing anyway. Now he gave a series of awfully good bangs and the Navaho people felt it in their beings and showed it in the movement of their bodies, their feet. Even the whites were beginning to circle in now—even the missionary. Go easy on him, My Prayer thought. He's got a life to lead.

My Prayer turned over the drums to an assistant, a boy who had never been to Gallup—Paris—a boy without sufficient training to release his creativity but with sufficient knowledge to imitate genius. My Prayer turned over the drums to him—his name was Andy Alltogether—and slithered through the Navahos until he got to the missionary, Mr. Sanders.

"I wouldn't do it," he said.

"What?"

"Dance."

"Why not?"

"I wouldn't do it," My Prayer said.

"Why?"

"You've got a life to lead," My Prayer said.

The whites were standing at the periphery of the circle watching the serpentine pattern of the dance. They all seemed unconscious of My Prayer; even Mr. Sanders, who was supposed to be talking to My Prayer seemed unconscious of the Indian in their midst.

"Why?" Mr. Sanders said again.

"Because you've got to live with your people, not with my people," My Prayer said.

"Do I?" Mr. Sanders said.

The Indian in their midst looked perplexed.

"So is your old man," Mr. Sanders said. This was a phrase from his childhood, Mr. Sanders thought. This was something he had not said since 1922. "Says you," Mr. Sanders said, and then he said carefully, looking closely at the face of the Indian in their midst, "Yes, we have no bananas." That was his childhood, 1920 maybe, long before he entered the seminary. "Yes," Mr. Sanders agreed.

"Yes what?"

"Yes, we have no bananas," Mr. Sanders said carefully to the Indian.

Well, My Prayer thought, something has been added to the brew. Have I got to cope with a nut?

"Have you got all your arrows okay?" My Prayer said.

"Have I got all my marbles?" Mr. Sanders said, translating. "Have I lost some of my marbles? Maybe I did for the last fifteen years. Maybe I did lose some of my marbles but now I'm beginning to collect them again. My Prayer, I don't want to go into all this. My Prayer, I simply want to dance with your dancers."

"No good," My Prayer said.

"What My Prayer's trying to indicate is that it's a question of your loss of status pattern among the whites."

204

Mr. Sanders looked down, looking for Alastair. There he was looking up. There, too, alongside, was Little Sant and the old Indian fighter.

"Yes," Alastair said, "he's worried about your loss of symbol status among your own people. It would be traumatic in the context of white mores for you to accept, by dancing, a primitive symbol pattern other than the cross—other than the Christian."

"It's legal," Little Sant said. "He got it from a book."

"He said it very nicely," My Prayer said. "What did he say?"

"No good," Mr. Sanders said. "In his childish way he said exactly what you said. No good."

"In a very vulgar way from where I stood," Millie Sant said. "Do men have to be vulgar for the sake of being vulgar? Where's that small dark crock—" She reached over to give Alastair a jerk but he had retreated safely in back of Mr. Peersall. "But he's awfully cute," Millie said. Now Millie turned on the missionary. "You can't dance that heathen dance," she said. "If that's what My Prayer said, he's right."

"That's what I said," My Prayer said.

"And if that's what Alastair tried to say, he's right," Millie said.

"That's what his book said," Little Sant said.

"You see," Millie said quickly into the face of the preacher. "You do see, don't you?"

"Yes, I do see finally," Mr. Sanders said and he left for the dancing with a dusky Indian girl who had been tugging on his arm all this while. But first he paid ten cents, as was the Indian custom at sweetie sweeties.

"I see," he said.

PART III

TWELVE Inca doves that for weeks had been building quick and wide circles around the Circle Heart were now at last ready to shoot south. The young that were still young could at last keep pace with the flight. Not too well; they faltered and got out of line and sometimes they tried to take the lead when they were too young to take the lead. Sometimes the small Inca doves would not join the practice flights, as though they had no intention of leaving here at all. Nothing wrong with the Circle Heart. But they went finally. The young doves could not survive to come back to the warm summer of the Circle Heart unless they fled it during the long winter. One day they were gone. Gone so they could come back stronger to the summer of the Circle Heart.

"The cottonwoods have not lost their leaves so early this year."

"That's because we've had some good rains."

"I'm going to go away," Little Sant said.

Apropos of nothing, Alastair thought. He is so full of *non sequiturs*. Well, I have got a few myself.

They were both sitting, hanging, on the corral fence on a pleasant Sunday morning two years after the funeral of President Taft, and Alastair thought he would continue the conversation by branding with a pencil on the fence board $E=mc_2$.

"Is that going to be your brand?" Little Sant said.

"It's going to be the brand of everyone in the twentieth century unless I do something about it."

"So you're going to save everybody?"

209

"I guess so."

"With your education you're going to save everybody."

"I guess so."

"That's some of what I'm running away from."

"What?"

"Education."

Alastair had to think about this for a while, had to try to imagine somebody that would run away from an education. He couldn't.

"I can't," Alastair said. "I can't even imagine anyone hypothetically."

"Who said hypothetically?"

"I did."

"Then you run away from it. I am running away from an education."

"Why?"

"Well, that's better," Sant said. "Well, I'll tell you exactly why. Because I am."

"Why?"

"Because I am a bronc man."

"That's just a saying."

"Well, I got something to prove it."

"Everybody's got to have an education," Alastair said.

"Now that *is* just a saying," Sant said.

"Oh?"

"Yes. If everybody spent their time studying and nobody doing, what would the studying people be studying?"

"Oh? Yes. But I'm still going to get an education."

"Yes, it's right for you, Alley. Some people are not fit for anything else. It's not the way they were brought up or who their parents were, it's just that they're kind of all thumbs and they can't do anything so they have to say I'm educated. Nobody can do anything to help them, they are just the way God made them— helpless. Yes," Sant said, "like Reverend Peavey of the Holy Rollers said when he was against putting a sewer system in Cuba, 'If God wanted the people to have sewers he would have put them there.' Yes," Sant said, "if God didn't love education he wouldn't have invented so many helpless people."

"You think God's got a sense of humor?"

"I can think of no other explanation."

"Don't talk about this to grownups. They'll say we're getting out of line."

"Don't worry. You can't talk to them exactly."

They thought about this for a while and then both wondered what they were thinking about, exactly.

"Well," Alastair said finally. "When exactly are you going to leave?"

"Tomorrow early."

"What's going to happen to me?"

"You'll get educated."

"I mean me without you. I can't imagine it."

"You'll get used to it."

"I don't think I ever can."

"In time you can. I'll write."

"I don't think I ever can."

"I'll write."

"I don't think I ever can get used to it."

They both sat sadly on the fence thinking about it. Alastair retraced the brand, $E=mc_2$, but he was not thinking about that.

"Why exactly do you have to leave so suddenly, Santo?"

"It's not so suddenly, Alley. I have been planning and thinking about it a long time now."

"Ever since you got that piece of paper from Lemaitre."

"That's right. But it's what's behind a piece of paper, Alley."

"That's right. You know, Santo," Alastair said, turning on the fence toward Sant, "I think what's indicated for you—"

"What?"

"I think what's indicated for you is that you've got to have a go at this running away, ride at bronc shows and find out that what was behind that piece of paper is a lot of baloney."

Sant thought about this.

"And what's behind your piece of paper, your diploma they'll give you for studying—that piece of paper? What's behind that piece of paper is a lot of books written by somebody else."

"Maybe. We'll see."

"Don't you think, Alley, if a man tries hard enough he'll make it?"

"That depends."

"Then you don't think there's any justice?"

"Only the justice we make."

"Another book?"

"No, that's my own reckoning."

"I'm still going to leave tomorrow early. Alley, is there something you want to say to me before I go?"

"Yes, there's a lot I want to say. But nothing in particular."

"Nothing particular about my father and your father?"

"Nothing particular."

"How your father died?" Sant said.

"He was killed by your father. But it was an accident."

"You're sure it was an accident?"

"It's always an accident."

"You mean it always is? Even war?"

"That's right. And don't forget your father had a jury trial."

"Yes," Sant said, and then he looked around at everything before he said, "But there weren't any black people on the jury."

"No, but there were some red ones."

"What's that got to do with it? You mean the reds will see that the blacks get justice?"

"No, not necessarily."

"It's a pretty good theory."

"Yes. But that's not what I know."

"What do you know?"

"I'd rather not talk about it."

"I tell you, Alley," Sant said. "I can't leave unless I talk about it."

"Then stay."

"I can't stay, Alley, unless I talk about it."

"Then leave."

"I can't do nothing, Alley, unless I know."

"All right," Alastair said. "The black took from the red by accident and the white took from the black by accident."

"What do you mean?"

"I mean my father, the one they call the Gran Negrito, came out here and he needed land and a wife. He had a gun and a legal book. There was a dead Indian and in the end the Gran Negrito had land and a wife, Indian land and Indian wife. Then it all died, first my mother, then the land, and the Gran Negrito himself. Us. Like we got it, we lost it. All an accident again. The law proved it was all an accident, the same as the way we got it."

"How do you know?"

"That's the story the drums told at President Taft's funeral."

"How do you know?"

"I followed My Prayer home. I would not leave his hogan. He said I was a ghost; he had seen me flee from a burning hogan way back—and I must leave. I told him I would leave forever if he told me all. I would never harm him again. Then he told me how I came out of the burning hogan like a ghost and how they hid me from the other Indians who might destroy a ghost until they made a long trip in their wagon and left me on the steps of a white orphanage because I was not red. And he told me how my father stole the land by accident. And I told him I would not haunt him any more, and I left."

"Alley, are you going to haunt us?"

"No. I have decided to try to bury the dead, as your father decided to try to bury the dead by taking me in. I walked all that night, when I left My Prayer's hogan. I walked like a ghost, thinking of all the accidents ghosts can cause, wondering what caused my father to do it, wondering what happened to him to make him do it—why he had to do it. Then I realized it would never end, that ghosts would haunt ghosts forever, that accidents would never end. Then I suddenly realized that there was nothing I could do about it, that I had to have revenge, as my father must have had to have revenge, that I could not walk in the daylight any more, couldn't look in the mirror any more, until I had revenge. I got your father's gun and went into his bedroom."

"Yes?" Sant said.

213

"He woke up and saw me standing there with the gun and he said he understood."

"Understood what?"

"That there had to be another accident."

"And then what?"

"Then I told him I couldn't do it."

"And then what?"

"Then we decided to kill his horse."

"Did you?"

"Yes."

"So that's what happened to Indian Country. I thought he traded him. What did killing Father's horse do? Did it help?"

"Yes. It ended something."

"It was a beautiful horse."

"I suppose they were all beautiful—all those people the accidents happened to. I don't remember."

"Do you want to?"

"No. I don't have to remember anything now. Something is ended. I think I can take on what comes now okay."

Sant reached over and touched Alastair on the back.

"Yes, I think it will be okay now, Alley."

THIRTEEN **I**n the middle of the night, a moon-filled New Mexican night where the owls can see Old Mexico and wild animals move gently and call suddenly, something like the coyote calling will happen or the departing bugle of an elk from on top, moving down country, will happen and shock. In the middle of a moon-filled New Mexican night there are all these arriving and departing sounds to quicken, to startle you.

"What was that?" Millie said.

"Little Sant," Big Sant said.

"Where is he going this time of night?"

"I guess he's moving down country."

"What do you mean?"

"He's leaving us."

"What do you mean?"

"He's going to hunt on his own. He's sixteen now."

"What do you mean?"

"He's leaving."

"For good?"

"For good or for worse. That's what he's got to find out."

"We've got to stop him."

"No, Millie, he's got to find something out."

"But we've got to stop him."

"We can't stop him, Millie. We can only be here if he can't make it there."

"Where?" she said, rising on her elbow and staring down at the face of the reclining figure. "Where?"

"Cortez."

"Why Cortez?"

"That's where the rodeo is."

"And why didn't he tell us?"

"Because it's none of our business."

Millie relaxed back into the bed and stared up at the viga-beamed, moon-lit ceiling. Now she sobbed gently. Big Sant took her hand that lay limp on top of the gray four-point blanket.

"A boy has got to cut out something new, Millie. A boy has got to try."

"Like you did. Cut out something new."

"I made it, Millie."

"You're making this worse," she said.

"I made it, Millie, the only way I knew. Maybe he doesn't like my way, maybe this land is wrong for him. Education's wrong too. We've got to let him go."

They both lay there silent now save for a quiet sobbing.

"I put fifty dollars in his wallet, Millie, last night. I saw this coming. He kind of told me in a silent way. He can always make it back here with that money."

"But supposing—" Then what she said was lost again in the sounds of her grief.

"He can always make it back," Big Sant insisted.

Now the boy moved down valley on his horse, his movement joining in with all the other gentle moves on the slope. On his flank a prong-horned elk was moving unseen and downward too. His horns were at the straight stage before they branch out, at a stage where it is legal for hunters to kill them but at a phase in the development of their fighting antlers when it is difficult for them to make it on their own. But for this elk there was nothing else to do. He picked up the horse and man scent now and paused to let them get down to the low country first.

Sant touched the horse with his heel to quicken it. He would ride as far as the missionary's, leave the horse there, and go on to the Greyhound stop on the highway by foot.

Now a tall burst of flame lighted in a glare all the country

216

ahead. The fire had not suddenly risen—the horse and rider had just topped out over a hogback ridge of jack pine and there was all this brightening country below. The wild animals, making their final move before dawn caught them exposed, made a wide, frightened circle around the fire. The horse and rider made toward it, it was directly in their path. As a matter of fact, Sant realized suddenly, it was their destination. The fire was at the mission. The mission was on fire.

Sant tried to speed the horse by rein-slapping his flank but the horse was not having any. He was broken enough to go toward a fire if he had to but no horse is ever busted sufficiently to move toward a fire quickly. If the Indians have done this, Sant thought, it is not a very nice thing for the Indians to do. As Alastair would say, Sant thought, burning down the mission is not a very subtle way to say something. I hope the missionary got out alive. It is supposed to be funny, Sant thought, burning a missionary. That is, cooking him in a pot so you don't waste anything. According to the cartoon jokes in the magazines it's supposed to be quite funny. Alastair would have the cause for humor in the fact that no one invited the missionary to come—he invited himself and if he insists he might as well come to dinner and bring his own dinner, or, to keep things neat, *be* the dinner. But Alastair wasn't here any more. It was all over with Alastair now and he must begin to figure out things all by himself. The way to figure this was that it wasn't funny at all. Mr. Sanders had come here with the best of intentions. I wonder if the best of intentions excuses an invasion—if you can violate any nation's—the Navaho Nation's—beliefs with the best of intentions. Alastair would like the word "violate." He would like the whole phrase "violate a people's traditions." To hell with Alastair. I think that you can't violate another nation's traditions. You can't and expect to get away with it. But here you have got a mitigating circumstance. You've got the missionary's best of intentions. "Mitigating" is good. To hell with Alastair. To hell with all those phony words.

Sant tried to get the horse to move faster by kneeing and heeling and turning his ear, but it wasn't any good. A fire is still always a thing an animal doesn't like very much. So they proceeded toward the burning mission at the horse's pace. You could tell it was the mission now. It made a beautiful fire. It was built of foreign materials, thin clapboard, and it was three stories high, higher than anything in Indian Country. The three stories would give the fire a splendid draft, and nothing burns better than New England kindling wood. Nothing burns better than two-by-four studs, joists, and rafters on sixteen-inch centers, that the New England building code calls for. It calls for the best fire Indian Country ever had. It is too much of a temptation for a poor Indian. You cannot tempt even an Indian too much. Even a Navaho. No, Sant thought, they should not have done it, but if they had to do it I hope they let him out of his New England house first. It seems only fair. I wish this damn horse would get a little bit of a move on. What's he scared of? What are we all scared of, I wonder?

Now as the dark horse and young rider got closer you could see clearly the giant sage and the scrub oak and weird cholla cactus all emblazoned against the black sky. It made a much better fire than the Indians were ever able to build for a *yebechai*. The mission was going out in a blaze of gory. Glory, Sant had meant to think. He dropped off his horse and made toward the blaze. It was very hot against his face and when it got unbearably hot he began to circle, watching for some kind of opening to dash in, but the fire was going good all the way through and up, crowning and billowing and easily sixty feet above the house. Sant began to retreat now. If the missionary was in there there wasn't any hope at all. God damn those Indians. What did they think it was—1840, 1860 or what? Indians aren't supposed to behave this way now. All the money the government has spent to civilize them. All the money the government has stolen from them to spend on them to civilize them. Do they still think they're savages or what? Indians will still be Indians no matter what you steal from them to civilize them. Maybe they all ought to be rounded up and put in a camp where they can be civilized and watched, but that was tried once. I guess there's nothing you can do about Indians.

Sant sat down on a burned log a safe distance from the fire and was joined by his horse, who finally arrived. "I guess there's nothing can be done with Indians."

218

Sant realized he was sitting on a burned log from the old hogan. The whole place was burned down now—there wasn't anything left at all of the mission. "I wonder if there is anything left of the missionary."

Now Sant could make out some activity in back of an enormous rock that his circle of the fire had been too small to observe. There were people arriving. Indians. There were many Indians arriving and all going to say something to a man standing there, protected in back of the rock. It was the missionary, Mr. Sanders. God protects the protected. Sant edged in close and so did the horse. The horse was very brave now. Sant could hear that the Indians were all saying the same thing and all with a touch of awe in their voices. Where there had been a touch of contempt before now there was a touch of awe in their voices.

"Why really, this is the tallest fire. Oh, why really, this is the fire that very well, really, might end all fires. We have really never seen such a fire and none of our ancestors have either. Really, they haven't."

There was awe in their eyes, too, as they stepped back from congratulating the missionary. They looked at him with an awe-filled expression. Sant knew that there is nothing an Indian respects more than a man who is responsible for a good fire and this one was the finest fire the Indians had seen, including their ancestors and their children and their children's children. Who else would or will ever trouble or afford to import the makings of such a fire? Build a house and have such a respect for fire as to burn it down? That was why the awe was in the Indians' eyes. Here was one man who, why really, understood, and he was a white man. A white man who beat the red man at his own game. Their own religion. Why really, this is some white man. Why really, did you say he was from Boston? Why really, what a loss to the nation of Boston, his coming here was. To a red man this fire was what a globe-circling satellite would be to a white, and put up by a private individual and not one containing a mere dog, but a satellite ringing the earth, containing a herd of elephants. That's what the missionary's fire was to the Indians. That's about it, Sant thought. The man, I guess, is a kind of genius, Mr. Sanders is.

Sant went back and sat on his burned hogan log until the fire had died down to a respectable pile of glowing coals and there was nothing left standing but a very respectable and straight New England, kiln-brick chimney, the only thing that had withstood the outraging fire. The tall black chimney of foreign and manufactured stones was the only thing brought that would stay, all that would endure.

"I suppose," Sant said, sitting alongside the missionary after all the Indians had gone, "I suppose in a couple of days they will pull that down too."

"What?"

"The chimney. All that's left."

"No," Mr. Sanders said, watching it. "They allow things to fall of their own weight, their own absurdity."

"Oh?"

"Yes," Mr. Sanders fanned himself against the heat with his pith helmet, then he tossed that into the glowing fire with a large gesture. "Yes," Mr. Sanders said. "Their own contradictions. I remember," Mr. Sanders said in a tired voice and yet looking around him with a kind of glee, "I remember at Concord, at the Bethlehem Seminary—that's where I studied in my youth. My youth." Mr. Sanders stared into the fire. "My youth. Well," Mr. Sanders said, snapping out of it and looking up suddenly. "They gave a course—Mr. Perklers—a course on the understanding of the red man, on our problems with our savage brothers. Are you interested?"

"Kind of."

"Well, the main part of the course was based on a diary, a book called *Brother Smelzer among the Indians.* That title for Brother Smelzer's diary didn't sound so foolish then. The Rover Boys and Teddy Roosevelt were very popular then. You were always among somebody or up some river then. Well, anyway—" Mr. Sanders caught himself suffering total recall and got to the point. "Brother Smelzer's diary among the Indians was four thousand pages long. He must have written half of each night in that jungle among those savages by lantern up some lost tributary of the Amazon, I'm sure it was. Anyway, only a fourth of it had been printed by the Society, which was a lot. Mr. Perklers, who gave the course, told us to go to original sources. Maybe I was the only one who did or maybe I was the only one who ever read to the end of the four thousand pages. You know what the last words in that diary were?"

"No."

" 'I must get downriver before they convert *me*.' "

"Wow!" Sant said.

"Yes, that's the only word now," Mr. Sanders said. "In my youth I didn't understand. I thought maybe it was insanity, that Brother Smelzer had gone insane. Now I will always wonder."

"Wonder what?"

"Whether they did."

"Did what?"

"Converted him," Mr. Sanders said. They both sat silent a long time looking into the dying fire. "But I suppose you have your own problems," Mr. Sanders said.

"I sure have," Sant said.

"What?"

"Some place to leave my horse."

"Leave it here at my place."

"You haven't got a place," Sant said.

Mr. Sanders looked around slowly at the cactus and sage; holding on to one he raised back from his sitting position. "I never thought of that before."

"You always had a place before," Sant said.

"No, I never had a place before," Mr. Sanders said. Mr. Sanders looked more intently now at the surrounding country in this first cold light of morning. "Now I have got a place. Until now I've been moving around a piece of Boston. Now I've got a place." Mr. Sanders motioned at Sant. "You can leave your horse at my place."

"Thank you," Sant said.

"Por nada," Mr. Sanders said. "For nothing." They both sat silently watching the morning break.

"What do you know about women?" Mr. Sanders said.

"Very little," Sant said. "Next to nothing."

221

"Where are you going?"

"To join the bronc people," Sant said.

"Where are you going?"

"Cortez. They're in Cortez now, the bronc people. They've got a show in Cortez. The rodeo's in Cortez."

Mr. Sanders watched the fire. "And you know nothing about women?"

"Next to nothing," Sant said.

"Me neither," Mr. Sanders said.

Mr. Sanders fished around in back of where he was sitting until he came up with a box. "You know what this is, son?"

"It's an adobe form. You make adobes with it," Sant said watching.

"The Indians just gave it to me," Mr. Sanders said. "I thought it was very nice of them."

"Yes, it was," Sant said, waiting for his chance to leave politely, watching the gathering day.

Mr. Sanders laid down the adobe form gently. "You say you know very little about women. How little?"

"Very little," Sant said.

"Do you know what an affair means?"

"No, but I guess Alastair does," Sant said.

"You mean Alastair's had an affair?"

"Very little," Sant said.

Mr. Sanders looked impatient and tapped the box again. "An affair means intercourse."

"I've had that with a lot of people," Sant said.

"You still don't understand," the missionary said. Now he looked at the sky in thought. *Edesh il,*" he said.

"With Indian girls, yes," Sant said. "Does that count?"

"Yes, it does," Mr. Sanders said. "Was it good?"

"Very good," Sant said.

"Good," Mr. Sanders said definitely. "I'm not a dirty old man. I only want the facts of life. I'm a child. I am the child in this conversation. I know the words but not the facts, not the acts. I was a puritan, now I've seen my first morning and there's nothing dirty about it. There was something dirty about the puritan but

222

there's nothing dirty about the morning." Mr. Sanders picked up the box, the adobe form, and examined it carefully. "I'm sorry you had to be the first person to come along, that I had to pick on you."

"That's perfectly all right, Mr. Sanders," Sant said.

"I'm sorry that the puritans had dirty minds."

"That's perfectly all right, Mr. Sanders." Sant wanted to get on with his own business but he could not resist the last statement. "What do you mean, had?"

"Why did we make God a dirty-minded puritan?" the minister said.

"That's very strong language," Sant said.

"Well, eighteen years in a cast is a long time. I would use stronger language but I'm very poorly equipped with my New England background. But I'm sorry you had to happen along."

"I tell you it's perfectly all right, Mr. Sanders. And I came here on purpose to leave my horse."

"Okay," Mr. Sanders said.

"I presume you'll take him back to the ranch."

"I presume I will. Yes, of course," Mr. Sanders said.

"If you'll turn him loose he'll go back by himself."

"No, he might roll off the saddle. I'll take him back. I promise," Mr. Sanders said. "What ever happened to Alastair Benjamin?"

"He's going to get educated."

"Worse things could happen. Did Alastair ever resolve what happened to him?"

"Yes. And he thinks things will stop happening now."

"Why? Has he forgiven everything that happened?"

"No. He killed my father's horse."

"Well." Mr. Sanders thought about this a moment, watching the last fire. "Yes. That's all right. That could stop the chain letter of killing people. That could finish the old West, the old revenge."

"Alastair feels so," Sant said.

"Well, if he feels it, doesn't presume it, I guess he will make it now."

"I believe he will," Sant said. "I think maybe we can all make it now. But I want to ask you about my trip."

"What about it?"

"You think I'll make it as a bronc rider?"

"No."

Sant looked around at everything and then back to Mr. Sanders.

"Because if you don't know, who the hell does?" Mr. Sanders said.

"Well," Sant said, "you see, I've arranged it so I've got no way to come back. I've got only enough money to get there."

"You could crawl back," Mr. Sanders said.

"I don't think I can," Sant said.

They both rose now as though at a signal, as though the sun, finally appearing now after faking a long false dawn, as though this were a signal, they both got up. Mr. Sanders rose, still holding the adobe form the Indians had given him, and Sant went over and unloosed the cowhide suitcase from the horse.

"I'll flag down the Cortez Greyhound on La Ventana Hill."

"You do that," Mr. Sanders said. "And never a borrower or a lender be, and above all things, don't get killed."

Sant winked at Mr. Sanders.

"By the time you get back I will have learned to walk," Mr. Sanders said. "I have got to learn everything from the beginning as though I were born yesterday."

"I hope it works out," Sant said.

"It will be exciting," Mr. Sanders said.

"I mean, I hope the Indians don't hand you a line," Sant said, slinging the cowhide suitcase over his shoulder.

"Well, I guess if anybody can hand out a line I can."

"True," Sant said, striding off.

Well, Mr. Sanders thought, watching Sant move off, he didn't have to be quite so definite. By God, I was never that bad.

Mr. Sanders sat down now to figure out how the adobe forms worked, to figure out how you make bricks without straw.

224

FOURTEEN **S**ant found the suitcase much heavier than a suitcase should be and the Tex-Tan saddle, which weighed about thirty-eight pounds, much heavier than thirty-eight pounds ever was. Altogether he was lugging one hundred pounds, give or take ten, up and down every rise and fall in the slightly tilted escarpment that was the eleven miles that stood between the mission and the road. Every now and then, actually at the top of each rise, he would set it all down and sit on top of it and contemplate the things that Spinoza thought about but from a more "really" point of view. That is, how far are the stars and how near the moon; but mostly he wondered if someone had moved the highway farther over toward Santa Fe. Take during antelope season, he had hunted this distance easy in this same country but then he was carrying a 1903 Springfield with a Weaver four-power scope which would add up to maybe nine and one half pounds. It's funny what a difference ninety pounds makes. It's funny, too, what a difference it makes whether you're riding a horse or not.

I hope they never do away with the horse permanent, even if it's only kept for what its ancestors have done. Never in the history of affairs have so little done so much for so few—or something like that. Anyway let us start a Save the Horse Week. Anyway let us try to make it on this last hill. There she is—the highway. Now, that's nice, they haven't moved it so awfully much at that.

Sant pulled down to the highway, dragging the suitcase until he reached the edge of the pavement and a lemita bush, then he put the saddle on top of the suitcase and then sat on this as though he were horsed and watched down the highway for the Greyhound.

I wonder if the Greyhound will stop. I wonder if there's a regulation against it or I wonder if maybe the Greyhound just can't be bothered to stop for one little stove-in cowpuncher. I wonder if maybe the Greyhound will think I'm a highwayman and not stop. I wonder if the Greyhound will think I'm a gun-slinger. No, the Greyhound will think I'm too little to be a gun-slinger. Still, Billy the Kid was very little too. I wonder what I could do to make myself look less like Billy the Kid. I wonder what Alastair would do. I wonder what Lemaitre would do. I must see if Lemaitre will keep his promise. I wonder if he will remember me and what he promised. I wonder what I could do to make myself look less like Billy the Kid to the Greyhound.

While Sant was figuring this the Greyhound loomed suddenly on a rise and bore down quickly, began to roar and run to make a hill, then jammed on all the air and came to a stop just in front of Sant. Sant lugged all his stuff on board and then asked the Greyhound man how much.

"Where you going?"

"Cortez."

The driver looked around at the country. "How far north are we from the Tinian Trading Post turnoff?"

"About twenty-five miles," Sant said.

The driver thought a while. "That makes it eight ninety," the driver said.

Sant paid him and got his change and the Greyhound started off but Sant didn't move.

I've got two twenty-dollar bills and a ten here in my wallet I can't account for. My father could have slipped one of them in and maybe it was the missionary who gave me the other. But how could he have done it? Maybe it was Alastair. Do they think I won't make it out there?

He looked for some place to toss the money and then noticed that people were staring so he put it in his wallet and looked for a place to sit. He pulled his stuff down the aisle looking for a familiar face but he didn't see one till he got to where the Indians sit in the back. Indians always sit in the back. Now he saw a

226

Navaho he had seen around and he threw up his stuff on the rack above Tso.

"Where you going, Tso?"

"Anyplace."

"No place in particular?"

"That's right."

"Well, you're sure to end up some place." Sant sat alongside Tso.

"That's right."

"You know you're going north."

"Thanks," Tso said.

"Do you want to go north?"

"I wanted to go north since I was this high."

"What will you do when you get there?"

"I'll go see the Hurry-down boys," Tso said.

"Who are they?"

"They're always on the trader's radio," Tso said. "They want everybody to hurry down to their place. They want us all to hurry down while there's a few days left. Ever since I was this high the Hurry-down boys have wanted me to hurry down. Now that I'm going north I guess maybe while I'm there I'll hurry down to the Hurry-down boys."

"Don't forget the Tomorrow-for-sure boys."

"Hurry down tonight, tomorrow for sure. No, I won't forget them."

"You got to give them all a chance at an Indian who's sold his sheep."

"They're all equal."

"What do they charge, Tso, to carry an Indian?"

"Interest? Six per cent a month."

"That's seventy-two per cent. The Hurry-down boys are charging you Indians seventy-two per cent a year."

"The Tomorrow-for-sure boys too?"

"I guess so."

"Well," Tso said, putting a brown finger on his high cheekbone, "is that good or bad? Does it mean the season is open or closed on Indians?"

"Open season."

"Well."

"I guess the season will always be open on Indians," Sant said.

"Well." Tso seemed to be thinking about this as he adjusted the band around his head, but he wasn't. "Where you going, Santo?"

"I'm going to work the shows."

"What does the rodeo pay?"

"Casey Tibbs already made two hundred thousand dollars. I guess Lemaitre made about half a million in his lifetime."

"Is Lemaitre dead?"

"No, he's just resting up."

"I heard he was dead."

"No."

"I heard he got hurt so bad so many times he's about dead."

"No. He's just resting up."

"I hear he can't walk."

"How do you know that?"

"We got Indian guys who follow the shows, get all those show magazines."

"The rodeo magazines don't know what they're talking about. I take them too. It's just an opinion."

"They say he's paralyzed."

"You get paralyzed, well, you can get unparalyzed. Everything else is an opinion."

"They say Lemaitre will never ride again."

Sant got up and walked to the front of the bus and looked out at everything going by up there and then he walked to the back of the bus and checked everything that was going by back there. Then he returned to his seat and looked over at Tso.

"He will ride again okay," Sant said and he looked over at Tso. "He'll ride again okay," Sant said. But the Indian was asleep.

Everyone except the sleeping Tso got out to rest when the Greyhound made a rest stop in Cuba. There was one Zia Indian, though, that got out but he didn't rest inside the hotel. He just walked around to the rear of the Greyhound and when Sant passed him on his way to the hotel the Zia was directing his stream of rest

228

against the hood of the rear Greyhound engine, which cooled the Greyhound and made it steam nicely.

Inside the adobe and log hotel a lot of Indians, Navaho and Apache mostly, were sitting on the circular steps of the sunken fireplace, not speaking. Piñon logs were burning in the fireplace and gave the adobes and the hanging Indian rugs a good smell. Mr. Boker, the ancient Anglo owner of the hotel who knew everything that happened, was better than a newspaper for Indian Country because he didn't consider the advertisers, didn't consider the outside world.

"Well, Mr. Bowman," Mr. Boker said. "You going someplace?"

It was the first time Mr. Boker, anyone, had called him Mr. Bowman. It felt all right.

"Cortez maybe," Mr. Boker said, looking at the posters on the wall.

"Yes," Sant said.

"Well, I hope you do all right."

Sant nodded. Mr. Boker looked at him carefully. "You hear your friend Lemaitre got his?" Sant nodded again. Mr. Boker took out a pencil and began making meaningless scratches on the register.

"Right here in New Mexico. He starts right here in Indian Country, goes all over the world, presidents and kings, New York City, New York, Paris, France, a million dollars, and he come right back here where he started to get it."

"Where was it, Mr. Boker?"

"Ratón."

"Is it bad?"

"Murder." Mr. Boker paused. "The horse murdered him. An older horse too. Tricked him off and then stomped him to death. They couldn't pull the horse off."

"Is he dead?"

"The papers say he's alive. They call it living."

"Was it a local horse?"

"Local horse, local boy," Mr. Boker said. "Imagine Lemaitre starting right here in Indian Country, goes all over the world, presidents and kings, New York City, New York, Paris, France, a million dollars, and he comes right back here to get it. It's as though the horse were waiting—waiting to claim him for where he belonged. Waiting to trap him here finally where he belonged. Indian Country," Mr. Boker said.

"Was it the horse—? Was it from Coyote?"

"Yes," Mr. Boker said. "Local horse, local boy. Wait!"

"I can't keep them waiting," Sant said.

Back in the Greyhound Tso woke up as they went over the Cuba bridge. "Are we there yet?" Tso said.

"Where?"

"Anyplace."

"No, we're not anyplace yet," Sant said.

Tso watched up at the ceiling of the Greyhound and Sant watched out at the land. It had snowed in the high country during the night and everything above seven thousand feet was scintillant in the early sun. The deer now would work their way down to the mesas where they would try to make it during the long winter. The elk would move down too, but not so far. They would drift down to where the big mountain benched below the sharp-white granite tailings, where the mountain spread out before it fell off into the long valleys. You could make a living there.

"Tell me, Tso," Sant said, "what ever happened to Afraid Of His Own Horses and The Other Indian?"

"They drifted out of the country."

"Oh?"

"Yes. One of those government projects to relocate the Indians in Chicago."

"Then they're gone?"

"No. They drifted back again."

"Wasn't the feed any good?"

"The feed was okay but it wasn't here."

"Wasn't the money any good?"

"The money was okay but it wasn't here."

"How you going to please an Indian?"

"Leave him alone," Tso said.

Sant looked out again at the land. The highway leaves the

230

foothills of the Jemez Mountains not too far north of Cuba and now they were in the wide flat country of the Jicarilla Apaches. The Jicarilla Apaches work sheep mostly and they live in tents. Now the tents had all been folded and the Apaches were working their way back to the Indian agency at Dulce where the railhead was, where the government was, where the Department of the Interior was handing things out. You could make a kind of living there.

"Tso, have you seen this year's new horses?"

"They're too big," Tso said.

"Then they've brought the new horses into the agency?"

"Yes," Tso said. "And they're too big."

"It's about time the Indians got some new breeding horses."

"Maybe," Tso said. "But these are too big."

"The Indians' horses are too small."

"Maybe," Tso said. "But the new ones are too big."

"You mean they can't make a living here?"

"Not the both of us," Tso said.

"They burn too much hay?"

"And they won't fit our stalls," Tso said.

"I didn't think the Indians had stalls. I thought they left them under the trees."

"They won't fit under the trees."

"Or between them either?"

"That's right," Tso said.

"Then the horse trader will have a bad year."

"I hope so," Tso said. "Santo, do you have to go out and break your neck in this rodeo business?"

"It's what I want to do."

"Break your neck?"

"I want to work the shows."

"But you're going to see Lemaitre first?"

"I'm going to get off in Durango to say hello."

"I'll settle for that," Tso said.

"You must think he's in awfully bad shape."

"I know. I know what big horses can do," Tso said.

When Sant got off the Greyhound at Durango, Tso was again asleep. The first thing Sant had to do was find where Lemaitre was. The man at the Greyhound depot in a green eyeshade told him to try the Saddle and Bar.

"Where's that?" Sant asked.

"Mountain and Fourth. You're at Mountain now."

Sant went up Mountain Street toward Fourth feeling trapped. Durango, Colorado, lies within the deep fold of a mountain. The business section of town is on faulted rock. It moves slightly each year. But it was not this that Sant sensed. He sensed the oppression of the overwhelming mountains. It was a place where you couldn't see out. You had the feeling, without ever being able to see the horizon, that this was it, that if you couldn't see it you would never feel it, never know anything more than Durango. He had had the same feeling at the bottom of deep canyons on hunting trips. City people must have it always. It makes no difference that people are close. You are lost.

Sant watched into the windows of all the cowboys' shops, making a note of all the things he needed to buy at the Tomorrow-for-sure, at all the cowboy Hurry-down boys, shops he passed, all the important, unessential things a small triumph in the ring could buy. If Durango were not so mountained in there'd be other dreams of other worlds a small triumph could buy.

Now he was at the Saddle and Bar and he pushed in before reflection. Any thinking at this point he knew would send him back to the Greyhound, so Sant pushed in and found himself in a nice, clean, simple room with a very long bar with saddles for stools. Down where the bar made a short L there were two cowboy gentlemen watching the bartender, who was watching the ceiling. It was very quiet.

"I would like to see Lemaitre," Sant said.

The bartender walked down to the middle of the bar where Sant was and leaned over and slightly down and said, "Lemaitre's not seeing anybody." The bartender had a crew haircut.

"It will do him good to see people," Sant said.

The bartender only smiled.

"Tell him it's a friend."

The bartender smiled again and winked down at the two cowboy gentlemen at the L of the bar. They made no sign. Their expressions were frozen. They were very fancy-dressed. They must have had many triumphs.

Sant unfolded his arms. "Tell Lemaitre it's me. Tell him it's Sant." Sant removed his wallet and passed a card up to the bartender. "Sant Bowman."

The bartender went into the back of the room and then into another room through a solid oak door with a horseshoe on it. Sant folded his arms again and waited. The two cowboy gentlemen watched Sant with the same expression they had used in watching the bartender—nothing.

The bartender came back wearing a surprised look.

"Lemaitre will see you," he said.

Sant went through the oak door and the two cowboy gentlemen looked at each other very surprised.

Lemaitre was seated, propped up, in the dealer's chair in front of a huge and round green card table. The only light came from a fierce shaded lamp that spotted the table and nothing more. Sant was in the room a whole minute before he saw anything more of Lemaitre than his hands.

"Sit down," Lemaitre said.

Sant took a seat at the opposite of Lemaitre's at the concentric green stark table with the hard light.

"What is it?"

"Do you remember that?" Sant said, pointing to the worn white card that lay on the green table in front of Lemaitre.

"I remember," Lemaitre said.

Now Sant saw more than Lemaitre's hands and it was awfully bad.

"You promised."

"I know," Lemaitre said. "But—"

"But you promised," Sant said.

"To let you break your neck?"

"That's what I want to do."

"Break your neck?"

"I want to work the shows."

Lemaitre didn't say anything.

"Was it fun?" Sant said.

Lemaitre made a cigarette with the fingers of one hand without moving his arm, flashing an emerald as big and bright as an arena. He dipped his head and snatched the cigarette quickly, then swung back his hard, taut, pained face and blew out perfect blue rings, concealing the jewels of Ophir, the memories. Some distant night, a knight—a knight dying, felled in Samarkand.

"Yes," Lemaitre said.

"Was it worth it?"

"Yes," Lemaitre said. Lemaitre paused and drummed his fingers on the green table, the only movement he seemed able to make. "But don't tell anyone." He paused again. "They'll lock us up."

Twenty minutes later Sant got on the same bus. He had expected he would have to take the next bus but the same bus was still there. So was Tso.

"Tell me this, Santo," Tso said. "What did he say?"

"Well, he said they'd lock us up."

"And they should too," Tso said. "What did he say next?"

"Lots of things," Sant said. Sant watched the bus try to make its way through a town that was caught in the crevice of a mountain.

"You can tell me all," Tso said. "I'm just another Indian."

"You mean no one would believe you?"

"That's right."

"Tso, it was very funny."

"Funny?"

"Tragic."

"Tragic?"

"It was weird."

"Funny, tragic, or weird?"

"Weird is the closest."

"Then it was weird."

"Not exactly. He's got dignity. *Dignidad.*"

"How did he get that?"

"He was born with it, I guess."

"Is it good or bad?"

234

"Very good, Tso."

"I never went to school."

"It's when a man can take a funny tragic weird situation and still remain a man. A guy can be smashed and remain a man."

"Is that dignity?"

"Yes."

"You seem very sure of yourself."

"I'm sure of myself now."

The bus began to wind through a Mormon town now. You can always tell a Mormon town by its name. It has no style. When a Western town has a name like Farmington, Fruitland, Kirtland, Peachblossom, it's probably Mormon. Names without style. Not Aztec or Cuba or Tierra Amarilla. These names have style and were not named by Mormons. You can tell by the buildings too. If they're kiln-fired red brick, two stories, ugly, with the ring of money, you just went through Peachton. Capulin is slash and adobe, falling down in style. Coyote, too, it has style.

"He's still got style."

"Who?"

"Lemaitre."

"This town hasn't, I guess."

"What was it?"

"Blockton."

"No, it hasn't at all."

"What good is style if he's falling to pieces?"

"Oh, it helps an awful lot," Sant said.

"It got him into it."

"And it will get him out."

"How will it get him out?"

"It will, that's all," Sant said.

They rode up now a rich green valley with snow above them on both sides.

"I wish you would think it over, Santo," Tso said.

Sant was quite a while watching out the window at the high snow on both sides before he said, "No. It's all right now, Tso."

On the outskirts of Cortez they both got off the Greyhound

where all the cars were turning off the asphalt into the very dusty road that led to the rodeo ring.

"Why did you get off here, Tso?"

"This place looks as good as any place."

"Do you want to carry the saddle?"

"Sure, I'll carry the saddle."

They lugged all their stuff down the road that sprayed them with a continuous fall of dust from a steady line of cars going toward the stadium. Sant carried the cowhide suitcase and about every hundred yards he would sit on the suitcase and Tso on the saddle and rest.

"I've ridden at Dulce and Windowrock," Tso said. "It wouldn't hurt me to try again."

Sant spat out some of the dust and looked over toward a sign that was beginning to appear through the haze.

"I see they got Jim Shoulders riding here."

"Who's he?" Tso said from his seat on the saddle.

"He'll be the next all-around champion."

"What about you?"

"It takes time, Tso."

"You know what George Washington said?"

"I don't care, Tso. Let's get moving."

They got started down the road on the last lap.

"This George Washington's an Indian," Tso said.

"All right, what did George Washington say?"

"George Washington said the next champion would be you."

"I'm sure George Washington meant well," Sant said.

They went around to the back of the stadium where the riders and the animals made their entrances and their exits, where they had all the stock corralled and penned and tied. Tso minded their gear while Sant looked around for someone who seemed important. He found a man finally who wore a tight, small, snap-brim black hat and a bow tie.

"I've come to ride," Sant said.

"I've got enough troubles," the man said.

"I've come from Lemaitre."

236

"I told you I have enough troubles," the man said and he continued to hurry, disappearing into the dust and horses.

Sant went back and sat next to Tso.

"Did I ever tell you what Thomas Jefferson said?" Tso said.

"I don't care," Sant said.

"This Thomas Jefferson was an Indian. He's dead now."

"I know Jefferson's dead," Sant said.

"He got killed in a rodeo in Salt Lake," Tso said. "They brought him back to Penesteja before he died. Do you know what his farewell address was?"

"I don't care."

"What Jefferson had to say?"

"Someone probably wrote it for him," Sant said.

They both looked quite sad and both quite forlorn there, sitting in the middle of all that motion alone and gathering dust. Especially Sant, the white boy, seemed to show more dust than the red boy, who seemed to take dust better, and Sant seemed to look much more forlorn than the forlorn Indian. As a matter of fact, the Indian was taking their defeat fine. They sat in the middle of all the commotion and falling dust for maybe twenty minutes watching out quietly but not seeing anything. They came but they could not see, and Sant was wondering whether anything would be conquered now.

"Who the hell wants to ride?"

"Me," Sant said. It was the man in the snap-brim black hat towering above where they sat.

"Who the hell said you could ride?"

Sant undid his wallet and passed up a letter.

"Lemaitre," the man said. "It's his writing all right." The man tapped his knuckles with the letter. "I'm short of riders." There was a lifting of the dust now and they could see two cowboys lying recumbent. "Are you ready?"

"Yes," Sant said.

"The other boy?" the producer said.

"No. No, I don't think so," Tso said.

"You came to ride, didn't you? Didn't he?" the producer said to Sant.

"Yes, but—"

"Yes, but what?"

"Yes, but he's a Jeffersonian."

"I've got enough trouble," the producer said. "You, boy, follow me."

"Yes, sir," Sant said.

"What's the name?"

"Sant's the name. Sant Bowman."

"Never heard of you."

"You will," Sant said.

"I've got too much trouble already," the producer said. "Are you ready."

"Is the horse ready?"

"Of course."

"Then we shouldn't keep him waiting."

"Oh, God!"

"It wouldn't be polite," Sant said.

They were moving through the darkness of the passageway that ran under the stadium toward the arena.

"I've got a tough one for you to go with," the producer said up ahead in the darkness. "I can't help it."

"A local horse?" Sant said.

"Yes. A local bastard."

"Local horse, local boy," Sant said.

There was a sudden burst of violent daylight as they hit the arena and a sudden burst of awful noise.

As they made the turn for the chutes the producer grabbed a telephone from a red box marked "Private" while Sant knelt down in the sand of the arena to buckle on spurs.

"I got one," the producer said into the phone while watching up at the press and announcer's box that jutted out high over the stadium. "I got a Sant Bowman next on Flamethrower. Where from?" He spoke down to Sant.

"Indian Country," Sant said. "Same town as Lemaitre." Sant made the final tie on his spurs. "Say I'm riding for Lemaitre."

The producer repeated this on the phone and Sant trotted across the big open stretch that had suddenly gone very quiet and tight. He made a quick leap to the top of the chute that was ready and held Flamethrower. Flamethrower was a big black and trembling to go.

"What are we waiting for?" Sant told the restraining cowboys. "Let him go!" and Sant dropped onto the horse, twisting the points of the razor spurs behind the shoulders of Flamethrower and as deep as he could sink them. The horse shot out. Flamethrower was both a shooter and a twister. He took several long shooting leaps and then went into a sudden twist. It never failed. It failed this time.

"Always go relaxed," Lemaitre had said across the poker table. "Become part of the horse."

Flamethrower was a shooter and a twister and a scraper. When he failed at all else he would tear you off against the boards.

"Let him know who's the master." This was not Lemaitre. Sant had figured this himself.

Sant shoved in the spurs brutally as far as they would go and the horse went into a tight spin. This was not the technique of Flamethrower, only an agonized attempt to kill the thing on his back and, like everything without technique, it failed and the horse began to give out. Sant gave it one more final spur that set the horse gyrating straight up, and then Flamethrower was finished. When Sant realized the horse was about to fail he gauged the distance between himself and the catching horse and rider but instead of allowing the catcher to help him he placed his hand on the rump of the catching horse behind the rider and vaulted over the horse and came up running on his own feet alongside the running horses. He gradually came down to a trot and pulled up at the railing. He still had on his hat.

The stadium was making an awfully loud noise now. At the other end of the stadium the producer was on the phone again.

"Sant Bowman," he said.

Now above all of the noise of the stadium the loud-speakers were trying to say "Sant Bowman."

Outside, the waiting Indian could hear it too. He kicked into the dirt and then looked up into the wide sky.

"That's our boy," Tso said. "Sant Bowman."

FIFTEEN   Alastair Benjamin had been gone now from the Circle Heart three weeks. He had been sent away by the Bowmans to be educated. They missed him very much. The house was empty. The house was quiet. The whole ranch was without sound. This morning they had gotten a letter from Big Sant's brother, to whose house Alastair had been sent to stay while he got educated. The letter had said that Alastair had disappeared. They had gotten a note from Alastair one week before this saying, "This is not an education, it's a war. This is not a school, it's a battlefield."

"We should not have sent him there," Millie Sant said. "There were other places to send him. We could have sent him to Albuquerque."

"We had to send him where we could afford to send him."

"Did it have to be there?"

"That's where my brother was."

"Will he come back now?" Millie Sant was sewing on a sock but now she quit. "Will he come back here now?"

Big Sant was on his knees putting a log on the fire. "I don't know," he said.

"Well, isn't there something we can do?"

"We're doing it," Sant said, and he dropped the log, cracking the hearth, making the only noise that had been made in the house for a long while now.

"Now I've done it."

"It can be fixed," Millie said.

"We'll see."

240

"He'll come back."

"We'll wait and see," Sant said and he began to wrestle again with the log that had broken the hearth.

When he got off the train Alastair Benjamin had decided to walk the very long distance from Albuquerque to the Circle Heart. It was not that he had run out of money. He had that much money. It was that he had run out of something else. He had run out of the ability to go home. Like any soldier in defeat he would have liked it very much if there were a long interval of nothing. If several years would run by quickly so that he might find something that he had lost before he went home. The thing was, he had reckoned, the thing was that no one had ever let on there was a war. The war that must have been on since forever had always been concealed from him in this corner of New Mexico. They had always kept this war very carefully undeclared here.

Now he topped a rise in the cattle trail he was following and there was Cuba, the heart of the country where war was undeclared.

He had been rolled back now, he figured, almost five hundred miles and it was a very queer thing that all along the way everyone along the way seemed to sense they were talking to, or watching, a man who was running from something. He seemed to be carrying his body, moving along, like a flag of failure.

He was careful to follow the cattle trails that went around Cuba. He did not want to meet anyone from there now. He did not want to see anyone yet. Maybe he had been hoping he would have walked it off before he got to Cuba. That he would have forgotten what happened and it would not show like a flag when he got this close to the Circle Heart.

The mountains around the town looked black now and much taller than when he went away only a few weeks ago. The snow always makes pines look black at a distance and the snow always makes mountains appear taller, but something else made them look tall and black now, and he wanted it to go away but you cannot remove a mountain by thinking about it. You could not remove the black trees either, the pines in funeral rows that led up into the clouds.

The animals were not talking, coming up from Albuquerque—the wild animals he had seen while walking the back trails that ran along the west base of the Jemez. He had met quite a few animals that seemed surprised to have met him. "Very surprised to meet you." They had all bounded away quickly. The animals were not talking. Take another time, take an ordinary time, take the average time when the hunting season is well over, and you walk this much distance in the back trails of the slippery Jemez and you will find animals to watch while they watch back. They ordinarily have a healthy animal curiosity about such a weird animal as you. But today the animals were not talking. It is a comfort to have a rapport with animals without the report of a gun. It is a comfort when you are very lonely to see wild animals who seem very lonely too. Alastair wiped his cheek in the immemorial gesture of sweating something out and sat on a juniper log and watched the sky whiz by, the white clouds moving rapidly across the all blue. Animals should not have feared him. Alastair broke a twig. You can always marry a Pueblo girl, but then you can't live in the pueblo. They have a law against it. No whites are allowed to live in the pueblo even if they marry a Pueblo girl. We Pueblos have got a restrictive covenant leveled against everyone but us. This includes any shade of white at all, including black. The Navahos are okay and Apaches are okay too and maybe Utes. With Utes it never came up. But everyone else can take a flying jerk for themselves. This is not nice but it is the American the Pueblos have been taught to talk and I suppose it's nice that a Pueblo can talk at all, bad words and restrictive covenants falling where they may.

Alastair stood up and dismissed all this. After all, he was not trying to crash a pueblo and he had not either been trying to crash the white world. He did not want to sleep with their white daughters. He only wanted a small education.

Alastair stretched his arms and tried to think more relevantly. A relevant way of thinking would be to decide where he was going. It's always nice to know where you are going even when you are retreating. But of course the main thing about a retreat is that you are going nowhere. The very name must derive from nowhere.

Obviously he was making toward the Circle Heart, but a while ago he was making toward Cuba and he had gone around that. Now would he go around the Circle Heart?

"I don't know," he thought aloud, and he lifted the suitcase to his shoulder.

He could have gone around Cuba by swinging west out into the Indian Country, the trading-post country, the flat country, the country without water that they gave to the Indians. The chances were he would meet someone out there who was not interested. The trader would be trading and the Indians would be resting against the work their wives were doing. But instead of swinging west he had swung east. With luck he would meet no one at all on the trails that ran along the foothills of the vast mountain. The trail that had been crowded before with the footmarks of the wild animals, the doglike paws of the coyote and the smaller same paw of the fox and the cloven foot of the deer and the same larger foot of the elk now gave way to the mark of cattle and the hoofprints of the shod horse. He was close to civilization. He was on the ranchers' trail where the cattlemen brought down their stock through the Señorito cut. There was danger now of meeting someone.

"What passes, friend?"

Someone, Arturo Cipriano de Godoy, had ridden up soundlessly from the rear and waited now alongside.

"*Ninguno novedad,*" Alastair said, putting down his load. "Nothing much. What with you?"

"Nothing at all," Arturo said.

"How is the cattle business?"

"Terrible, you wouldn't believe it." Arturo used this phrase interchangeably with "Wonderful, you wouldn't believe it." Not depending on business, which was unimportant, but on his morale.

"Remember we met in the Valle Grande," Arturo said.

"We met in the Great Valley," Alastair agreed.

"New Mexico Cattle and Timber Keep Out."

"Yeah."

Arturo made a cigarette. "I decided to let them go broke on

their own." Arturo finished the cigarette with a flourish and applied the sharp end to his mouth.

God, he's dressed gaudy, Alastair thought.

"In the Great Valley you were with Sant Bowman." Arturo lit the cigarette with a large match. "You were very young, *muy joven,* and I lied to you because I did not want him to get killed. He wanted me to remember that he had ridden with Lemaitre and I remembered it well but I lied to him because I did not want him to go out there to some other place and get killed. There is nothing more dangerous than the broncs and I thought I would save his life. But I was wrong. He has made a life."

"Made a life?"

"Yes. Don't you read the papers? He is defeating all the broncos. Yesterday he had an enormous success in Salt Lake. Back there in the Great Valley I didn't know what big courage he had."

"I've got to be going, Arturo."

"Some of us have it and some of us don't."

"I've got to be going, Arturo." Arturo had worked his huge brown horse across the path.

"Some of us talk big and some of us act."

"I've got to be going, Arturo."

"Some of us use big words to hide the word coward."

Alastair reached up to grab the bit of the big brown, and the horse wheeled, frightened and violent, striking Alastair as it rose and pivoted. Alastair felt his own suitcase hit him as he fell down through the white aspens into the ravine. He lay there a while, not moving, listening to the Spanish horse and Spanish rider thunder off. They both seemed out of control.

Alastair got to a sitting position now and felt the blood, gentle and warm, running down his face. He wiped it off with a sock that hung on an aspen twig and then began with crippled motions to gather all his stuff and put it back in the suitcase. When he finished he sat on the suitcase a minute, not thinking, before he started the stiff climb back to the path. Thinking does not help much. You have got to do something. You've got to climb back up. It's a long way up. It's strange how easy it is to come down. You come down without thinking and I guess that's the best way up. Thinking doesn't help much I guess, unless, as Santo would say, you are climbing at one and the same time.

From where the Bowmans sat they could watch all of the vast Jemez, clear almost from Coyote to San Ysidro. They were sitting on a leather couch made from Angus steer hides, black matching the black-and-white Indian rugs, and looking out through a five-by-five window encased with heavy timbers in the three-foot-thick adobe and mud wall which gave out on the Jemez, turning all red now. Even the long white reaches of the thick-with-snow Mimbres Haunch that ran all the way down into the Vacas were burning in the thin bright shadow of a dying New Mexican day.

"A wild Spaniard runs through here on a wild horse and wants us to believe he saw Alastair on the Jemez." Big Sant shook his head. "I tell you, Millie, what would Alastair be doing wandering the mountains when, to reach the Circle Heart, he only has to follow down the Señorito cut?"

"It's getting dark," Millie said. "He could have hit a box canyon. Hunters get lost on the Jemez every year. There's not a year goes by a hunter doesn't die on the mountain, and it's getting dark now."

"City hunters," Sant said. "No, we got a message from a wild horse, wild rider. Arturo has not been quite right in the head since he got fired by the Keep Out outfit."

"I think Alastair's lost," she said.

The sun went out. Darkness comes suddenly in northern New Mexico. Now all the light was gone on the Jemez. The lighted stage of mountain they were watching through the wide proscenium of mud bricks darkened quickly until there was nothing to watch. Just before this happened they could see the dark groves of pine following the deepest folds of the mountains lighted all the way to thirteen thousand feet. This display was different from any other. Each night something new happens because the mountain is always lighted differently. Each night the mountain gives a different performance.

"I will put some candles in the window," Millie said. "Because Alastair is lost up there." And she went about doing it.

245

"Wild horse, wild rider," Sant said. "You can't trust Arturo since he got fired by the Keep Out. Did you ever see such an outfit like he wears?"

"He wore that outfit when he still had his senses." She lit the candles. "It's his *pasó por aquí* outfit. With that outfit everyone will know that Arturo Lucero Cipriano de Godoy passed here."

"They certainly will. Do you think your candles will do any good?"

"Certainly."

Sant knew that the dim yellow light of the candles could not be seen for more than a few hundred yards but he said nothing. There was nothing to watch now but the candles and neither had anything to say so they watched the faint yellowness glistening against the blackness of the window and said nothing for a long while.

"You presume—you think Alastair got himself purposely lost?"

Sant touched his chin in the faint light. "Why? Why would he do that?"

"Yes," Millie said. "Why?"

And they both were silent again as they looked out at the silent and dark mountain.

"Why?"

Why is anything? Why is everything so much the exact total of what we do? Why is so much black and white and why is it the mountain always says things so well, silently, and we in a whole lifetime of brilliance only manage to level the wrong gun at the wrong bird in the wrong season? And on the wrong mountain, Sant thought. Why? The candles flickered as though they might go out, and Sant and Millie Sant wondered as Alastair wandered the mountain they had just seen go out.

"Maybe," Big Sant said, "Alastair could not quite make it back here now."

"The snow?"

"No. Something else."

"What else?"

"Unfinished business," Big Sant said. "I think before he

246

comes home he's got something to finish. Something we'd want him to finish. Something he wants to finish."

"In our country?"

"No. Another country," Big Sant said.

Alastair made it back up the steep aspen-clogged ravine into which he had fallen but when he reached the path it was black dark. Alastair felt his way quickly along the path in the matching darkness. He did not like the feeling, the knowledge now, that the path was slanting up the mountain. The strategy would be to turn down the next ravine and hope that it would follow all the way down and not box, not dead-end into a high ridge of stone, not slant sideways finally instead of down, not lose him up there in the beginning snow. The ravine he was in boxed quickly and it took him a good hour to climb up the saddle of the ridge in the now thickening snow. Just one more mistake like that, lugging the suitcase with absolutely numbed hands up the sheer frozen cliffs in a now hard-driving snow, just one more impossible climb to reach the saddle of one more barrier ridge, and he knew he would have had it. He would then know exactly why he had come home. He would have come home to do something he could have done just as nicely where he had been. Where had he been? He had been involved in some nightmare. He put down the suitcase and clung to a thin pine with his arms to keep the wind from toppling him down the cliff below, the cliff that began two feet from his left foot. He had been to the outside world and now he was near home. It does not seem that nightmares are restricted to the outside world. I bet nightmares can be had in heaven. I bet that all of the natives here who swear they know this mountain as well as they know the palm of their rear end could, in a sudden snow, find themselves, or someone else could find them here, frozen to a pine tree on the next bright morning. Where? No, they would find him in some frozen attitude of movement. He would keep moving here, walking, climbing, crawling, over every mountain between here and the Pacific Ocean. *Pasó por aquí,* Alastair Benjamin on his march to the sea.

Alastair had not been many hours on his march to the Pacific

Ocean when he topped out over a crest of wind-screaming oak and saw ahead and below a fire swirling high into the night. He might have lost his mind now. He was not certain he was seeing a true fire. But you might as well walk toward an imagined fire, toward a crazy glare. A crazy fire is better than none. He approached the fire now, down a barren hogback ridge. The fire still swerved up madly, and now, out of the clearing where the fire was, there rushed a bearded madman. Mad because he grabbed Alastair and carried him like a board toward the warm fire. Mad because he was white and did not belong to a mob. But mostly mad because Alastair had fixed in his mind a march to the sea. *Pasó por aquí,* Alastair Benjamin on his march to the sea.

The white man who was all alone—imagine a white man all alone—had him wrapped in blankets and was bringing some feeling into his arms and legs by rubbing and now forced something to his mouth.

"Drink this."

Something scalding went down through his insides and he saw the fire again. It was not such a big fire now and the man was not so mad. It was Mr. Sanders, the missionary.

"Try to move those arms and legs," Mr. Sanders said.

Alastair sat up and Mr. Sanders screwed back the bottle top. "Something I got from Mr. Peersall."

"I saw them go by up there," Alastair said.

"Who?"

"The bank robbers. The ones that got killed that robbed that bank in Durango. They went by. They were lost."

"Where?"

"On the mountain in the blizzard when I was holding onto the pine tree."

"You had a hallucination," Mr. Sanders said, unscrewing the bottle again.

"Is it a hallucination that we all seem bent on killing each other off?"

"No, that's not a hallucination," and the former divine took a quick drink.

"And I saw the death of Sant."

248

"How was he killed?"

"In an arena. They bore him out like a Roman hero."

"That was a hallucination again." Mr. Sanders tapped the bottle. "He's still going very big."

"But they wanted him killed."

"Now you're talking normally again." Mr. Sanders touched back Alastair with ruthless kindness. "Keep those blankets on."

"And I got to figuring," Alastair said, "that you can't solve anything by killing a man's horse."

"Yes, you can if you think you can," Mr. Sanders said.

"Aren't you practicing religion any more, Mr. Sanders?"

"Yes, I'm practicing it now," Mr. Sanders said. They sat there hushed for a while with only Mr. Sanders' tapping on the bottle audible.

"There are still some hunters lost on the mountain," Mr. Sanders said. "I'll keep this fire going until they report in someplace. It could be they've topped down over the Los Alamos side and are already saved."

"Saved?"

"For this season," Mr. Sanders said. Mr. Sanders looked into the darkness. "Starting next month I'll be able to ship three carloads of adobes a month to Boston."

"Why Boston?"

"They got me into this and now I'll get them out."

"It doesn't make sense," Alastair said, and then his eyes seemed to awaken. "Let's not be bitter, men," he said. The former divine remained quiet, seeming to be studying something out in the darkness where the adobes must be stacked.

"I pay the Indians a dollar ten cents an hour and I've organized them into a baseball team. They like to call themselves the Braves. The Boston Braves. And who am I to raise my hand against them?"

"Who indeed," Alastair said. "But then you're not practicing religion any more?"

"You can take the missionary out of the mission but you can never take the mission out of the missionary. But you can't storm the Indians and you can't ambush them."

"Can't ambush them?"

"No," the missionary said. "You've just got to quietly appear in their midst as just another Indian."

"Just another Indian?"

"That's right," Mr. Sanders said thoughtfully. "But we'd better be getting you home."

"Home?"

"Yes. I gather you're running away back home."

"Not exactly. I was on the mountain."

"Well, you can stay the night here and sleep on it," Mr. Sanders said.

Alastair rose at the first false dawn to a world of adobes. The adobes seemed stacked high and wide to infinity. Actually they covered four good acres in the middle of the sage. Mr. Sanders had builded another mesa alongside a true mesa.

"Boy, you certainly can sell adobes, Mr. Sanders," Alastair said over *tortillas* and eggs.

"No," Mr. Sanders said, "but, by God, those Indians certainly can make them."

They quickly finished their *tortillas* and eggs and Alastair studied Mr. Sanders' mesa of adobes again.

"Actually I sell two truckloads a day in Albuquerque and one in Gallup," the former divine said. "The rest I'm stockpiling for Boston."

"You certainly are going to get even with Boston."

"Yes, I am," Mr. Sanders said. "Did you figure out last night where you're going?"

"I figure I better see Mr. Peersall first," Alastair said.

"Mr. Peersall is dying." Mr. Sanders rubbed his chin. "I don't think he can help."

"I think he gave Sant something."

"Mr. Peersall is dying," Mr. Sanders said. "I don't think he has anything more to give."

"Well, *vamos a ver*. We'll see," Alastair said, rising in a corridor of adobes and raising his suitcase to his shoulder. Alastair put out his free hand. "I hope your Braves have luck."

250

"They'll need it," Mr. Sanders said, rising and taking the hand and then releasing it. "They play lousy ball."

"They'll improve with age," Alastair said, walking away through the brick maze.

"We'll all hope" were Mr. Sanders' final words.

When Alastair got to Mr. Peersall's log shack Mr. Peersall was sitting in the sun tending his weeds. The weeds of the West are cactus and sage and such as this that grow violently everywhere where there's not much water. An Anglo and a Spanish-American will usually plant a rug of lawn and surround the rug with things that won't grow here—tame roses and other Eastern exotics that do not want to live in a strange country. Mr. Peersall cheated somewhat. He brought up lower desert plants to his high altitude in spite of the experts.

"They told me she would not bloom at seven thousand feet," Mr. Peersall said, pointing his Sharps at a red-blooming cholla. The three-foot plant seemed one of nature's experiments with abstract art. It was composed of sausage-shaped balloons stuck together at weird and odd angles with extruding needle and razor points to discourage the critics—and the cattle that want to eat it up, Alastair thought.

"But I've come about something important," Alastair said.

"Sit down," Mr. Peersall said, pointing to a rock. "Now, what is so important about your running away back home? I ran away from my first battle—my first fracas is a better word. You're very aware of words, aren't you, son?"

"I was, but I found they're not much help."

"Well anyway, I ran. Like you, I ran."

"You believe everything Arturo de Godoy says?"

"I believe this. I recognize the symptoms."

"Well, you don't know what it was like."

"Maybe I don't then."

"You mean I should have stayed in there?"

"I don't know who else is going to fight your battles, son."

Mr. Peersall used his Sharps rifle like a hoe and from his sitting position nurtured a small bur sage.

"I guess you think you're quite a sage yourself," Alastair said.

251

"I've learned a good deal." Mr. Peersall had gotten so good he could turn over a leaf or twist a bloom toward him with the forward sight of his Sharps.

"Well, I guess you gave Sant something."

"I didn't give Sant anything. I guess maybe that's what I learned, that you can't give anyone anything. You maybe can hint at what they've got that they can try to give to others. And that's about all."

"What have I got to give, Mr. Peersall?"

Mr. Peersall had sharpened the back edge of his forward sight so that he could yank off dead wood with it. He did this now to a failing twig and then put the gun across his knees and looked at Alastair.

"Nothing," Mr. Peersall said. "I suppose you've got nothing to give yet." Mr. Peersall removed the bolt.

"But you gave Sant something."

After Mr. Peersall removed the bolt he looked through the bore.

"When you talked, Sant would always listen. I was always thinking of bigger things."

"This thing's a better plow now than it is a weapon," Mr. Peersall said, watching through the bore.

"Am I boring you, Mr. Peersall?"

"No, son. It's simply that Sant—well—" Mr. Peersall paused.

"You mean I've got to do it alone?"

"Yes."

"But the missionary used to say no man is an island."

"Well, he is."

"You think he just got that from another preacher?"

"Yes."

"We've got to go it all alone?"

"Yes, we do."

Alastair thought about this while Mr. Peersall waited patiently. Then Alastair thought some more, watching down the valley, rubbing his neck and looking down the long valley.

"So you want me to go back to where I just came from. Do

you know where my father came from, Mr. Peersall? You knew him as the Gran Negrito."

"That's how we knew him."

"Well, I found out from Big Sant's brother where my father came from before he came here and stole the land from the Indians—drove them out."

"Yes?"

"Well, my father was driven out from down there. 'A smart book nigger.' They drove him out down there and when he got up here he did the only thing he knew, the only way he'd been taught —he drove an Indian out."

"Yes," Mr. Peersall said. "And now they've got you afraid. They've got you afraid to claim the education that belongs rightly to you. The circle has begun all over again just when the Circle Heart thought they had it stopped."

"Belongs rightly to me?" Alastair rubbed his chin in thought about this. "Belongs rightly to me?" Alastair looked straight at Mr. Peersall. "Well, I guess we can't let the curse start all over again just when we thought we had it stopped with Mr. Sant's horse." Alastair picked up some stones and stared down valley. "Well, I don't know but I think I'm ready to try it again, back where it all began—catch it back there before it gets loose again, Mr. Peersall."

"All alone?"

"Yes."

"Well, it will take me a little time to get ready," Mr. Peersall said.

"But you just said—"

"I said we had to go it alone, but I didn't say there would not be others. Other fools to join the battle too. And old fools as well," Mr. Peersall said.

"Don't try to get up, Mr. Peersall."

"I *am* up," Mr. Peersall said, leaning on his stick of gun. "Now, in which direction does the smoke of battle lie?" Mr. Peersall exchanged the stick to the other hand. "Where's the trouble, son?"

After one hour of scurrying around they both got started off

253

together. Mr. Peersall took the lead and set a very good pace. Then Mr. Peersall ended all at once. He faltered, stumbled only half a minute, and then went down all at once like a shot deer. He had time to mumble in Alastair's arms that he had had only a few more days left to tend the weeds in his garden, that he had been only waiting around for the last weeks for an opportunity to quit the world like this—to quit it going somewhere and to be taken from behind and quickly. Like a fallen wild deer, to go quickly.

Alastair found a kind of plaque for the tomb of gathered rocks that he put the body under—large field stones to protect the body from wild animals. When Mr. Peersall had faltered and fallen they had just topped the crest of the Piedras fault, a jutting Mesaverde formation that outcrops coal. After Alastair finished with the grave of Mr. Peersall he pried a piece of coal from a pure-black ledge and wrote these words on the flat sandstone concretion plaque:

WILLIAM PEERSALL. WHO WILL MOURN HIM?

Alastair tried again on another concretion.

PASO POR AQUI BLUE-EYED BILLY PEERSALL ON HIS WAY TO JOIN BATTLE. 186- —1958. IN BELOVED MEMORY.
ALASTAIR P. BENJAMIN.

Alastair got up from his job and began moving down. The P.—the Peersall—Alastair had just added to his own name on the plaque made him feel that he had a great deal in back of him now to go on—a great deal, he guessed, to kind of live up to. Indian Country. A wild free country. *El pais de los broncos.* The country of the Bronc People.

Alastair picked up the pace, passed beneath a tremulous aspen shattered brilliant with light, walked beside a mesa brushed in fiery cloud, then descended into a long valley that led to another country.

254